ROCKET MAN

VON BRAUN: NAZI AT NASA

PAULA ASTRIDGE

Woodslane Press Pty Ltd
10 Apollo Street
Warriewood, NSW 2102
Email: info@woodslane.com.au
Tel: 02 8445 2300 Website: www.woodslane.com.au

First published in Australia in 2018 by Woodslane Press
© 2018 Paula Astridge

A catalogue record for this book is available from the National Library of Australia

Printed in Australia by McPhersons
Design by: The Mighty Pen @mightythepen

For my dear friend,

Leone

Other books by Paula Astridge

Kill The Fuhrer

Golden Boy

In the Way of the Reich

Waltzing Dixie

Bad Hand

Scallywag

5

The world makes way for the man
who knows where he is going.
— Ralph Waldo Emerson

PROLOGUE

THEY WERE TAKING TOO LONG TO DIE and the SS officer watching their hanging came close to passing out.

"Who is he?" the prisoners from Dora concentration camp wondered when they saw the young man in black uniform look faint and waver on his feet.

He had stood steady when the executions began, with his square jaw and blue eyes set hard on the six men wearing nooses around their necks; but as the fast drop-kill he expected turned to a sadistic, slow garrotte, he felt sick and suddenly turned to leave.

A firm hand clamped around his wrist to stop him.

"Where do you think you're going, von Braun?" SS General Hans Kammler demanded.

As commandant of the Third Reich's underground armaments factory, Kammler had final say as to how it functioned, but von Braun had more the ethics of a scientist than soldier and was appalled.

"I will not be a party to this," he answered, trying to wrench his arm free. But the vice-like grip tightened.

"If you're not for us," Kammler said with an alarming calm, "then you are against us and can hang with the rest."

He was a man of his word, and out of respect for his brutal reputation Baron Wernher von Braun stopped protesting and turned a blind eye to the vile proceedings in this man-made hell being burrowed into the depths of Germany's Kohnstein Hill. In the Third Reich's hurry to hide their new secret weapon from the enemy, they were supplementing their earthmoving equipment with prisoners' bare hands – a half-starved work-force of thousands who crawled like living skeletons through its dark labyrinth of tunnels, scratching out a honeycomb complex of suffocating cubicles where they were to lie and die between labours.

Those prisoners being executed for daring to rebel had now done dying in acute distress and von Braun was free to go, but not before throwing the commandant a look of undisguised contempt.

"You've got no one but yourself to blame," Kammler called out after him.

Von Braun stopped dead in his tracks because it was true. His genius and insatiable ambition had created this monster: the V-2 rocket for which this facility was intended. Having revelled in the kudos of its invention, he now had to bear the shame of slaves being worked to death to produce it and for the millions of innocents it was destined to kill.

He hadn't planned it this way. As a doctor of physics and a single-minded space enthusiast, all he wanted was to fly rockets to the moon, but as his means to that end, he had given Hitler a new wonder weapon to win the war. Having set its apocalyptic wheels in motion, he was caught up in the cogs of the Nazi machine from which there was no escape. He had forgotten where to draw the line on morality and had totally lost sight of where it all began.

PART ONE

SONNY BOY

CHAPTER

ONE

"ARE YOU READY?"

Shielding his big brother from harm with the heroic sweep of his arm, 12-year-old Wernher von Braun lit the fuse on the six skyrockets strapped to his wooden coaster wagon and hopped on board for the ride.

A fizz of fuses exploded in a dazzling jet of white flame and he was off, hurtling down the Berlin city street with hands gripped tight to the wheel, fair hair blowing in the wind, and intense, blue eyes fired with excitement at the prospect of breaking the speed record.

The wagon, painted red for the occasion, careened crazily out of control, its rubber-rimmed wheels spitting sparks as it zigzagged down the main road, while the sporadic bang of exploding rockets punctuated a woman's screams as it whisked by, ripping her stockings, before crashing into a greengrocer's stand and coming to a hard, hissing halt.

As a pallet of apples rained down on his head, young Wernher looked up in ecstasy. It was worth every bit of the pocket money spent on fireworks. His rockets had performed beyond his wildest dreams and neither the fruit vendor's rage nor the fist-clenched fury of the irate bystanders made him the least bit repentant about the devastation his experiment caused. For it was just the first of many he intended to conduct to fly a rocket to the moon and no one was going to stop him.

When it came to his obsession with space, all else paled in comparison, while his lack of contrition was the product of his privileged upbringing. As a young baron with a noble lineage that stretched back to the knights of the Middle Ages, he needed to apologise to no one ... except his father; a father, who as Germany's Minister for Agriculture, did not appreciate being hauled out of an important meeting at the Reichstag to go to the police station where his would-be scientist son was being held under arrest. The fact that he had to pay a sizeable sum to bail him out was just the icing on the cake.

"For the sake of your reputation, sir, we are prepared to release your son into your custody for a month's house arrest."

The police officer addressed cabinet minister Magnus von Braun with suitable respect, but far from appreciating the man's discretion, the baron was too incensed to speak and could only nod his curt consent. For not only was he coping with the public disgrace of his family name being dragged through the mud, but it appeared his boy had rolled in it too. With filthy clothes, grazed knees and a face coated in soot, he looked more like a street urchin than the son of an aristocrat and prominent politician of the Weimar Republic.

As soon as they arrived home, Wernher was taken by the scruff of the neck to stand shame-faced before his mother – the beautiful, brilliant Baroness Emmy.

"He's confined to the house for four weeks," her husband instructed her.

She acknowledged his directive and with difficulty disguising her tongue-in-cheek reprimand, sent her son to his room.

There was nothing more to be said, and trusting that his wife would mete out the appropriate punishment, Baron Magnus went happily back to the halls of power.

There, he reigned supreme, but everyone agreed that it was really Emmy who ruled the roost. She was a loving wife and mother, who best understood how to handle their three boys. As such, she knew that no amount of time in solitary confinement would convince her middle son that he had done anything wrong. So rather than exercise a firm hand in physical punishment, she took him milk and biscuits and sat down to talk common sense.

"The world needs *live* scientists, not dead ones," she said point-blank.

This, he understood, as he did the fact that his accomplice in crime, older brother Sigismund, had already been forgiven for letting himself be led astray by his wayward, year-younger sibling. It was not for the first time, nor, the baroness was sure, would it be for the last.

There was no doubt in her mind that Wernher was to blame, because she could read him like a book. With their shared sharp intellect, artistic talent and charm, they were much alike and would have been identical were it not for the one glaring difference between them – Wernher's peculiar compulsion to constantly want to build things. It was a fascination for a more hands-on way of life that puzzled the family when centuries of von Braun boys had been content with the benefits of their blue blood and the careers cut out for them: the Prussian military, a legal career with a view to politics, or simply settling on their baronial estates.

Somewhere along the line, the genes of their elite heritage had been infiltrated by an imposter; a diligent ancestor with a blue-collar bent, who branched off the family tree with a maverick genius that had sprouted again in Wernher. But for this 20th century baron to again break ranks and realise his dreams, he had to be brave enough to pursue them at all costs; and if need be, at others' expense.

"Well that's the last gift he's getting from *me!*" Wernher's indignant aunt declared, when on his seventh birthday, he put the expensive books she bought him into his wooden wagon to trade for the timber he needed to finish building his tree house.

For that, he received a sharp slap on the leg when his mother collected him from the village shop where he had gone to barter his goods.

"That was a *terrible* thing to do! You've hurt your aunt's feelings," she scolded, but Wernher was unmoved when, to him, it just made good sense. He had a tree house to build, he had run out of wood and his aunt would be none the wiser.

She would have remained that way had the shopkeeper not phoned Baroness Emmy, suspicious and highly amused by the small boy in sailor suit who wheeled his wagon full of leather-bound classics into the shop to swing a deal. Because the episode was so funny, young Wernher got away with it and quickly learnt his lesson – that there were benefits to being beguiling and that he could always rely on his bold charm to get what he wanted.

"We shouldn't have let him off the hook," Baron Magnus said in hindsight.

"No, but I didn't want to stifle his initiative," Emmy was quick to reply, when she had been thwarted by as much her entire life. As an extremely clever woman, her scientific aspirations were never taken seriously, and she was not about to let her son suffer the same. "Our Wernher is capable of great things and nothing must stand in his way."

"*All* our sons are clever," the baron boasted defensively.

With this, she heartily agreed. Both Sigismund and her youngest, five-year-old Magnus Junior had far above-average intelligence.

"But *Wernher's* a genius," she clarified with a calm objectivity that had nothing to do with favouritism. It was just the truth, albeit tainted by the flattery of him following in her footsteps.

Like her, Wernher could turn his hand to anything. Before he was five, he could read an entire newspaper, right way up and upside down. At nine, he was proficient on the cello, and within a year of learning the piano at age ten, he could play Beethoven's five concertos by heart and had composed his own works. Although, at 12, he was fluent in only three languages compared with her six, he matched her stride for stride in their passion for the arts and the fledgling field of astronomy. To both, nothing was impossible, and with their creative minds forever striving for the unachievable, neither believed the sky was the limit.

That lofty concept was beyond Baron Magnus, who preferred to stay more grounded in his goals. If Wernher chose to go where only angels dared tread, he still had two exceptional sons primed to pursue their Papa's path in politics.

"And at least all three get their strong looks and builds from me," his vanity stepped in to say, but never out loud, because it was enough to see his attributes mirrored in theirs; Wernher's, admittedly, to a slightly greater degree, which was a fact neither denied nor resented by his brothers, who had too many outstanding attributes of their own to begrudge any Wernher had in excess.

As displayed in their exceptional offspring, Magnus and Emmy made the perfect pair and they knew it the second they set eyes on each other.

… oOo …

"An orphan you say?" Baron Magnus repeated to the Prussian Trade Minister, Clemens Delbrueck, back in 1909.

As the politician's young adjutant, Magnus had been obliged to attend the social function and was very glad he did, for it was there he first saw the elegant, blue-eyed blonde, Emmy von Quistorp. Like all fertile, young females of the aristocracy, she had been put on the marriage market and as if a broodmare, was being paraded around the ballrooms of Berlin in search of the highest bidder.

"It's not as tragic as it sounds," Delbrueck replied, swilling down his champagne. "Her brother inherited their family estate, of course, but she has a substantial dowry."

Here, Delbrueck put practicality aside, along with the oyster canapé a second sniff warned him off. "Not that she hasn't earned it, poor girl."

Having piqued Magnus' interest, he continued:

"She was pulled out of her English finishing school at just 16 because her mother died suddenly and her father needed help to get through the crisis. Not many girls of that age would be willing or capable of giving it, but she not only acted as his secretary for their estate, but assisted him with all his ornithological experiments."

"So, not just a pretty face," Magnus said, even more intrigued.

"Certainly not . . . and then to top it off, her father died soon after, leaving her to continue his scientific studies alone. Amazingly enough she did, but it's beyond me why she bothered. As far as I'm concerned, it's strictly for the birds."

Pleased with his quip, the Minister moved on to socialise elsewhere, while Magnus watched on with fascination, biding his time between Strauss waltzes for his opportunity to cut in and sweep the beautiful Emmy off her feet. From the moment he did, they both knew it was forever.

... oOo ...

"Although it was hard for me to adapt to being the mere housewife of a county commissioner," Emmy told her sons years later when referring to her husband's first political promotion, "I was so intense about life – always soaring up and falling down. It took me years to discipline myself into a woman's mundane routine."

Yet, as far as her husband and boys were concerned, there was nothing in the least mundane about her.

I've never known a finer woman, Baron Magnus wrote fondly to a friend. *She was born into privilege, but is as much at ease in distinguished society as in the company of her servants. When any of them fall ill, she nurses them like a mother, because she truly believes in the equality of man, and daily puts it into practice.*

Apart from their shared love of music and languages, it was this liberal attitude of hers that rubbed off most strongly on Wernher. Throughout his coming years of spectacular success during war and peace, and despite the adulation those in power rushed to shower on him, he was to remain a man who exuded class by never distinguishing between its ranks.

TWO

I T WAS 1926, and while Germany enjoyed a brief break between world wars, depression and violent civil unrest, Baron Magnus was climbing the political ladder. He was flourishing as a minister in von Hindenburg's government and had secured a spot on the Reichsbank's board of directors. There was every reason to be full of hope for his family's future, for unlike the millions of his fellow countrymen struggling with the harsh penalties of the Versailles Treaty, all augured well for the von Brauns, bar Wernher's serious trouble at school.

"He's lazy and doesn't apply himself," the headmaster wrote on his report card. "He's an asocial element and misfit who doesn't belong in this school. If he is to remain here, he must repeat the 8th Grade."

More baffled than angry, the baron thrust the report at his wife.

"I don't understand," he said. "How could such a clever boy manage to only scrape through basic grammar and history and fail mathematics and physics outright?"

"He's bored," Emmy answered, as she scanned the report card's array of Cs and red, underlined Fs before calmly turning her attention back to the magazine she was reading. "If something doesn't interest Wernher, he simply doesn't bother."

At this astounding revelation, the baron tried to compose himself, but couldn't.

"Well, he'll damn well *have* to if he's to amount to anything," he blustered. "He can't just pick and choose as he pleases for the rest of his life. You shouldn't have given him that wretched telescope for his birthday. His obsession with astronomy has blinded him to all else."

This was disappointing for the baron when he had instilled his own passion for hunting and sailing into Wernher's psyche and was lately so proud of his boy for having followed through on his aviation interests by bravely flying in an open-cockpit Junkers13. Sadly, the baron had just found out that it had more to do with Wernher's need for speed, than his desire to bond with his father.

With this, Emmy secretly agreed, so in answer to her husband's question, she merely shrugged.

"Perhaps, but what's to be done?"

She was deriving a certain pleasure from teasing him for she hadn't the slightest concern about Wernher's academic prowess. He could do anything he set his mind to. It was just that right now it was tuned in to the heavens . . . far, far away from the tedium school was inflicting on him.

"What's the point . . . ," Wernher had complained to her only the day before, "of endlessly translating Latin and French when I could be working on exploring new frontiers?"

At the age of 14, however, he was not old enough to be indulged to that extent and had to train his non-conformist self to obey the rules until he earned the privilege. In the meantime, trying to force his hand was pointless when neither the embarrassment of his previous arrest nor his continual detentions at school deterred him.

Since the wagon-and-rockets incident two years before, his experiments had continued to cause chaos. One of his rockets blew up in a fellow student's face and started a fire on the school grounds; another was launched into the greenhouse at home, splintering glass throughout their prize cauliflower collection; and two more were shot, for good measure, into a hardware store and a bakery on the main street. Fortunately, there were no fatalities, but his father's wallet was considerably thinner for paying the hefty compensation.

"What the boy needs is a dashed good thrashing," the baron said as he paced the floor, patting the pocket where the lump in his wallet used to be.

Yet, even as he said it, he knew it would never happen while Wernher had the knack of talking his way around any situation. Brimful of confidence and personality, he had everyone wrapped around his little finger, but it was against the grain for the baron to weakly give way. Suddenly hot under the collar at the thought, he looked out the window to see Wernher and his American school friend working away in the back shed.

"Well what tomfoolery is he up to now?" he demanded. "After that appalling report, he should be in his room studying."

Emmy casually stubbed out her cigarette: "He's building an automobile."

That was the last straw.

"Stuff and nonsense!" the baron blustered. "The boy's quite out of control. Why can't he be like his big brother, Sigismund, and follow the rules? If he hasn't enough respect for his parents to do so, he can go without his monthly allowance and let's just see how far that gets him."

Realising her husband was overwrought Emmy got up and walked to the window to console him.

"There's no need to worry," she said, linking her arm through his as they watched their son in the garden below. "Problems have a way of working themselves out, but never as one expects. I'm sure something will happen to set him straight."

That stroke God was holding in reserve fell the very next day, the minute the mail arrived. Wernher had waited three, long weeks for the parcel he ordered and was so excited when he pulled it from the letterbox that he could barely untie the string. When he finally unwrapped the book inside, however, his thrill turned to mind-numbing devastation.

"I can't understand a word of it!" he exclaimed, dismayed by its hundred pages of tightly packed mathematical formulae. And worse . . . that there was not a single picture of a spaceship to be seen.

When he had stumbled on the advertisement for Hermann Oberth's latest book in an obscure astronomy magazine, he could hardly believe his luck. His eyes lingered on its title with a romantic longing: *The Rocket Into Interplanetary Space*. Here, at his fingertips was a revolutionary work by the Romanian physics pioneer who was destined to become his mentor. Its promise was to unlock the mysteries of the universe with two electrifying claims: *That machines could be built to reach beyond Earth's atmosphere and that they could carry human cargo.*

"And all within the next few decades," Wernher had marveled when he filled in the application form and gazed in wonder at the logo of a rocket ship shooting for the stars. It was of no concern that Oberth's theories had been rejected by the Astronomers' Institute, because experts of the like had done exactly the same when Columbus said that the world was round.

Yet, at this very disappointing moment, it was hard for Wernher to be a believer when all he had in hand was a book full of gibberish.

"It's beyond *me*," his mother lied when he went to her for a translation. "You'll have to ask your headmaster for help."

Before giving it, the man laughed out loud.

"Well it serves you right von Braun. If you want to understand it, you'll just have to get stuck into your physics and mathematics."

The headmaster expected his troublesome student to rebel at the thought, and was astounded when Wernher did just that with a passion that excluded all else.

"All I want to do, one day, is fly a rocket to the moon," Wernher explained. "If this is what it takes, then this is what I'll do."

Along with his new-found conviction came his request to transfer to another school better equipped to handle the heights to which he aspired. That school was the Lietz Progressive Boarding Academy based at ancient Ettersburg Castle. Its advanced teaching techniques combined strong academics with practical working-class crafts, and thriving on the routine, Wernher was not bothered about the school's founder being a flagrant anti-Semite. It did seem a bit odd that in an institution for the outstanding there were no Jews who were renowned for as much, but happy among his fellow Protestants and tolerated sprinkling of Catholics, he never missed mingling with them and learned that it was *infra dig* to do so.

It had nothing to do with bigotry. It was just that he didn't care when his priority was to push for knowledge at top speed without getting side-tracked. He had a lot of catching up to do and with his head down, working like a fury; he was soon topping his class in mathematics and physics, tutoring more senior students in the same and impressing his professors with his attempts at writing science fiction.

It was for this reason, along with being daunted by von Braun's rapidly growing expertise, that the teachers let him have his head; encouraging his endless hours of star-gazing and his monitoring of each lunar eclipse, while waiting in awed anticipation for him to complete his carefully measured diagram of Mercury's transit across the sun.

For a short, heady time, he and everyone around him seemed

to be in seventh heaven. While Wernher was raising his friends' aspirations to *'what could be'*, Germany was flying high on hopes not experienced since the Great War, because Charles Lindbergh's first transatlantic flight had lifted it out of its international humiliation. Though an American, the celebrated aviator backed the controversial views of the fledgling Nazi regime and made it clear that if another war were to come, Germany would win.

Ominous rumblings, but with his mind set on space, young Baron von Braun stayed oblivious to what was going on in the real world . . . right here on planet Earth in his hometown of Berlin.

A MALEVOLENT MIST, thick as a London pea-souper, shrouded the German capital. Strange things were happening behind its beautiful Baroque walls, and the streets were seething with sin after hosting three astonishing firsts: the first open attacks on Jews; the first bloody gun battles between the Nazi Brownshirts and communists; and the disturbing news of Adolf Hitler's first Nuremberg rally.

As yet, in 1927, few Berliners took him and his peculiar splinter group seriously. Most wrote them off as thugs who would never amount to much, but warning bells were ringing because the party's roughneck roots were mutating into a national movement at alarming speed, all courtesy of their fanatical leader, who had a feral instinct for sniffing out suffering. As an embittered veteran from the World War I trenches, Hitler knew exactly how to manipulate the masses, mustering their hopes and fears into a common hate so that he could steer their sheep-like herds into a frenzied stampede of bloodlust against the Jewish people.

"Mark my words . . . that man will be the end of Germany," Baron Magnus said, when he read the news in the morning paper of Berlin's latest bloodshed.

Showing an uncharacteristic lack of insight, Emmy continued to sip at her tea, more worried about her middle son than the mounting Nazi threat.

"Hitler's just a fad," she answered dismissively. "How many times have we seen his like come and go? If I were you, I'd be more concerned about Wernher's letter."

It had been sitting on the mantelpiece for the past hour while the baron mulled over his son's written request to transfer from his Lietz school to its new, specialist branch on Spiekeroog Island, where he would accelerate his studies and graduate a year early. The school was situated on an East Frisian barrier island, which was little more than a giant sand dune in the North Sea. But its white-capped waves, wild winds and wealth of water sports were enough to stir any boy's blood.

You'd love it! Wernher wrote to win over his father. *Now that I'm sixteen, it's time for a change and I can't see why you'd object when it's my chance to better myself during the school's 1928 semester. But if that's not enough to sway you, dear Papa, then just think of all the glorious sailing!*

He was playing his trump card referencing the nautical, because he knew it was his father's weak spot.

"The boy's nothing short of a scoundrel!" the baron declared, amused by his son's transparent attempt to hoodwink him, for they both shared an obsession for boats and a flair for handling them. While Wernher, despite his youth, was at home at the helm through the worst of storms, there was nothing the baron loved more than being at the wheel on a clear-skied, summer day watching the sharp prow of his yacht slice the blue sea into white water.

Deal done, nothing more to be said. The baron signed his approval.

... oOo ...

"Dedication is what I admire most," the headmaster at Spiekeroog said when he found young von Braun working back, as usual, after class. "But surely you'd rather be at the local dance with your friends?"

Wernher put down his pen and looked up with an engaging smile.

"No sir. I'd prefer to get on with my work."

"Singular," the headmaster replied, leaving him in peace. Yet he wondered, as he walked away, whether he should have advised him otherwise when the boy's good looks would have assured him the pick of partners.

As to that, Wernher hadn't the slightest interest. Although he was at the age to spread his wings and try his luck, he could not see beyond his ultimate goal and, as yet, was completely blind to conceit. He rarely looked in a mirror to admire his handsome reflection and was more frustrated than flattered by the constant adulation of friends and females when he longed to be alone.

Hanker as he did, however, for a hermit's existence, he could not stop his innate magnetism attracting all and sundry. It seemed that the more he sought solitude, the more he fascinated others, each of them trying to break down his walls of resistance and become his best friend. None of them understood that they were interrupting his dreams of space and that he needed to be alone to achieve them.

Such single-minded conviction was beyond most teenagers' comprehension and sometimes, Wernher had to admit, beyond his own when only two days before, he knocked back the advances of a beautiful girl on the beach. Although admiring her soft, brown eyes and shapely, tanned legs, he did not respond to her flirting in expectation of being asked to the dance. She was disappointed and had to console herself with the other boys' whistles as she walked away in her pretty, pink costume and polka-dot scarf.

"Are you *mad!*" one of his friends hurled at him, along with a wet tennis ball.

In hindsight, Wernher thought that perhaps he was, when sitting at his desk under a flickering lamp, the memory of her curvaceous figure was suddenly winning out against those in his algebraic equations. It was 10pm and with the 'x's, 'y's and square roots starting to dart erratically before his eyes, he realised he was overtired and needed to go to bed; little wonder when he was working himself into the ground. He had opted not to go home for the school holidays and had spent his entire summer break studying in his room, not having the time to go outside in the sun, or for that matter, to take a bath.

"*Hell's teeth!*" his roommate, Helmut Albrecht, exclaimed. Fresh back for the new term he'd opened the dorm door and been knocked back by the stench.

The room reeked of sweat and hard-edged determination. Dirty clothes and scrunched-up paper carpeted the floor and Wernher's hair, now inches too long, was lacquered to his head with grease.

"I'll clean up tomorrow," he said in response to his friend's dismay, as he threw himself down on his bunk in exhaustion. "Just toss my books off your bed."

"You don't honestly think I'm going to sleep here?" Helmut answered, holding his nose as he backed out the door, before going to confer with other classmates about their friend von Braun: "We've got to do something about him."

They all agreed and when they burst open Wernher's door at midnight he woke in shock as 10 of them descended upon him in the dark, four holding him down, while the others gagged and hog-tied him to a metal pole pilfered from the school gym. With three of them shouldering the load fore and aft, they marched, as if to a medieval feast, across the sand dunes to the beach, slid him off the beam, and at the count of three, swung him into the surf.

"We'd better untie his hands and feet or he'll drown," was their first afterthought when he came spluttering to the surface for air. The second was to throw him a bar of soap.

He should have held it against them, but with his usual good humour, Wernher walked from the waves laughing, waterlogged from head to toe, but smelling a whole lot sweeter.

This ability to take it on the chin was yet another attribute to add to his list. By rights, someone in possession of so many should have aroused jealousy, but no one seemed to mind walking in von Braun's shadow. Despite the fact that his physical presence and mental prowess cast such a large one, his exuberance for life and genuine liking for others, made him hard to hate.

One exception was a substitute teacher, who Wernher corrected in front of the class. When the man finished scribbling his complicated equations on the blackboard, he was annoyed to find that von Braun was not paying attention.

"*You there*, sitting at the back!" he said, pointing an accusing finger at the student who had been ignoring the lesson to work on something more advanced.

Snapped from his concentration, Wernher looked up with a start amid his classmates' chuckling.

"I wonder, young sir," the teacher continued as he tapped his chalk on the board, "if you would extend us the courtesy of explaining how I achieved the result I have here?"

Wernher had completely lost track of the tutorial and had to think fast as he walked to the front of the room. He quickly scanned the blackboard, picked up the duster and in one fell swoop wiped the smile from the teacher's face, along with the equation he had chalked. Replacing it with another, he explained to the man where he went wrong.

It was no coincidence that the teacher called in sick the next day, but it came as a total surprise when Wernher was asked to lecture his own class in the man's stead. It was an enormous compliment, but it made him uneasy. The last thing he wanted was to appear a show-off, so he tackled the problem with a joke.

"Could I possibly be more obnoxious?" he quipped as he stood in front of his friends and was instantly relieved by their boisterous laughter.

Thus, his pattern was set for life: To cover all contingencies with humour.

It was pure power of leadership, however, that won his class-mates' support when he suggested that they buck in to build a state-of-the-art observatory for the school. Although his private dream, they all rushed to make it their own, offering him whatever help he needed.

The small telescope Wernher's mother had given him no longer served his purpose and he had convinced the headmaster to buy a new refractor with a 95mm objective lens. The plan was to construct a hut for the new telescope where they could carry out serious observations of the vast North Sea sky. But the weather was against them; the moment they began digging the foundations for the square building with its removable roof, winter storms set in with a vengeance and high tides lapped scarily on school land. The ice build-up was so severe that the ferry could not reach them with supplies and it wasn't until the summer thaw of '29 that they were able to lay the concrete slab and finish the wooden structure.

Its completion made Wernher a legend at the school, but his parents saw it differently . . . that he was getting too big for his boots. Proud as they were of his achievements, they felt that the family was being left behind in the process.

"I don't like it," his mother said when he let them know he was not coming home for the summer holidays.

It was the first time the family hadn't holidayed together,

and Wernher breaking free from tradition did not sit well with Emmy with whom he had always been so close. Well, he had got away with it once, but as far as she was concerned, the moon would just have to wait until he fulfilled his more pressing family obligations.

He was halfway through handwriting his 300-page book on astronomy and was pasting in a picture of America's 100-inch telescope on Mt Wilson when his mother's letter arrived. Much as he loved her, he was reluctant to stop work to read it and was sorry that he did.

"Do I have to come?" he wrote in answer to her insistence that he attend the christening of his newborn cousin, little Maria von Quistorp.

"Yes, you do!" she immediately penned back, her reprimand made clear by a thick-inked exclamation mark.

So, it was off to the von Quistorp's Bauer Estate in Pomerania and then to the local Lutheran church where the extended family in full noble plumage filled the pews and surrounded the baptismal font. At 17, Wernher had two good reasons for feeling out of place: predictable teenage diffidence and his total disinterest in religion, which had earned him his nickname of the *Happy Heathen*. Even for his parents' sake, he could not appreciate the sanctity of the ceremony and felt surly about having to be a part of it. He tried to retreat by quietly melting into the congregation, but his mother had her eye firmly fixed on him and was determined to call him out.

"Perhaps Wernher could hold the baby," she said, making the sudden, unorthodox suggestion that he usurp the godparent's role.

When nobody objected, Wernher was suddenly more shy than belligerent and had a suggestion of his own.

"Let Siggy do it. He's the eldest."

Emmy flashed a warning glance at her eldest son, and recognising her ploy to restore Wernher to the fold, Sigismund passed the buck straight back to his brother. All were waiting in anticipation and with the minister's fingers already wet with holy water, Wernher had no choice. He stepped forward and took the baby in his arms, awkwardly adjusting the long, lacy lengths of her christening gown that were yellowed from centuries of use.

As the prayers proceeded, the tedium showed on his face, but catching the look of tight-lipped reproof from the aunt who had never forgiven him for flogging off her gift, he thought it was wise to focus on the infant in his arms.

The baby smiling up at him blinking big, blue eyes was not enough to make him smile back, but when her tiny, pink hand suddenly reached out to cling tight to his finger, his heart skipped a beat. It was a moment of revelation, a bonding of souls and somehow he knew that she was his and that he would look after her for the rest of his life.

FOUR

S CHOOL DAYS WERE OVER, and to satisfy their father's hope that at least one of his sons follow in his footsteps, Siggy was preparing for his civil service exams. That left Wernher free from the obligation, so he signed off from high school with honours, bound for the Technical University of Berlin.

"Let's celebrate!" he said to Siggy, having galloped ahead a year in his studies to make sure they graduated at the same time. "I can't wait to see the new science-fiction flick in town."

Siggy rolled his eyes at the thought. He didn't share Wernher's wild enthusiasm, but when it came to stories of space, he knew there was no point arguing. Here, Wernher was not alone when futuristic movies were all the rage in Germany. To capitalise on the craze, the studios were churning out the tawdry, B-graders at lightning speed.

"You can't honestly say you enjoyed that," Siggy scoffed, when he and Wernher walked from the theatre after sitting through two hours of cinematic bilge.

He was right. The production was indefensible. Throughout, Wernher had to work hard at taking it seriously; but even he, with his passion for space and forgiveness for all foolishness involved, could not get beyond the green-clad actors in tin-foil hats. To stop himself laughing, he sucked loudly on his straw to drain the last drops of his Coca-Cola.

"It's not the films I'm interested in," he justified, as he threw the empty bottle into the bin. "It's the people behind their production."

There was one he specifically had in mind – physicist and engineer. Hermann Oberth, who as one of the founding fathers of rocketry, had set Wernher's dreams of space on fire three years before. Now news had it that the famous filmmaker, Fritz Lang, had hired Oberth as technical advisor for his upcoming film *Woman in the Moon*. Lang wanted to produce a work of quality and had commissioned Oberth to build a liquid-fuel rocket for publicity, with the intention of launching it into the stratosphere at the movie's premiere. Such a project was before its time and way beyond Oberth's skills, but its prospect provided for a lavish, big-dollar extravaganza – Berlin's final, financial flourish before the world crashed into the 1929 Depression.

Unaware of the impending doom, Wernher was elated to hear that Oberth was hiring space enthusiasts to help him with the venture. Although he was hell-bent on being one of them, he was a bit shy about pleading his case face to face with his hero, so he settled on using the side door, insinuating himself into the favour of Oberth's associate – science writer Willy Ley, a young man, not much older than himself, who shared his yen for rocketry and seemed far more approachable.

Like him, Ley was an explorer of the unknown – a university graduate in astronomy and physics, who had been inspired by Oberth's theories and was working tirelessly to prove them. As vice president of the Society of Spaceflight, he was filling the pages of its in-house publication, *The Rocket*, with sensational stories of space that were kindling the imagination of millions. At the same time, he was helping Lang by making space models to exhibit at large spectator events; creating displays so real that they were exciting the public with future possibilities of space travel and opening a window for new 'weapons of wonder' that would revive their glorious German Empire.

For such a man of energy and vision, however, his home looked remarkably mundane.

"I'm afraid Mr. Ley isn't in," the housekeeper said when Wernher knocked at the door.

It was a cold-call, but having dredged up the courage to arrive unannounced and brashly introduce himself, Wernher was not about to back down.

"That's quite all right. I'm happy to wait," he answered with a dashing smile, which he was fast learning made women more amenable.

"Well who may I say is calling?" she asked.

Standing with hat in hand, now close to coming of age, Wernher said with authority:

"Von Braun . . . Baron Wernher von Braun."

Using his aristocratic title was the surest way to get his foot in the door, and to inveigle his way into the privacy of the man's home. As if by right, he followed her into the parlour where in deference to his charm and peerage, she directed him to a chair and offered afternoon tea. While she made it, however, he preferred to wander around the room, browsing Ley's bookshelves and reams of written notes.

When Ley came home, having run from the railway station in the rain, he was alarmed to see the light on in his front room, but surprised even more, to hear the sound of classical music drifting through the window.

"There's a young gentleman here to see you," his housekeeper explained, helping him out of his wet trench coat while she leant forward to whisper: "A baron, no less."

Perplexed, Ley walked to the parlour, wiping the raindrops

from his black hair and round, rimless glasses. He should have been incensed to see the stranger playing his piano, but entranced by the sweet strains of *Beethoven's Moonlight Sonata*, he moved quietly into the room and signalled for von Braun to continue as he sat down to enjoy it. As soon as the last *pianissimo* chords were played, however, Wernher was up and out of his seat, rushing to apologise.

"Mr Ley, please let me say how sorry I am for this terrible intrusion, but it was imperative that I see you."

Short of someone having died, Ley could not imagine what could possibly have been so important, but the copy of Oberth's book the young man now had in hand, explained it all.

"My name is von Braun, sir," Wernher continued, clutching the treasured volume even tighter. "And I would do anything, including making an ass of myself, to be a part of Dr Oberth's rocket project. I was late hearing of it and was afraid I'd miss the boat if I didn't come directly to see you."

Wernher's bright-eyed enthusiasm was appealing, but when he tripped over the rug and laughed on his way to shake hands, Ley was won over completely. Six hours later, having talked till midnight about the planets and stars, the deal was sealed and von Braun left the house having consolidated a friendship that would stand the test of time, not only in Germany, but across the other side of the world for the next 40 years. It started with Ley's promise to introduce him to Oberth and an invitation to join their Spaceflight Society. Its members, however, were quick to find one of von Braun's few faults.

"He's very clumsy with his hands," Oberth remarked privately to Ley when Wernher used a hammer rather than a precision tool for rocket assembly. "And there's a good deal of arrogance about him and his writing style."

As part of his resume, Wernher had presented his article on astronomy that had been published in his school newspaper.

It was a complex subject, and although impressed, Oberth suspected that its punchy simplicity was not a mark of good journalism, but von Braun's inference that there was no point going into greater detail with readers who could not possibly understand it.

That was presumptuous, and with their society preferring not to patronise the public, Oberth was weighing up von Braun's worth. His silence was disturbing, and construing it as genuine concern, Ley spoke up quickly on their recruit's behalf.

"We have to remember that it's just the arrogance of youth. You needn't worry. Life's bound to knock it out of him soon enough."

"Oh, I'm not worried," Oberth leapt in to say. "I was just thinking we might make good use of it."

Apart from conquering space, the rocketeers' priority was always money. They had none and were forever seeking financial support. The difficulty was that as introverted academics, none of them had the necessary flair to drum up public interest and donations, but Oberth was sure that this good looking, young aristocrat with his fast-talking panache would solve the problem.

It was not, however, what von Braun had in mind.

"One of Berlin's department stores wants us to set up a window display of interplanetary rockets and I need your help," Oberth put to him as his first assignment.

It was disappointing when von Braun was expecting deep and meaningful discussions about space. But like all else in life, money came first.

"Are you *sure* there's nothing more important I could do?" he said dispiritedly after his first few days of tedious duty.

In answer, Oberth slapped him companionably on the back.

"No, my boy, you're doing a splendid job just where you are. Keep up the good work."

As to that, von Braun had to wonder why he bothered enrolling at Charlottensberg Institute of Technology to attain his mechanical and aircraft engineering degree, when acting as Oberth's assistant meant merely being a street beggar. So far, he had stood eight hours a day, forefront of the display, doing nothing but scrounge money from housewives as they shopped.

"Did you know that just one of these interplanetary rockets will cost 7000 marks and take a year to build?" he said to every woman who walked past. When they invariably stopped to chat, he would continue: "But it's worth every penny for the sake of our Germany's future and we were hoping you might like to donate."

The contribution tin he was holding in his hand continually rang with the clank of coins; none of the ladies understanding a word he was saying about space, but happy to help because of his handsome face.

For von Braun, however, it took longer for the penny to drop – to understand that Oberth was using him; not for his brain, but for his effusive, arrogance-edged charm that women found so attractive.

More offended than flattered, he finally confronted Oberth.

"I'm not studying physics to be a salesman."

His small outburst of pride did little more than raise Oberth's eyebrows: "Well, of course you're not, dear boy. But I say . . . why limit yourself to being good at just one thing, when you obviously excel at both?"

To this, von Braun had no logical answer, so he let Oberth keep talking.

"Don't think, for one moment, that I underestimate your intelligence. I intend to make good use of it just as soon as we get enough money in our coffers. Thanks to you, it's pouring in by the bucket load, but remember – we dreamers have to be practical. Before we conquer space, we have to sell it to the public and I'll wager you'll always be the best man for the job."

Thus encouraged, von Braun got into the swing of his department store pitch.

"I bet that the first man to walk on the moon is alive today somewhere on this Earth!" he said with fresh gusto to the next person passing.

It was a shot in the dark to grab their attention. He had no idea as he spoke that a boy named Neil had just been born to the Armstrongs of Wapakoneta, Ohio.

CHAPTER

FIVE

THE PRESSURE WAS MOUNTING as the premiere of Lang's movie approached. Nothing was ready and Oberth suddenly disappeared. Having realised that, as yet, a liquid-fuel rocket was beyond him, he made himself scarce and foisted the upcoming failure of the rocket launch on his second-in-command, Rudolf Nebel – a former fighter pilot and engineer who had pioneered the use of unguided air-launched signal rockets from his WWI bi-plane.

Although the rocketeers' respect for Oberth remained intact, von Braun was shocked to find his mentor's office empty.

"Where is he?" he asked in dismay.

"Gone back to Romania and his old teaching job," Nebel replied, having had more time to digest the desertion. "But don't worry, he's left us his notes."

Those notes were little to go on having proved inadequate for Oberth, but with the movie opening in two weeks, the men who remained had no choice but to band together and do their best.

WHAT A FIZZER!

the newspaper headline read when their rocket launch proved a disaster.

Yet, far from being discouraged, they decided to stay together and work on Oberth's concept until they got it right.

It was hard to do without money. Due to the worldwide Depression, there was a terrible lack of it, and with the public's mood swinging from science-fiction to surviving starvation, The Spaceflight Society was hanging by a thread. The diminishing group of diehard rocketeers among them, however, pushed on and formed a small company to continue Oberth's experiments alone. It all sounded so grand, but the reality really wasn't.

"Well what do you think of it?" Nebel said when he showed von Braun their new facility.

As the senior of the group, Nebel had worked a miracle by talking the municipal authorities into letting them lease very cheaply an abandoned ammunition storage depot on the outskirts of Berlin. It was no more than a field full of rusty airplane hangars sprouting among knee-high weeds, but it was theirs in which to work their magic.

Von Braun patted his hand proudly on its sagging gates.

"It's fantastic!" he said, standing back to admire the freshly painted sign Nebel had hung above them:

ROCKET FLIGHT FIELD
BERLIN

It was a bold, new name befitting what they believed would be the immensity of their achievements. Here, they would be working, quite literally, at the grassroots of a new age, and Wernher was thrilled.

... oOo ...

"It's a dump!" his father disagreed, when he came to inspect the new site.

He could never understand his son's mad obsession with rockets and was embarrassed to see him socialise with the city's riff-raff – that new breed of unemployed businessmen in rags who had hit rock bottom due to the Depression and were now occupying the Rocket Field premises as a free workforce. They were a peculiar bunch of seeming ne'er-do-wells with only their joblessness and fascination for rocketry in common; all of them expending what was left of their dignity on this new-fangled field of science.

At least he was relieved that Wernher was keeping his options open by continuing his university studies while lending his rocketeer friends a hand during his every spare moment. It was a luxury that few, like sons of aristocrats, could afford and one which earned Wernher his nickname of *Sonny Boy*. As the junior among the erudite group of unemployed scientists, mechanics and engineers, he had no choice but to grin and bear it, all the while aware that the border-line term of affection implied that they appreciated his tireless work, but begrudged the fact that, for him, times weren't *quite* so hard and were not costing him his pride.

"With their brains, you'd think they'd be able to get a proper job," the baron said, shaking his head in disbelief as he watched the sad stream of shabby scientists shuffle through the Rocket Field gates.

"They're not down and outs!" Wernher flashed back defensively when he saw the disapproval on his father's' face. "They're all brilliant professionals reduced to poverty thanks to lesser men's misjudgement."

The baron considered taking exception to his tone but was so impressed by the conviction behind his son's argument that he let him continue.

"We're offering them nothing but food and shelter for their expertise, which in better times, we could never afford. Without it, we'd be lost and I find it hard to comprehend what they must be suffering. As far as I'm concerned . . . if we achieve nothing else with these rocket experiments of ours, at least we'll know we've done some good by giving them a roof over their heads."

Suddenly ashamed and extremely proud of his boy, the baron reached for his wallet.

"Will this help?" he asked, handing him the large wad of money.

And Wernher smiled, because despite his father's pompous pretensions and professed disdain for democracy, he could always be relied upon to do the right thing.

"It will, indeed . . . thank you, father," he replied, moved to the extent that water welled in his eyes.

At the sight of it, Baron Magnus baulked. "Well that's enough of that!" he growled, rushing to stop sentiment shattering his hard shell. "Now show me the rest of this facility of yours."

... oOo ...

In the adjoining field, Wernher could see three of his associates – Klaus Riedel, Willy Ley and Nebel standing ready to conduct their latest rocket ignition test.

"Ah, perfect timing," he said, guiding his father in their direction. "Come on over with me and I'll introduce you."

Unfortunately, it was a meeting minus social pleasantries. By the time they reached the three men on the other side of the compound, Riedel already had a gasoline-soaked rag in hand and was about to light it.

"Open the valves and let the propellants into the motor!" he called out to Nebel with sudden urgency, before he hurled the lighted torch over the motor's mouth and shouted: *"Take cover!"*

The three of them ducked behind a barrier, while taken totally by surprise, Wernher only had time to push his bewildered father to the ground and fling himself flat on top of him for protection.

Sparks flew and the jet ignited with an ear-rupturing thunderclap that roared around them for 90 seconds before the rocket-motor's fuel ran out and left them lying stunned in the reverberating silence. When they coughed their way clear of the fumes, all five men were beside themselves: four of them with immeasurable joy and Baron Magnus with red-hot rage.

"This is a *death trap!*" he exclaimed as he struggled to his feet and brushed the dust from his pin-stripe suit. "Are you fools!"

Scooping the baron's hat from the dirt, Ley handed it back to him and replied:

"Close to, I'm afraid, sir, but we're sorry you got caught up in it."

Baron Magnus was not appeased by the apology.

"You should be arrested for attempted murder," he fired back, "or for committing suicide yourselves . . . hardly the responsible actions of sensible men."

"There's always danger in the unknown," Wernher jumped in to say. "But don't you see that's what makes it so exciting? Being sensible doesn't come into the equation."

"*What* equation?" the baron scoffed, as he shook the soot from his homburg and put it firmly back on his head.

"Oberth's!" all four men in their lab coats chorused, while Nebel went on to say:

"And its three-part premise: that machines can be built to go beyond our atmosphere; that man can leave Earth's gravity and survive in space; and that its exploration can be profitable."

At last, this was a word the baron understood and as a banker by trade, his interest was piqued.

"Well that's the first rational thing you've said and the only reason I'll allow my son to continue with this project."

That being said, he took himself off in his black Mercedes, not saying a polite 'goodbye' or stopping to wish them well.

"Sorry about that, Sonny Boy," Nebel said as they watched him go, but Wernher could not believe his luck.

For as furious as his father was, he had not forbidden him to stay or demanded his money back, despite the fact that they had just come close to killing him.

CHAPTER

SIX

THE MONEY HE GAVE THEM HELPED, but the 5000 marks donated soon after by Lieutenant Colonel Karl Becker, head of army ballistics and munitions, went even further.

"I'm interested in the military potential of your solid and liquid-fuel rockets for assembly-line production," he said when he secretly kicked the money their way.

It was not his habit to rort the system, but as a forward-thinking artillery engineer, he believed it was for Germany's benefit and the best way to skirt any red tape that might hinder the process. In him, at last, the rocketeers had a key supporter and funding source to validate their dreams; sadly, not as they would have wished – as a means to wing their way to the moon, but for a new weapon of mass destruction. It posed a moral dilemma, but beggars could not be choosers.

When Becker's black sedan first drove into their compound and circled to a stop in front of them, it had all been very suspicious, He and his offsider, Captain Walter Dornberger, got out of the car dressed in civilian clothes, but their soldier's air and technical talk of thrust balance and test data left no doubt in the rocket men's minds that they were military experts with an agenda.

Becker explained when he went with them to their office:

"Our mission must remain top secret because we are acting in direct defiance of the Versailles Treaty which forbids Germany's production of arms."

Here, he paused to throw them a wink. "But nobody said anything about rockets."

The trust he was putting in them was gratifying, so Nebel and von Braun gave him and his assistant a guided tour of the Rocket Field grounds and treated them to a sample of their experiments. They were faulty in the extreme, but showed promise, and Becker was determined to get in on the ground floor.

Dornberger, however, had second thoughts when one of the rocket blasts knocked him off his feet.

"Are you hurt?" Becker asked as he helped him back up onto them.

"No, sir," he lied, shaking his head clear of its ear-ringing disorientation, "but my pride's taken a bit of a beating."

For this reason, Becker felt he owed his junior officer an explanation.

"I don't like the state of Germany's affairs," he whispered to exclude Nebel and von Braun from the conversation. "When our crumbling Weimar Republic finally falls, it'll leave a gaping hole for something far worse to fill. From here on in, it's every faction for itself and *this* . . . ," he said, gesturing towards the small Mirak1 rocket fizzling out in front of them, "is going to be our way of staying a step ahead."

As always, Becker had the army's best interests at heart. Its forces had held firm through the republic's ups and downs and it was now ready to take a more assertive role in order to achieve its aims: to finally quash the Versailles Treaty, rearm the nation and catapult their country back up to where it belonged as a lead player on the world stage.

The failed Kapp Putsch to oust the republic back in 1920 had taught the army to distance itself from extremist groups, but now there was a new boy on the block whose shrill and surprisingly popular Nazi Party was forcing them to sit up and take notice; and more importantly, to grab an advantage that would see them powerfully placed in Hitler's inevitable regime. If they couldn't do it with brute force, then they would achieve it with technology.

It was a brains-over-brawn strategy that would have worked had it not been based on a lie; had Nebel not boasted prematurely that Oberth's rocket was almost perfected.

"But it's nowhere *near it!* You'll have us all cited for fraud," Ley warned when Nebel's lecture at Berlin's Post Office auditorium provoked a flurry of excitement among the assembly of army officers and members of the press.

Although it was Nebel's job to drum up interest in their work, he had been selling it like a sideshow of late and the rocketeers were concerned.

"Don't worry. It's all just a game," he said glibly. "I'm merely positioning us to best play it."

None of this sat well with his fellow rocket pioneers who were anxious about total commitment to the military and the brutal consequences of breaking promises to powerful people.

Despite the failure of their rocket launch at Lang's movie premiere, Nebel had continued to seek sponsorship from the influential – a mixed bag of good and bad. There had been no harm in him approaching Albert Einstein, but to ask for help from such bloody-minded enforcers as Adolf Hitler and Dr Joseph Goebbels was extremely unwise. Already, Ley, von Braun and renowned science writer Max Valier were mumbling among themselves about Nebel's showcasing of false hopes and the danger involved.

"Since when have *you* been afraid of *anything?*" Nebel

interrupted to challenge Valier, who had recently made the 1930 headlines for test-driving a rocket car prototype powered by unstable liquid fuel. "Being blown apart in the name of science has never fazed you before."

A month later, Nebel was very sorry he said it because his prediction came true.

"He's dead!" young engineers, Arthur Rudolph and Walter Riedel came from their Heylandt laboratory to tell them. But still pale and visibly shaken, they found it hard to speak. Riedel took a deep breath and finally managed to stammer:

"One of his alcohol-fuelled rockets exploded in his face. He died in my arms not more than an hour ago."

Riedel was devastated by the experience. He had never seen death at such close quarters and was overwhelmed at the prospect of Rudolph and he having to continue their work at the liquid-oxygen-equipment laboratory alone.

While all at the Rocket Field stood in stunned silence, machinist Klaus Riedel, related to Walter Riedel only through their shared love of rocketry, took advantage of the sad situation to ram home his point.

"Which only goes to prove the very volatile nature of our work and how *imperative* it is not to rush it."

At that poignant moment, a rebuttal from Nebel was not appropriate, but it came two days later at Valier's funeral.

"Nevertheless, we have to move it along before we're all dead," he said, knowing that what little was left of Valier's body to mourn was working against him and his efforts to push their rocket group forward.

The problem was that Nebel had trouble telling the truth and his growing reputation as a conman was destroying the rocketeers' credibility. He had fast-talked his way into high places by promising immediate results at the expense of safety and now, having underplayed essential experiments and their inherent dangers, his hard-sell was backfiring, and those who were once bluffed by it were no longer taking his claims seriously.

There was no question of Nebel's dedication, but now knowing that his good intentions were doing them damage, a gloomy mood prevailed as they stood at Valier's grave.

"What will you do now?" von Braun quietly pulled Arthur Rudolph aside to ask.

It was obvious that 25-year-old mechanical engineer Rudolph was unnerved by his mentor's death. His pallid face still showed the strain of feeling physically sick at the gruesome memory of their blood-splattered laboratory.

"Well, one thing's for sure," he rallied to say as they strolled from the cemetery. "I don't intend to give up. Valier wouldn't want me to."

More than that, Valier would have been extremely proud of him for soon after developing a safer version of his engine that successfully powered the newly invented Heylandt Rocket Car.

"I only wish Valier were here to see it," von Braun said, congratulating Rudolph when the vehicle and its ground-breaking engine were exhibited at Berlin's Tempelhof Airport in August 1930.

To this, however, Rudolph merely shrugged.

"So what if it's a technical triumph? Its prohibitive fuel costs make it totally impractical."

When the rocket car's production was discontinued, Rudolph felt dejected, but soon decided to pour his passion into something far greater. In 1931, long before it was opportunistic to do so, he signed up with the Nazi Party with a zeal that matched his love of rocketry and a pledge of undying devotion.

"Why?" von Braun asked in astonishment when they were all on the brink of such exciting advances in science and Hitler, with his band of street thugs, seemed so backward.

Wernher had not, nor ever would have the vaguest interest in politics and even if he did, he was sure he would never rest his hopes on such a pack of Neanderthals. Still naïve at the age of 19, he had no idea of Rudolph's dual agenda: his determination, as an engineer, to retain the subsidy his and Riedel's experiments were receiving from Hitler's SA Brownshirts; and his secret guilt for not being averse to their ethnic-cleansing policy.

It was a little disturbing for von Braun to now have a friend firmly ensconced in their ranks. Certainly, his 'old school' family would not approve, but the strong, practical streak in his nature told him not to cut ties with anyone who might come in handy someday. If Hitler proved to be all he professed at his manic rallies, he could well turn out to be a blessing and the Rocket Field's best source of funding for the future.

Expediency was the key for all concerned, and backing Nebel's view that they must move ahead, Becker started by slowly easing him out of the picture in favour of von Braun, whose selling skills and similar enthusiasm for the subject seemed tempered with better sense. Although still wet behind the ears, von Braun had adopted only the best of Nebel's entrepreneurial style, and Becker saw in him the seeds of something great.

CHAPTER

SEVEN

HIS PARTIALITY WAS PERHAPS HELPED along by von Braun's pedigree and the fact that it facilitated a finer education. It was still a work in progress and von Braun was squeezing his mechanical engineering degree in between helping out at the Rocket Field.

When first setting up their headquarters at the old ammunition dump, Nebel and Klaus Riedel had been forced to bunker down for the winter, cooking on an old potbelly stove and sleeping on freezing floorboards while they strived to develop their pint-sized, liquid-fuel rocket dubbed The Mirak.

Back then, all von Braun had time to do was help them set up shop and clean the place on weekends, because he was committed to work at Borsig Automotive Factory as part of his 'practical workshop' studies at Berlin's Royal Technical College. For this reason, many on site begrudged him playing such a key role at their rocket facility and being considered one of its central figures.

"He's just a rich kid living on his father's money," said those associates less fortunate, who had already achieved their engineering degrees and were less popular and poorer as a result.

Yet, as much as they resented Wernher's good fortune, they found him difficult to dislike with his bright-eyed enthusiasm, charm and constant willingness to share a joke. No one could deny that his mere presence pepped up the place and made him the perfect spokesman whenever important people came to peruse their work.

"I'd love to stay and chat with you a little longer, but I'm afraid I have to go," von Braun said, when midway through showing one such guest around the facility, he realized he was running late for work.

To compensate for leaving the visiting VIP in the lurch, he handed him the display model of their Mirak rocket and turned to leave.

"*Young man!*" the dignitary called out after him, shocked to be given such short shrift. "Are you or are you not wanting to sell this project of yours to me?"

Courtesy had Wernher stop to answer: "I am indeed, sir, but I'm obliged to work a second job and can't imagine that you, as a businessman, would appreciate an employee who was not prepared to honour his commitments. I am, however, here again tomorrow if you'd care to continue our conversation."

"Well I *never!*" the man huffed in disbelief as Wernher then ran to catch the tram taking off from its stop outside the Rocket Field gates.

Left standing dumbfounded in the middle of the rocket firing range, his guest wasn't sure whether to be incensed or impressed by his audacity, but when von Braun leapt on the passing streetcar and then turned with a wide smile to wave goodbye, he decided not to hold it against him and to return the next day as the beguiling young baron suggested.

Wernher had pushed his luck to stick to his strict schedule. He bought a ticket from the conductor and took his seat on the streetcar bound for the suburb of Tegel. Most days his trip to the Borsig factory there was much longer because it started from his family home in the far more exclusive Tiergarten district; but either way, it was a bit of a bore for someone who liked sleeping in and was now forced to get up before the crack of dawn each day. All his life Wernher loathed doing it, yet it never crossed his mind that the family's servants, who had to rise at 4am to prepare his breakfast and pack his lunch, might feel the same way.

Fortunately, it was a burden they had to bear for only six months longer because Wernher was already halfway through his obligatory stint at the Locomotive and Heavy Machinery works. There, he was expected to punch in at 7am and work till 4pm and to do it on the dot to appease its foreman, who was a stickler for punctuality, among other more tedious procedures.

"You won't be treated any differently from our other apprentices," he warned von Braun from the start. "And you'll have to join our metalworkers' union."

Being the only baron to bless its ranks did not bother Wernher, but the way the foreman spoke to him about his work did.

"What in the hell do you call this von Braun!" he demanded, having earlier in the day handed his new apprentice a lump of iron the size of a soccer ball and ordered him to file it, by hand, into a perfect cube.

Apparently Wernher had failed and had to continue the exercise for eight weeks until he got it right.

"Go on . . . do better!" was his daily incentive from the foreman, until he whittled it down to the size of a perfectly proportioned die and his project was declared complete.

What a monumental waste of time, von Braun thought, but refrained from saying, when he saw the look of smug satisfaction on the foreman's face; for he had taught his apprentice the valuable lesson of patience, perseverance and fine craftsmanship which would serve von Braun well for the rest of his life.

"I really enjoyed getting down to brass tacks and working with the men on the floor," he confessed to his parents at the end of his factory training.

His liberal thinking pleased his mother, but his father rolled his eyes when he saw that his son's were filled with new-found fire at the prospect of becoming a blue-collar worker.

"It's dirty-hands engineering and I *love* it!" Wernher went on, rubbing his own together at the thought of all they could create.

CHAPTER

EIGHT

WITH ALL HE HAD GOING ON, those hands of his were full, but that was the way von Braun liked it – living life hard and fast, never wasting a single second or rejecting any far-fetched idea; and because he was obsessed with speed and all things aviation, he decided to add yet another string to his bow.

"I want to learn to fly," he told his parents when he visited them at their new country manor.

The 1932 German presidential elections had made the von Brauns reassess their real estate. With the news that the Nazis had won more than 100 seats in parliament, an alarming excitement beset Berlin. Despite the fact that it did not secure them the majority and von Hindenburg still scraped into power, it was obvious that a second round of votes would soon see Hitler take over as Chancellor, and Baron Magnus felt downright depressed.

With his ethics firmly rooted in proud Prussian tradition, he could no longer ignore the murderous German era in which they were all now embroiled. Especially when every step his son Wernher was taking seemed to be moving him towards involvement with the National Socialists and the building of their military might.

"Oh come now father, none of us take Hitler seriously with his little Charlie Chaplin moustache," Wernher reassured him. But the baron was not convinced when he knew that wiser men had succumbed to the dangerous Nazi leader's charms.

Already, Wernher's colleague Rudolf Nebel had applied to Hitler for financial help and had been refused. But Baron Magnus had no doubt that the up-and-coming dictator would soon make the rocketeers' ground-breaking work his focus, because despite his claims to the contrary, his main agenda was war. There was nothing the baron could do to stop his son getting caught up in it, other than try to divert his attention back to the simple life before it was too late.

"It's a lovely old Silesian estate," he announced to his family when he bought the large farm and adjoining village at Oberwiesenthal. "I suddenly had a yen to return to the country and I think it's now proper that we take a second family home away from Berlin."

For him, the timing was perfect – not only to remove his son from a volatile hot-spot, but to reconcile himself to being out of a job. Although still Germany's Minister for Agriculture, one of the *Raiffeisen* agrarian associations on whose board he sat had merged with another and made him redundant. While he licked his wounds, the wholesome, country life was the answer. Yet, Wernher had other ideas and chose not to live there permanently. Unlike his father, he was far from being fed up with the fast lane and could hardly wait to get on it.

It was handy, however, that their new family farm was so close to the Sailplane School at Grunau where Wernher planned to do his gilder plane training, so he decided to stay there for the three weeks it took to get his licence.

"Well your birthday's in a few days. Perhaps we can pay for your lessons as a present," his mother suggested, thrilled to see him and happier still to know that he'd lost none of his zest for life and learning.

Now that both he and Sigismund lived full-time in Berlin, Emmy had only her youngest, Magnus, living permanently at home and she missed her two older boys terribly. It did not surprise her, though, that Wernher wanted to strike out on his own.

"Thank you Mama, but I've managed to save the money myself over the last few months."

That was quite a feat, his parents realised, when the freelance articles on rocketry he was writing for the newspapers paid a pittance. For Wernher, however, it was now a point of principle that he pay his own way, if for no other reason but to prove that he could to those hardcore critics of his back at the Rocket Field.

Like all else he did in life, he went at it full-throttle, determined to be the best.

"Sorry I'm late," he apologised to his parents, when with a face glowing red from excitement and a day's dose of winter sun, he burst into the dining room to find that he had missed the family meal for the third time. "I wanted to stick around and help the other students' bungee-assisted takeoffs in the snow."

As always, he was just as interested in the dynamics of flight as the flying itself, and by the end of his course he mastered both. He would have indulged himself longer in the sport, had he not been obliged to fulfil his two-year national military training requirement. Now that he had his glider pilot licence, his choice of services was simple.

"I'm going to do it in two separate-year stints with the air force," he informed his father, who thoroughly approved as it was the only true option for aristocrats.

All augured well, and within several weeks Wernher was flying high and well on his way to winning his wings when he suddenly fell back to earth with a thud.

Conceit, for him, had never been an issue, but for the first time he found himself looking in the mirror and wondering why he wasn't measuring up. He had never lacked confidence before, but since meeting fellow flying student Hanna Reitsch, he was stumbling over himself and his words, and he could not think straight.

"*Wow!* Who is she?" he asked one of the other students when he first saw her stride onto the airfield rigged out in her leather jacket, with flying helmet and goggles in hand. The fact that she was a woman playing a man's game was astounding in itself, but her thick thatch of blonde hair and pretty, blue eyes made her phenomenal.

"Way out of *your* league," the student swiftly replied, knowing that Hanna was destined for great things and was already a favourite with flying aces far finer than them.

Wernher, however, was completely smitten and undeterred. For the first time, he spurned his own strong views to claim interest in Hitler because of her obsession with the man, figuring that if the moustachioed fanatic had won her over, he couldn't be all bad. Blind to reality, von Braun was bedazzled and on the back foot.

"Would you like to come out for drinks with me?" he asked her after they landed their respective planes and were off on weekend leave.

Seeing the tell-tale signs of infatuation in his eyes, Hanna took off her leather helmet and let loose a cascade of golden hair.

"I don't think so Wernher," she said with a sisterly smile. "But thanks all the same."

To be knocked back by the opposite sex was a new experience for von Braun. He had always held the upper hand in such matters and was thrown off by having lost it. He was never one to give up, however, so he tried his luck three more times before finally conceding defeat.

"You're barking up the wrong tree with that one," a wiser friend advised him. "And all this time I thought you were smart."

Being clever, however, did not necessarily mean worldly, and Wernher's blank expression begged for an explanation. Yet, in a day when speculation over such things stayed unspoken, it was hard for his friend to find the words.

"Let's just say . . . " he began awkwardly, "that she's the best man among us and probably shares our interests in every way."

It took a few moments for his implication to sink in and when it finally did, Wernher felt deeply embarrassed – not only about his own naivety, but for having put Hanna on the spot.

"Friends?" he said, stopping to shake her hand the next day before they again took to the skies. And at this, her pretty smile broadened with relief and the prospect of counting herself as one of his closest companions for many years to come.

That was, until they went their separate ways – von Braun tackling the heavens beyond the stratosphere, while Hanna mastered the sky beneath it; later to become Germany's most famous female aviator and test pilot, so trusted by Hitler that she was to make an eleventh-hour landing near his bunker to be near him when he died, before taking off again, amid Armageddon, to fly the last plane out of WWII Berlin.

But long before that future, von Braun had to laugh off having loved and lost, and although he did it with style, something about him changed. Perhaps it was a hardening of self against hurt, perhaps a shift to a new level of sophistication, or simply the fact that he had grown up and was feeling frustrated about still not being able to work on his rocketry on a full-time basis. Whatever it was made him restless, and with Berlin so unsettled, he decided to transfer from its technical university to the Swiss Institute of Technology in Zurich.

"I don't understand why," his mother argued, not having heard that his university had temporarily closed its doors due to the savage brawling between its Nazi and communist factions; and that now, as the hub of National Socialist agitation, it was no longer safe to be on campus.

This, however, did not seem to worry Wernher as much as his own gloomy mood. It was rare for someone with his optimistic nature to be in such a funk and he was eager to pull himself out of it.

"I don't know," he said with a shrug. "I just think the change might do me and my studies good."

For him to crave something new was not unusual, but Emmy was not convinced. She knew her son better than she knew herself and could see a subtle difference in him that threatened to put a distance between them, not only in the physical kilometres he was suggesting, but in his emotions. The certain arrogance he had adopted from his flying training did not bother her, but she was concerned that he was sounding more clipped and cold-minded. It was hard for her to admit, but the time had come to let him go and to trust that he would take the right path.

CHAPTER

NINE

"**J**UST GIVE ME A COUPLE OF SAUSAGES and some mashed potato," von Braun said in English to the Irish woman serving behind the counter of the Swiss institute's cafeteria.

Most people there were not so fluent in the language, so he was surprised when the stranger standing next to him suddenly turned in excitement to speak.

"Are you British?" the medical student asked with an American twang, tinged by a touch of the Mediterranean.

"No!" von Braun denied emphatically. "I'm German."

"Ah, then that explains it . . . I *thought* your English was too good."

They laughed together in response and soon, he and Greek-born Constantine Generales from New York became fast friends.

"But all this talk about rockets and space is ridiculous," Generales said over lunch a week later.

As a Harvard graduate, four years older than von Braun, he was keen to set him straight. Wernher, however, was nowhere near being put in his place and had a persuasive argument to make sure he wasn't.

"I think someone other than I might disagree with you," he replied, taking the letter he recently received from Albert Einstein out of his pocket and putting it down in front of his friend.

It had been written in reply to the one Wernher had audaciously sent the professor two weeks earlier in which he discussed his theories of space travel and asked for Einstein's input.

As Generales scanned the note's indecipherable formulae for rocket propulsion, his eyebrows knitted in confusion, before shooting up an inch in surprise when he saw who signed it. Not only was he impressed by the famous man's signature, but by the fact that von Braun actually understood his unintelligible scribbling. He handed the letter back to his young German friend, suitably contrite and resolved to take him more seriously.

"Granted . . . I can't win 'em all," he conceded, "but if you're set on putting people on lunar flights, Wernher, you'd better try it out on mice as passengers first."

It was pragmatic thinking from a man whose medical training in cutting up cadavers made him immune to gore, but such cold-blooded experimentation was new territory for von Braun. Strangely enough, it did not seem to trouble him.

... oOo ...

"What do you think you're *doing!*" his landlady demanded, dropping her tea tray in dismay when she saw the blood-splattered walls in von Braun's room.

Generales stepped in quickly to explain, citing his medical studies as their excuse.

"Don't worry ma'am," he said, bending to pick up the broken china. "It's nothing sinister, I can assure you."

As an animal lover, however, she was mortified by the raw remnants of white mice clinging to the windows and wallpaper; their brutal deaths having been brought about by the specially mounted bicycle the two men had designed as a homemade centrifuge to simulate rocket takeoffs. On it, they had been sacrificing the lives of the tiny creatures by spinning the wheel on which they were running, faster and faster until their bodies burst apart and sprayed around the room.

"Monsters! Murderers of innocents!" she screamed, shaking her fist at them in an unholy fury.

In response to her attack, von Braun stood stunned. He had been so carried away with his experiments that he had completely forgotten himself and his standards and was shocked by her vile accusation. He never dreamed that in the years to come, the same would be levelled at him again, not merely blaming him for the murder of mice, but of men.

... oOo ...

The episode took the edge off his stay in Zurich and after only the first semester, he re-applied to his alma mater in Berlin as soon as the all-clear was given on its campus.

"But don't go straight back," Generales said, not wanting to lose contact with his new friend so soon. "Take a bit of a break and come to Greece with me for some fun."

To most young men, that equated to girls, but for the time being, von Braun had sworn off them. Not due to his failed dalliance with Hanna, but because they ranked low, at the moment, on his ladder of priorities.

"So, it's neither God nor girls for you," Generales said as he and Wernher sped down the road towards Athens in Generales' ancient open-top Opel.

"I don't like anyone or *anything* clipping my wings," Wernher confirmed, feeling exhilarated by the crisp wind whipping his face and the moral freedom of being an atheist. Both females and faith would come in abundance in the years to come, but for now, he had no time for either.

Why burden myself with the like when it's far more fun free-wheeling; he reasoned.

Or at least it would have been had their trip turned out better.

"Where did you get this broken down, old jalopy anyway?" he asked when the battered, green Opel broke down for the fourth time as they crossed The Alps.

Well used to his car's problems and finding their practical solutions, Generales continued to check the vehicle for leaks and barely batted an eye.

"Just shove some snow in the radiator to cool it down," he instructed.

Wernher shrugged off the simplicity of the remedy, collected a clump of snow from the roadside and fed it into the radiator. The impact was instant and he jerked his head out of harm's way when a hot, hissing shot of steam spewed out in revolt.

"Christ Almighty!" he yelped at having cut it so fine; and seeing him suck his scalded fingers as he petitioned The Divine, Generales laughed out loud.

"You can't have it both ways, you hypocrite. How can *He* help you if *He* doesn't exist?"

"Yes, well I like to keep Him on the back-burner, just in case," Wernher answered with a sheepish grin. But already his focus had shifted from his burnt fingers to his friend's application of basic mechanics, because without the benefit of more complicated procedures, the car bounced back to life at the turn of the key, when by rights its rusty remains should have been relegated to the junkyard.

Lesson learned, Wernher thought, pressing himself to remember it when it came to building rockets. If all else fails and clever facts and figures don't add up, simplicity could well be the answer. However, in their dilapidated, green Opel's case, it was only a short-term fix.

"Good ol' girl," Generales said, patting the cracked leather dashboard with affection after the engine obligingly turned over, but only 30 kilometres down the track, Wernher disagreed and called the car the Devil itself.

The first few times it broke down were amusing, but when one of its wheels fell off in Italy and they had to return to Rome in an unsuccessful hunt for a new bearing, both men lashed out and kicked it.

"We'll have to leave the heap of scrap metal at the garage here and pick it up on the way home," Generales grumbled as he bought tickets for the train to Brindisi and then for a boat to Corfu.

Fortunately, after two blissful weeks of Greek sun and hospitality, they were far more disposed to feel fondness for the vehicle again when they picked it up en route back to Berlin. It managed to stay in one piece and rattle its way home just in time to see the experimental Repulsor rocket launch at the flight field.

"It's spectacular!" Generales gasped in awe as they drove through the gates and saw the pencil-shaped projectile, fuelled by liquid oxygen, shoot up a record hundred metres and then descend with a small parachute attached to its tail.

Beside himself with joy at the sight, Wernher stood on his car seat and waved flat out to get Nebel and Riedel's attention.

"Come on . . . jump in the car," he called out to them. "It'll get us to its landing area faster."

There was no time for *'hellos'* and *'how was your holiday?'*, because when it came to the subject of missiles, all rocket men spoke the same language; not letting time spent apart stop them from getting straight back to business.

"That's launch No 87 and it was a *beaut*," Riedel boasted in a state close to ecstasy as they sped their way to where it touched down, the excitement on his face filling von Braun with envy for his studies and Mediterranean sojourn had made him miss them all.

Well to hell with the Greek Isles! he said to himself, for now he was sure that nothing . . . *nothing* compared to the sheer thrill and adventure of firing rockets into the unknown.

Although their test flights were still a case of hit and miss and the rockets themselves little more than workable toys, they were slowly making progress. Some of their launches over the past few months had sent their missiles, along with their spirits, soaring to all-time highs, while others, less successful, caused pandemonium.

"Cease and desist immediately!" Berlin's chief of police roared round in his Horch 400 squad car to bellow at them after one of their liquid-fuelled prototypes shot off course and landed slap-bang in the middle of his police headquarters down the road.

"It's not *funny*," the officer continued when he saw the smirk on Nebel's face.

Yet, with no one hurt, it was hard for the rocket men not to smile at the thought of all the startled faces at the police station, when a rocket suddenly crashed through their roof and lodged front and centre on the sergeant's desk.

The police chief, however, was not amused and wiped the smile off their faces by imposing a hefty fine on their premises and a ridiculous restriction on their rocket program. For an organisation as cash-poor as theirs, it posed a major problem.

"As does the fact that we need to work on a proper guidance system," Riedel said. "What's the point of achieving elevation and propulsion if our rockets are flying without direction?"

Lack of money, as always, was the issue, along with their dread of losing autonomy by relying solely on military funding. Unfortunately, without it, tackling expensive guidance systems and gyro stabilisation was not an option. The reality was that with their rockets roaming at will and their dreams of reaching space slowly dwindling, they had to accept the fact that their Rocket Field was no longer financially or technically viable.

"That is, unless we throw in our lot with Becker and totally commit to the army," von Braun put forward for the third time, because the writing was on the wall and he was frustrated by his colleagues' stubborn refusal to see it.

Each time, their response was the same: "We don't want to sell out our science to weaponry."

Von Braun felt the same way, but after thinking long and hard on the subject, he came down in favour of expediency. Yes, space was their ultimate goal, but they had no chance of ever reaching it unless they and their rockets changed trajectory. If a detour through war was their only road, he wanted to be the first to take it and was not prepared to let moral or political restraints get in his way.

69

PART TWO

ENGINEER OF WAR

CHAPTER

TEN

"**I** DARE YOU!" General Becker said to Nebel, Klaus Riedel and von Braun. "If you can successfully launch your Mirak II Repulsor rocket from our army's artillery range, I'll cover all expenses."

That was a tempting offer coming from the man who had just been promoted and put in charge of Germany's weapons development at the Kummersdorf testing facility just south of Berlin. In reality, Becker had little faith in the rocket's potential, but with Nebel constantly badgering him for army support and promising that their Mirak II could climb to an unbelievable altitude of eight kilometres, Becker decided to call his bluff.

"You'll have to transport the rocket to Kummersdorf by night," he insisted. "With Berlin's streets rife with civil unrest at the moment, a weapon being wheeled through them in blatant contravention of the Versailles Treaty will cause mayhem."

True to his order, the thin Mirak missile was strapped to the roof of a four-door sedan and driven through the city before dawn. Twenty-five kilometres further on, its tyres crackled to a quiet halt on Kummersdorf's gravel drive and an air of forbidden excitement pervaded.

"It better work," Becker mumbled, as he and Major Dornberger braced themselves against the winter chill. Huddled with hands in their coat pockets and huffing white steam as they spoke, they were not in the mood to be disappointed.

"And there it goes!" Nebel announced jubilantly after von Braun ignited the rocket with a flaming gasoline can at the end of a four-metre pole and stood back to avoid the burning flash.

Up it went in a gassy blaze of glory as the men cast their eyes skyward and collectively held their breath.

"Watch it *fly!*" Nebel continued in a running commentary as if the sheer weight of his sales pitch was making it perform.

Sadly, his next sentence was cut short, when having reached only an altitude of 30 metres, the missile suddenly swerved left and in horizontal mode sped with pinpoint accuracy to crash into the unused barracks at the far end of the facility.

Becker and Dornberger stood without emotion watching their building explode in a roaring ball of flame, before they turned and walked away without a word.

"Well, what happens now?" von Braun said, cringing at the possible consequences.

Two days later, the army officers put them in writing:

> *Our ordnance experts at Kummersdorf Weapons*
> *Development Centre have decided that the Mirak II*
> *is too unpredictable to meet our needs. Your services*
> *will no longer be required.*

"Please don't be so hasty," Nebel rushed to reassure them, but Becker was fed up – not only with their failed launch attempts, but with Nebel and his constant publicity-seeking that was jeopardising the army's strict confidentiality code. In regard to their secret military rearmament and its breeching of the

Versailles Treaty, the man was a loose cannon and they were glad to see the back of him.

They were prepared, however, to strike a compromise.

"We're willing to maintain minimal ties with your organisation," Major Dornberger got up from his desk to say, having only hours before been put in charge of Kummersdorf in lieu of Becker, who was needed further up the ranks of military hierarchy.

"And that tie . . . ," Dornberger went on to say, "will be with your fellow, von Braun."

If Nebel were offended, his pride did not allow him to show it, but the army's choice of candidates to carry on communications between them came as a shock to all the rocketeers who were older and more experienced.

"We want you," Becker and Dornberger later confirmed to von Braun in person, because from the very first time they visited the Rocket Field, their sights had been set on him. Not only was he young enough to be moulded in their military image, but he had the brains to match their expectations, not to mention a father whose position as the Reich Minister for Agriculture carried weight and social prestige, both of which augured well for the army and the upcoming dictator, Adolf Hitler.

"And we'll pay for your doctorate studies in physics at Berlin University as part of the deal," Becker added for further incentive.

Becker was an honorary professor of military sciences and technical physics there and was eager for von Braun to transfer from Charlottenburg Technical Institute so that he could keep him under his wing. It was too big an opportunity to knock back, so with some sense of guilt, von Braun signed the army ordnance contract to help develop liquid-fuel rocket motors and then quit his friends at the Rocket Field to move on to bigger things.

For a young man of 20 it was exciting, but scary territory, so von Braun was pleased to see a familiar face.

"I can't believe it!" he exclaimed with genuine joy when his old friend from the Heylandt Laboratory, Arthur Rudolph, walked in the door with Major Dornberger. He had not seen him since Valier's funeral and had no idea he was working at Kummersdorf.

"I thought you'd be happy to see each other," Dornberger said, sounding almost more pleased than they were by the reunion.

For far from being just a military expert in engineering, the major had quickly become the father figure of the Kummersdorf community, intent on running a tight ship that functioned like a family. Everyone respected him for that and liked him even more because he secretly shared their enthusiasm for future ventures in space.

"Dornberger's a top-notch engineer with the military clout and courage to push our dreams of space rocketry forward as soon as the time is right," physics student Ernst Stuhlinger said when he first welcomed von Braun to their Kummersdorf team.

Fresh-faced Stuhlinger was another clever candidate Dornberger had brought into the fold, and as an astute young man he had summed up the major's character perfectly, citing his strong qualities that would steer them successfully through the dark times ahead. For the time being, however, von Braun's future looked bright with Dornberger as his boss and friends, new and old, working at his side.

"So, what have you been up to?" he asked Rudolph when they were alone.

It was disappointing for him to hear only Nazi talk in response; a barrage of fighting words coming at him with a frenzied intensity that matched the fire in his old friend's eyes.

"Only Hitler has what it takes to push Germany back to its rightful place as world leader," Rudolph concluded with a fanatical flourish, which was a point von Braun was not prepared to argue when he found politics such a bore.

Instead, he lit a cigarette, calmly leant forward in his chair and answered:

"I couldn't care less about taking over the world, but if Hitler's interested in conquering the moon, he's got my vote."

ELEVEN

IT WAS IN THE DEPTH OF WINTER that President von Hindenburg reluctantly handed Germany over to Hitler. When he appointed him Chancellor in 1933, the country's parliamentary government effectively ceased and all went to hell.

The ruling class pretended not to see what was happening, but it could hardly fail to when Hitler's Blood War against the communists for having supposedly set fire to the Reichstag made headlines and the accounts of their brutal murders in Nazi revenge tripled newspaper circulation.

No intelligent man could plead innocence, particularly not Wernher, who was closer than most to the action, due to his father's political career. The Nazi torchlight parade went right past his Agricultural Ministry and no one could possibly have missed the news that the National Socialist Students' League marched straight to the stock exchange to scream their death threat at the brokers: *"Judah perish!"*

They were frightening times during which decent men's ideals could survive only if they did not scrutinise Hitler too closely; but by turning a blind eye, they tolerated him too long and were largely responsible for letting him run amok.

For the von Brauns, it got far more personal, because his rise to power put Baron Magnus out of a job.

"Here's to you, Papa," Siggy said, as he and Wernher lifted their glasses to toast their father's last day as a Reich minister.

Handing over his impressive portfolio to Hitler's agricultural activist, Walter Darré, should have been a sad affair, but the baron had never been a bitter man and was determined to make the most of it. Although he refused to join the Nazi Party on principle, he intended to take full advantage of its sway by staying at the hub of Germany's political and social scene.

"It means sacrificing my standards to hobnob with Hitler and his henchmen," he confessed to his family, "but if we're to ride out the storm, it's imperative that I do."

It was to this expedient school of thought that his son, Wernher, subscribed, more happily than his father, because barring morality, Hitler and his war machine looked the most likely to accommodate his dreams.

All in all, it was an auspicious time for von Braun to come of age. At 21, he had completed his obligatory two years of military service by attaining his glider and regular pilot licence. On top of which, he now had his bachelor's degree in mechanical engineering and was close to achieving a masters in aeronautical.

While he and his scientific companions went busily about their work at Kummersdorf, it was easy to ignore what was going on outside its apolitical walls. The boycott of Jewish stores and the purging of their people from the civil service, the judiciary and all theatres of learning and entertainment apparently escaped their notice, despite the fact that it brought a fair chunk of Germany's economy to its knees.

"That, however, will be remedied," the leader of the SS, Heinrich Himmler, assured the public in a radio broadcast. "For I am pleased to announce the grand opening of our first concentration camp at Dachau, which has been specially designed for political prisoners and other enemies of the state from whom we can expect an increase in production and an abundance of free labour."

The charade was over. Hitler discarded his non-threatening civilian clothes in favour of his SA brown shirt, and his Nazi hordes swarmed triumphantly into the streets, trampling the last remnants of the republic to death.

"The man's phenomenal," Wernher had to admit after battling his way through the milling Berlin crowds to meet his father for lunch.

The baron had been keen to catch up with his son on his fleeting visit to the city but was horrified to hear the sincerity behind Wernher's words.

"Don't tell me you've been brainwashed by that dangerous man," he admonished, as he signalled to the waiter for service. "I credited you, of *all* people, with more sense."

Wernher glanced at the menu and replied quite openly: "So did I and I'm as surprised as you. I was never one of Hitler's fans, but he's proved me wrong with the great strides he's already made to get Germany back on its feet."

"Admirable, I agree, if it stopped at that, but the man's after world domination and doesn't seem to care how he does it."

"That's ridiculous," Wernher scoffed. "You know as well as I that he's always been adamant about wanting peace, as do all veterans from the Great War trenches."

The baron stiffened in response. He did not care to be patronised and could not believe that his brilliant son had allowed himself to be misled. Yet, tempted as he was to call him a fool, he thought it wiser to water down his retort.

"You know, I've heard that the Berlin art gallery now has a huge portrait of Hitler in shining armour," he said, as he calmly flapped open his napkin and put it on his lap.

"Men don't wear armour, my boy, unless they intend to fight."

Sober words that snapped Wernher back to his senses. He was sorry, therefore, to hear that his old colleague Nebel had signed up with the Nazi Party when he, himself, decided to hang back; more so, from practicality than heeding his father's advice. With his army-related business trips picking up pace and his liquid-fuel experiments at Kummersdorf starting to pay off, he simply did not have time for swastikas and silly salutes.

… oOo …

"I've decided to use an alcohol concentration of 75 percent," he stated to his fellow engineers in regard to the development of their 330-pound thrust, liquid-oxygen/alcohol motor. "It's the obvious oxidiser and I believe, the only way to go."

"But it's dangerous and hard to handle," Ernst Stuhlinger argued back.

"Perhaps, but I'm familiar with it and feel more confident of its results."

On this point, von Braun would not budge, which was a quirk in his nature that baffled his colleagues. For the innovator they knew he was, it seemed odd that he often shied away from broaching new territory, insisting instead on treading the well-travelled path in rocket development. Whether it was out of loyalty to his hero Oberth's theories or fear of stepping out of his comfort zone, he refused to even consider the other nitric acid propellant combinations that other rocket experimenters around the world were soon to examine.

"It's best to stick with what you know," he said in validation, when to everyone's surprise, his first test with the new engine at Kummersdorf was a complete success.

Setbacks, however, were quick to follow, with frozen valves, ignition explosions and fire in the cable ducts posing a major problem. He was determined, though, not to let the team down, so while working on their solutions, he also put vigorous effort into developing test instrumentation for the charting of thrust-time curves, temperatures and pressures as Becker and Dornberger initially requested.

It was part of his job to keep them happy, but he became perturbed when they and the army, as a whole, suddenly took a hard line with all amateur rocket groups outside the Kummersdorf system. Because they were inciting unwanted publicity, the army resolved to harass them out of existence; and although von Braun had already deserted his friends at the old Rocket Field, he hated seeing it happen.

To keep the process civil while removing all signs of rocketry from public view, Becker herded most of von Braun's old colleagues into the aircraft instrument division of Siemens – the main player of the electrical industry that kept cordial relations with Kummersdorf. To know that they were safely employed and within reach if he should need them, went a long way to put von Braun's mind at ease.

Sadly, there was nothing he could do to stop Nebel being publicly discredited after he was caught embezzling money from the Rocket Field coffers, but when Wernher's ex-associate engineer Rolf Engel was arrested for treason, he saw red.

"All he did was try to set up a harmless, little rocket group of his own. What's wrong with that?" he blustered as he burst unannounced into Dornberger's office and slammed his angry fist down on his desk.

Dornberger was unmoved by his temper tantrum and merely moved his teacup out of harm's way.

"Not that simple, I'm afraid Wernher," he explained. "Your former associate is suspected of collaborating with the Soviets."

This, von Braun found hard to believe, but because he trusted Dornberger implicitly, he had to take his word for it. It came as a relief, however, when the evidence against Engel proved too flimsy and the judge dismissed his case.

"They're not going to get away with it that easily," Engel swore to von Braun on his release, because as a result of his six weeks spent in their rat-ridden jail, he had contracted jaundice and was gravely ill.

"I hold Becker and Dornberger personally responsible," he added with a hacking cough.

"Surely not?" Wernher answered, for as far as he was concerned, both men had always acted as gentlemen and treated him well. "If you like, I could speak to them on your behalf."

Engel gave a snort of contempt, as amused as he could be under the circumstances by his friend's naivety.

Wernher refrained from taking exception, for Engel was ill and deserved the benefit of the doubt. His sympathy, however, stopped at Engel's next words:

"I'm done with good intentions and I'm going to hit them where it hurts by taking all I know to the Nazis and signing up as an officer for the SS."

"Don't be an idiot!" Wernher threw at him derisively.

Such hard-line reproof coming from the ever-affable von Braun took Engel aback. Yet, hardly contrite, he instantly retaliated, pointing an accusing finger.

"Well you certainly can't talk, when you were happy enough prancing around in SS uniform yourself not so long ago."

Von Braun's brief stint with the SS Horseback Riding Unit had been nothing but a fleeting aberration. He was surprised that Engel even remembered it, let alone was prepared to use it against him.

"That was different . . . just a whim. Back then, I wasn't working with weapons," he said, stumbling over his reply and wondering whether he would ever live down the mistake he made at university by joining the riding school's affiliated ranks for a few, short weeks.

At the time, it seemed innocent enough as one of his obligatory, extra curricula activities. It had been hard to resist when SS Reichsfuhrer Himmler was going all out to woo Germany's young equestrian blue-bloods, appealing to their vanity by putting them in dashing uniform. Von Braun had taken the bait, but ever since, felt slightly ashamed. Certainly, his family did not approve and he was only glad that he destroyed the striking photograph of his SS-uniformed-self on horseback, which he considered sending them to take pride of place on their mantelpiece.

"I was there purely for riding lessons," he lied, knowing as soon as the words left his lips that they were laughable, for as a member of the aristocracy, horse riding ran in his veins and was mastered at the age of 10.

But why should I feel guilty von Braun then asked himself defensively. Most army officers and professors with whom he worked found Nazism acceptable and even General Becker, who he greatly admired, boasted about his good rapport with Hitler.

The young Baron von Braun, however, was rolling along with the Reich purely out of indifference and for a zealot like Engel that wasn't good enough.

"Well if you haven't got the guts to make a stand one way or the other, then *I have*," he cut through von Braun's introspection to say; and the fact that he said it, put a lifelong rift between them.

CHAPTER

TWELVE

FOR THE FIRST TIME IN HIS LIFE, von Braun was making enemies. Hitler's savage regime was forcing people to take sides, which made it hard for Wernher to remain his all-round, popular self. The extraordinary work he was doing and the brilliance it entailed put him in the spotlight, inciting envy and drawing attention from those waiting to see which way he would jump. All he really wanted was to run his own race, but with few having the luxury of fence-sitting, he had to protect his dreams of space by making it an art.

"It'd probably be better if we put you in army uniform," newly-promoted Colonel Dornberger suggested to him when Hitler was due to make his second inspection tour of Kummersdorf.

The first time he came, accompanied by Minister of the Interior Hermann Goering, von Braun was shuffled to the side and went completely unnoticed in his civilian attire. That was a strategic mistake, Dornberger now realised, for the Fuhrer seemed drawn to young men in uniform, and rigging von Braun out in military regalia might well prove their major drawcard.

"The only way we can secure the funds we need is to get the nod from the man at the top," Dornberger explained. "Hitler's it, so see what you can do to impress him."

After his encounter with Engel, however, von Braun came back with a flat refusal.

"I'll do anything that's required of me, but I won't do it in uniform," he stated and with the Fuhrer's cavalcade due to arrive at any minute, Dornberger had no time to argue.

It made no difference anyway, for Hitler was a hard nut to crack. With war not on the immediate horizon, liquid-fuel rockets were not his priority and as the master of 'talking up a storm', himself, he proved impervious to Dorberger's glib guarantees of their future importance.

"I'm not pouring money into a bottomless pit," Hitler decreed, thoroughly unenthused by the rocket show they put on and not swayed in the least by Deputy Fuhrer Rudolph Hess' opinion to the contrary.

For a second time, the Fuhrer and his entourage left the facility without even glancing in von Braun's direction.

"It's of no concern," Wernher said to Dornberger later. After singing Hitler's praises to his father and crediting him with more foresight, he had been disappointed when he saw the man in person. "I didn't realise he was such a shabby-looking character."

Von Braun genuinely did not understand what all the fuss over the Fuhrer was about. For a time, disillusion set in and after spending a year tinkering with liquid-fuel rockets in a concrete pit on Kummersdorf's artillery range, he had little success and began to flounder. Seeing his decline, Dornberger decided to do something about it.

"I'm bringing you in some help," he said, showing a new man to the testing ground.

When Wernher looked up from his work, his face broke into a radiant smile.

"No need for introductions," he said, striding over to shake hands with engineer Walter Riedel, who had worked closely with mutual friends, Arthur Rudolph and Max Valier on rocket car experiments. He had always admired Riedel's work and still had poignant memories of Valier dying in his arms.

Riedel was 10 years older than von Braun – a short, sedate man with a dry wit and serious expression. As polar opposites, Dornberger was betting they would strike the perfect balance.

"I'm hoping Riedel here will help guide your bubbling stream of ideas into steadier channels," he teased von Braun.

Rather than take umbrage, Wernher was amused and much relieved. He was more than happy to hand over his rocket hardware issues to Riedel so that he could concentrate on his combustion theory. It was an effective engineering partnership, which would soon see Riedel referred to as 'Papa' by the entire Kummersdorf crew; a fond familiarity under which, as von Braun's right-hand man, he would continue to work for the next 10 years.

It still wasn't smooth sailing, but after numerous experiments with the engine designed to drive their new A-1 rocket, they were ready in early 1934 for the full vehicle's first static test. Fortunately, at this point, it was not designed to fly, because its delayed ignition and the accumulation of an explosive propellant in the motor blew it apart where it stood.

So they tried again . . . and again and on their third attempt, von Braun and his team watched with baited breath as their rocket ignited. This time, though, its gyro vibrations cracked the oxygen tank, forcing fuel to leak and the missile to explode with an almighty bang. It made for an impressive fireworks display, but von Braun's mood was dismal:

"It took us exactly half a year to build that damn rocket and exactly half a second to blow it up!" he moaned to his crew, all of whom seemed as keen as he at that devastating moment to throw in the towel.

Yet, never one to stay down for long, von Braun bounced back cheerfully: "Oh well, back to the old drawing board."

Now that the basic design was discarded, however, he thought that taking a short break might do him and his ideas good. The first stop on his holiday was the von Quistorp Pomeranian Estate to check on the welfare of his little cousin Maria. Since her christening, he had become her self-appointed guardian, but a six-year-old child with freckled face and golden plaits could only hold his attention for so long, before he flew off to spend the last three weeks of his vacation in London.

Like his cousins' country manor, he thought of the city as a second home, because his parents once lived there happily and often chose it as their family holiday destination. Out of respect for the pleasant memories it evoked, Wernher felt akin to the place and was always at one with its history and stoic sense of tradition; which made it all the worse that one day he was destined to destroy it.

Luckily, as yet, the curtain had not risen on his fate and after returning rested and refreshed to Germany, his confidence was back in full swing. Not only was his brain brimful of new ideas in regard to rockets, but women had started to figure in his calculations because their statistics now seemed more appealing.

"And sometimes dating two at a time," his friend, Willy Ley remarked wryly, when Wernher turned up at a dinner party with a blonde beauty latched to each arm.

"One way or another, bombshells are part of my life," Wernher threw back with a wink, before leaning closer to whisper to his friend: "At least these ones perform on cue and are easier to get off the launch pad."

His sense of humour never failed and he used it to make the most of his peculiar social scene. Gregarious as he was, the secrecy of his project prohibited him associating with most of his friends. Even one of his best, Constantine Generales, had to be cut out of the equation despite having moved to Berlin to be near Wernher while he finished his medical degree. Although spring was in the air and romance was running rife, the army was prepared to tolerate von Braun's turned attention for only so long. Just a week after his return to Berlin, Dornberger called him to the conference table.

"We want you to do a total redesign of your rocket under the new designation of A-2," he said, giving an order that was seconded by the ring of military officers seated around it.

It was a huge task to set a man of just 22, but the army hierarchy knew he was exceptional and were determined to take advantage of his genius before any other branch of the armed services got the chance. While most students of his age were still struggling with their bachelors' degrees, von Braun had already achieved his PhD and had earned the title of Doctor due to his groundbreaking thesis on combustion theory.

"Effective today, your work status has changed," Dornberger informed him as he slid a contract and pen across the table. "You will no longer function as a private contractor, but as a full-time, civil service employee of the army's Ordnance Department. Just sign on the dotted line."

Still stunned by their demands and the speed at which they were made, von Braun did as he was told without reading the fine print. It stated that he now worked for the government, which he would continue to do for the next 40 years, during war and peace, and for enemies either side of the Atlantic.

THIRTEEN

NOW THAT HE WAS FORMALLY PART of the army's military machine, von Braun had to share in its trials and tribulations, the first of which involved his old colleague Rudolf Nebel getting arrested by the Gestapo.

"I wish that idiot would just shut up and stop causing trouble," Dornberger raged, for despite Propaganda Minister Goebbels' ban on any mention of military or technical aspects of rocketry, Nebel continued to talk, and had recently implicated von Braun by citing him as his 'inside man' at Army Ordnance.

As a result, Wernher was dragged from his bed in the middle of the night and put under interrogation at Berlin's Gestapo headquarters.

More alarmingly, it happened on the 'Night of the Long Knives', those dark hours of wholesale slaughter in June '34, when the Nazis turned on their own, murdering more than a hundred of the SA Brownshirt hierarchy. It was a blood-curdling purge staged by Hitler as a shrewd, political move and act of self-preservation. By ensuring that his old paramilitary associates were ripped apart by SS troops wielding any weapon that came to hand, the Fuhrer killed two birds with one stone: appeasing the army who feared the SA and killing any concern he had of having to play future power games with former compatriots who were every bit as brutal as him.

Like all sensible assassins, they lopped off the head of the snake by going straight to SA leader Ernst Rohm:

"Since you are the Fuhrer's friend and long-time ally, you are extended the courtesy of committing suicide," two SS officers said as they put a pistol down on the desk in front of him.

In a state of shock, Rohm leapt to his feet and ripped open his brown shirt.

"If I am to be killed, let Adolf do it himself." he exclaimed, hoping that a show of pride might hide his stark terror.

The officers, however, were unimpressed by his theatrics and left the room. When they returned 10 minutes later to find the deed not done and Rohm still standing in bare-chested bravado, they called him a coward and shot him dead themselves.

It came down to the survival of the most savage, which Hitler won hands down. Ironically, it earned him a more conservative image, marking him as the man who freed Berlin from bully-boy violence, while winning him the support of the traditional German military that was now minus the threat of being absorbed into SA ranks.

Such political pandemonium was completely beyond von Braun's sphere of activity and interest, so it was strange to find himself in the thick of it, handcuffed to a chair in the Gestapo interrogation chamber.

"You deny putting the Third Reich in jeopardy by conferring with Herr Nebel on top secret issues?"

"I do," von Braun answered categorically, given that Nebel's flamboyant antics had always been a source of contention and Army Ordnance had long since removed him from its confidence.

"I made it clear to Nebel that he must desist or face arrest for publicising details of our rockets' military applications," von Braun went on to clarify in a hurry when the man asking the questions suddenly strode towards him and slapped him across the face.

For an aristocrat unaccustomed to such treatment, the pain hurt less than the humiliation. So, von Braun struck back, with his hands impeded, kicking out hard at the man's shin. He stumbled, fell back and grabbed hold of his desk for support.

"And *that* . . . " von Braun continued, as the man advanced on him again with fists clenched, "was the sum total of Nebel's and my recent dealings together."

The interrogator put a full stop to that sentence with a solid punch to von Braun's jaw. It sent him sprawling sideways to the floor, but that was where his torture stopped. Before it became more severe, Army Ordnance stepped in to help, backing von Braun to the hilt and flexing its military muscle to free him from the Gestapo inquisition within 24 hours.

Most people in such dire circumstances were not so lucky, but despite being let off lightly, the experience of being helpless and at the mercy of bad men gave von Braun a taste of what might happen if he put a foot wrong. From here on in, he had to tread carefully.

... oOo ...

With every passing day, the rolling hills of our Silesia estate grow more inviting, Baron Magnus wrote to his son Wernher when the scandal of the SA slaughter hit the headlines.

Yet, even after his ordeal, Wernher was not tempted to leave Berlin and join his family there for longer than fleeting visits. He was eager, however, to hear their news and read on:

> *We're only glad that we pulled your little brother, Magnus, out of his Berlin school and enrolled him at your alma mater Spiekeroog, Like you, he flourishes there and you should be flattered that he has chosen to follow in your footsteps and pursue a career in chemical engineering, rather than shadow Siggy in the civil service.*

Many of the baron's Berlin friends had been arrested during the purge, so he felt fortunate in having moved with his wife and youngest son to the country where they were secure. The fear factor should have been enough to alienate them from the new regime, but thinking it safer to stay at its hub, he and Baroness Emmy continued to mingle with the best of Nazi society, frequenting dinner parties where the likes of Hitler and Hess would appear, while keeping up their close friendship with Hitler's Justice Minister, Franz Gurtner.

"He only stays in the job to prevent someone worse taking it over," the baron said to explain away his friend Gurtner's participation in the Third Reich and its atrocities.

Whether Gurtner's intentions were noble was a moot point when simply being in the position made him culpable. The upside was that he always had news of the Nazi network on his regular visits to the von Braun estate, and would speak of little else during their family fireside chats. To be made privy to such confidential information was a privilege, but it precluded Wernher pleading ignorance of the facts in the post-war years to come when he was fighting for his life and desperate to avoid blame.

"What did Gurtner mean when he talked about scores of murders?" Magnus Jr asked his older brothers after one of their armchair-and-fine-brandy gatherings.

For reasons of their own, neither Siggy nor Wernher answered: Wernher, because he was on the brink of great things and did not want to rock the boat; and Siggy, because he was fighting hard to rein in his rage.

He had been bitterly anti-Nazi from the start, but when, as a civil servant, he was forced to swear a personal oath to Hitler, he wrote in his diary.

I am now full of anxiety for my humanity.

His views were formed during his two-year absence from Germany. Studying at the University of Cincinnati in Ohio and then travelling the world opened his eyes to a broader, more civilised perspective on life, and he was horrified that his fellow countrymen had lost sight of it. He refused to shrug off his concerns about Hitler, as did Wernher, yet never held his younger brother accountable, because he knew Wernher's career and dreams for the future hinged on the man.

He feared more for 15-year-old Magnus, who was young enough to swallow heavier doses of indoctrination and who had just, this very night, happily informed his family of his new role as Junior Hitler Youth Leader at Speikeroog.

"And no one has any objection to this?" Siggy asked the family in the hope that at least one of them would stand up to be counted, but in Gurtner's presence, the room fell silent and young Magnus raced to his room to proudly put on his new uniform.

... oOo ...

Wernher, however, remained unenthused by military attire, for right now his life was one of studied indifference; of making the most of what was on offer without committing himself one way or the other.

"It was just an ill-advised test that had nothing to do with my line of development," he said, when a few days after his Gestapo interrogation, a liquid-fuel experiment killed three of his colleagues at Kummersdorf.

Still feeling thoroughly shaken by his own explosive Nazi experience, he was not prepared to involve himself in another.

"Unfortunately," he went on to explain to the press as Kummersdorf's spokesman, "Dr Wahmke and two of his students died as a result of a hydrogen peroxide and alcohol monopropellant which backfired and exploded on their test stand. We are all in mourning for three exceptional men."

Thankfully, come Christmas, the fog of failure lifted and there were cheers all round for von Braun's group when, from the North Sea island of Borkum, they successfully launched their new A-2 liquid-fuelled rocket.

"That's my baby . . . climb . . . *climb!*" von Braun whispered urgently under his breath, as he and his team watched it soar to an unprecedented altitude of two kilometres before trailing triumphantly back to earth.

"I bet that was better than any candy-stick in your Santa stocking," he quipped to his crew.

But the news got even better.

"Seems you're no longer considered small potatoes," Colonel Dornberger informed von Braun. "Your work's caught the Luftwaffe's attention and they're offering you and your group a two-million-mark contract to develop a rocket-powered fighter plane."

The enormity of the project left von Braun speechless – a rare occurrence for the chatterbox he was, which afforded Dornberger the opportunity to press on with the good tidings.

"You know what that means don't you? That you've hit the big-time and will have millions of marks at your beck and call."

Over the next two years, much of the money would be spent on planning and building a joint air force/army rocket research and development centre on the Baltic where financial support would wax and wane at Hitler's whim. As to that, however, von Braun was not worried, because he was on his way to where he wanted to go.

CHAPTER

FOURTEEN

"THAT'S OUTRAGEOUS!" General Becker said in regard to the Luftwaffe getting the bulk of the funding. "I know that as a pilot, the air force is close to your heart von Braun, but just remember that you and your rockets belong to the army and we deserve the bigger cut of the cake."

Becker and Dornberger had a battle on their hands securing it, because since Aviation Minister Hermann Goering had taken the Luftwaffe under his wing it was flying high on Hitler's priority list. Either way, von Braun won, for Goering's grandiose ambitions and the armed forces fighting over him were doing wonders for his career and the fuelling of rocket research momentum. When he stayed suspiciously silent on the subject, Becker read his thoughts and struck out to re-stake his territory:

"If Goering has his way, all will veer towards aircraft application and away from our development of ballistic missiles . . . and that wasn't the plan."

Now that the wheels of war were beginning to roll into motion, that 'plan' was all important. Although Hitler's ultimate goal was still under wraps, he had given a sneak preview by inaugurating the Luftwaffe, reviving compulsory military service and restoring

German sovereignty in military affairs; all the while, happily hoodwinking the world with promises of non-aggression pacts and peace. Scratch the surface and his battle cry rang clear, but at this point, the rivalry between his air force and army was more intense than any involving his prospective enemies.

It all started when Baron von Richthofen, head of Air Ministry Development and nephew of the famed WWI Red Baron, dropped into Kummersdorf to see what the army was up to. It was handshakes and smiles all round but sensing the loss of the army's monopoly on rocket research, Dornberger called von Braun to his office the instant the baron left.

"Richthofen told me . . . " he said, skipping polite preliminaries as soon as Wernher walked in the door, "that an official from the Junkers aircraft firm in Dessau was injured in a rocket engine explosion. I don't like him snooping round here, sniffing out other options. I want you to go to the Junkers factory, as *our* representative next week and sort it out."

Dornberger ran a real risk sending him there, because as a pilot von Braun was a member of the Air Force Reserve and always leant towards the Luftwaffe. Although he was exempt from regular service because of the importance of his work, there was a big chance that Goering's flashy fly-boys would win him over. To keep him on-side, the old army artillerists offered him a meteoric rise to power and made him the face of their rocket campaign, hoping it would stop him from defecting.

Nonetheless, Dornberger was fed up playing the popularity game and felt that sending him to the Junkers factory, at the very heart of all things that flew, would settle the matter once and for all. As it turned out, von Braun stayed true to his army colleagues despite running into a friend even older from his Rocket Field days at the factory – Johannes Winkler, who was experimenting with different rocket propellants on Junkers' behalf.

"I don't, however, see any dangerous form of duplication to worry about," von Braun rang Dornberger to report. "Winkler's work is small-scale and a fair bit behind ours at Kumersdorf, but I'm still interested to see the pulse-jet engine experiments the Air Ministry's showing me next week."

That particular experiment would eventually lead to the V1 buzz-bomb, and von Richthofen capitalised on Wernher's fascination with it while addressing the army's concerns about losing control.

"The Luftwaffe has a basic problem," he confessed to Dornberger over the phone. "The increasing speed and elevation of our bombers necessitates the creation of rapid-reaction interceptors, which can quickly zoom up to altitude. I have in mind a co-operative program between the army, the Luftwaffe and Junkers to produce a rocket fighter."

It seemed fair enough, and with Army Ordnance close to being convinced that the project did not step on its toes, it gave its support and invited representatives from Junkers and the Air Ministry to meet them at Kummersdorf 10 days later. The facts and figures were tabled and after a few grievances were aired, von Braun rounded off proceedings with the perfect compromise.

"As there's no difference in principle between a rocket engine for a missile and one for an aircraft, it makes sense to develop them both at the same time and place."

To seal the deal, however, Dornberger had the last word:

"Just so long as the army holds the upper hand."

For the army, it was as much a matter of pride as holding the purse strings, so to stay a step ahead of the Luftwaffe's new technology, Army Ordnance proceeded with its work on a much larger test vehicle – the A-3, for which it was given a budget of half a million marks.

"That includes a new office and furniture for you, von Braun." General Becker was pleased to inform him. "By the end of the year you'll have two dozen engineers and technicians working under you."

... oOo ...

"I'm impressed," Arthur Rudolph said, referring to both von Braun's new leather chair and his rapidly growing reputation. Having been friends for some time, however, he knew Wernher was having difficulty taking it all in.

"All I want to do is explore space," Wernher said when he saw his lavish new office. "I don't need all *this* to do it."

That, Rudolph believed, because von Braun was merely an astronomer at heart. After each day of designing rockets, the two of them would take their greatest pleasure in sitting up late at their Kummersdorf bachelor quarters, talking into the early hours of the morning about what lay 'out there', with little interest in what was happening on Earth. As far as they were concerned, inventing weapons was just a necessary evil getting in the way of their dreams.

"All this talk of war bores me," Wernher continued, as he fiddled with the freshly sharpened pencils on his fancy mahogany desk, suddenly getting a shock when a light started flashing on his newfangled phone.

The look of complete bewilderment on his face made Rudolph laugh out loud.

"Good God, man . . . you can configure the electronic intricacies of a missile, but a basic 'on' and 'off' switch has you stumped."

By nature, von Braun was the proverbial absent-minded professor. One side of his brain was pure genius, while the other half was perplexed by the simplest household gadget. It was a problem that would remain with him for the rest of his life, mystifying his friends and associates and making his wife roll her eyes each time he tinkered with her kitchen appliances.

"Well, no one's perfect," Wernher replied, happy to share the joke as he abandoned his desk and its paperwork to have a drink with his friend at the officers' club.

There, he and Rudolph stayed till dawn, both of them always hating to go to bed or get up early. In all things 'space' they were of one mind, bar the fact that Rudolph had a slightly better grasp on reality, while von Braun worked frenetically throughout his life to escape it.

"I'm willing to go along with all this military stuff," he said as they watched the sun come up, "but only if General Becker agrees to giving space exploration priority when it's over."

They drank a drunken toast to that, and then von Braun swilled down yet another to salute his friend, Rudolph, who understood him so well and was always at his side.

He was only sorry that another friend, with whom he was just as close, decided to walk out on him.

"You *can't* go," he protested, when fellow rocketeer Willy Ley, the man who had introduced him to Oberth and was with him from the beginning, told him he was leaving for America. "Wait till I get holidays and I'll go with you . . . at least for a few weeks."

Ley appeared agitated at the idea.

"I'm afraid it's more pressing than that," he replied, wiping beads of sweat from his brow. "It's bad enough that I'm part Jew, but it seems the Gestapo have also taken exception to some articles I've written for the foreign press discussing rocket technology. They say it's treason."

Here, Ley stopped to savour a short moment of triumph.

"And I guess . . . ," he then said, with a wry smile, "that they didn't take too kindly to the one I wrote referring to the Third Reich as a nest of rats. So, they're on my tail and I've got to get out of Berlin fast."

With the persecution of Jews intensifying, the shriek of SS sirens and gunfire in the streets had become commonplace. The men in black had already arrested many of Ley's breed and he knew it would not be long before they broke down his door. To leave the country, however, was no longer as simple as buying a ticket to New York. That luxury for Jews was disallowed, so it had to be done by stealth.

"Can I help?" Wernher asked.

Ley shook his head. He did not want to implicate his friend in his escape and stayed only long enough at von Braun's office to say goodbye and wish him well. From there, he went to his own place of business and used his journalist expertise to forge a letter on company stationery authorising his short vacation in London.

Within two hours, carrying just his three favourite books, some travel documents and a change of clothes, he closed the door on his Berlin home forever and fled to the United States via Great Britain.

"Will I ever see you again?" Wernher asked before he left.

To that, Ley had no answer, because whether von Braun knew it or not, he was being sucked into the Nazi network and would soon be his worst enemy.

CHAPTER

FIFTEEN

LEY'S LOSS WOULD HAVE BEEN MOURNED more if von Braun had the time, but Colonel Dornberger was now monopolising it.

"We have our orders," he leant across his desk to say decisively. "There's to be no more playing with toys and dreaming of the stars. Hitler wants weapons and expects us to come up with a rocket capable of carrying a large warhead beyond the range of standard artillery as soon as possible. That comes with a warning that if we keep on firing only experimental models, he'll put us out of business."

Things were getting serious, and for a fleeting moment von Braun wondered whether he would have been better off following his friend to America. For against the advice of the Reich's top generals, the Fuhrer had recently marched his troops into the Rhineland to remilitarise the region and excited over the easy victory, the army was keeping the ball rolling by being bountiful with funds.

"How much do you want?" they asked after Dornberger promised a state-of-the-art, long-range rocket with a one-ton payload and 30-ton thrust engine.

"A lot," he answered boldly, "because to build it, we'll need much bigger and better facilities."

He had in mind enough money to secure a large tract of land and to provision it with factories and housing, the like of which had never been seen.

While the army mulled over the idea, the Air Ministry pounced on it and leapt into action, sending an official that same day to buy the remote municipality of Peenemunde on the Baltic Sea island of Usedom. It was an isolated location selected with a view to the secrecy the project required. The boggy backcountry, with its thatched-cottage village and abundance of wild ducks and deer, was nothing but a haunt for hunters, but was to be transformed into a thriving rocket production centre destined to be the home of the deadly V-2 missile.

It meant that the rocket program and the Third Reich were now officially in business together. Yet still, its technical director, von Braun and his team had the strange notion that they could function untainted by politics.

Dornberger was more realistic.

"I'm going to push the secrecy aspect to stop as much political interference as possible, but just in case, I want you to wear this at all times," he said as he pinned a Nazi Party swastika button to von Braun's lapel.

"Is it absolutely necessary?" Wernher asked.

"It's certainly starting to look that way," Dornberger said grimly before he forced a smile and put a companionable hand on von Braun's shoulder. "But what will it hurt if it keeps the SS off our back?"

As the construction at Peenemunde began and the earth-moving machines cleared the way for its monumental buildings and looming stone swastika, von Braun, Dornberger and the head engineer of design, Walter Riedel, sat down to sketch out the preliminary specifications for the A-4 – the world's first ballistic missile later to be renamed the V-2.

"As I see it . . . ," von Braun said, as he rolled out his blueprint, "the largest rocket with a configuration similar to our A-3 that can be shipped without disassembly through railroad tunnels, would be capable of covering a range of 275 kilometres with a payload of one metric ton. The engine will need to have up to 25 metric tons of thrust, 17 times more than the A-3."

The figures were staggering but do-able, and Dornberger smiled with satisfaction. Together, they were working wonders: he, taking fatherly pride in 24-year-old Wernher's work, while in return, von Braun found himself functioning best under his colonel's paternal, but decisive command.

It seemed the Reich was on a winning streak, so it was full steam ahead and celebrations all round when Hitler opened the 1936 Olympic Games in Berlin. With the expectation that Germany would sweep the medal pool, the Fuhrer had every reason to be happy, but within days the smile fell from his face and he made no attempt to hide the fact that he was a very bad sport.

"Who is this Jesse Owens character anyway?" he demanded when the American sports star blitzed the field, winning a series of gold medals at record speed to destroy Hitler's boasts of Aryan supremacy.

Given half a chance, the Fuhrer would have pulled his pistol and shot him, but instead, had to sit through the humiliation of the American anthem being played over and over.

Von Braun was only sorry he missed it. On the day the Olympic Games started, he was busy moving from his Berlin apartment to a smaller unit in the town of Mellensee, closer to Kummersdorf, because the program he and Dornberger were putting in place left no time to waste on unnecessary travel between the office and home.

In between loading removal trucks, came the recruiting of staff for Peenemunde, and von Braun was excited about bringing old friends and new into the fold. He knew exactly who he wanted and precisely where to find them.

Chemical engineer Dr Walter Thiel, was the first on his list to take charge of developing a 25-ton thrust engine, which was destined to revolutionise rocket motors. Like von Braun, his specialty was combustion, while his strong physical presence and brain power were just as impressive.

"Looks like you've got competition," Dornberger teased when Thiel's talent for turning theory into practice quickly overtook what von Braun had accomplished with the A-1 and A-2 and made Thiel the driving force behind a myriad of improvements to the A-3 engine.

"It's a small price to pay for progress," von Braun replied, taking it on the chin, but bracing himself for in-house rivalry and the annoyance of having his methods questioned.

Dornberger sensed as much and cut straight through his bravado.

"Once in a while, it doesn't hurt to have to pull up your socks," he advised, before throwing his favourite a bone: "But then Thiel will never have your class or charisma."

It embarrassed von Braun that in being so transparent Dornberger felt the need to prop up his vanity, so he took a harder line when hiring Dr Rudolf Hermann. As just a young, assistant professor, Hermann claimed to be at the cutting edge of supersonic aerodynamics research, but Dornberger was not convinced.

"You'd never guess it," he commented after being introduced to the nebulous-looking man with pale complexion and currant-like eyes blinking behind thick-lens glasses.

"Don't be fooled by appearances," Wernher said quickly in his defence. "I know him well enough to take his word for it and we'd be unwise not to when we need someone like him to work on Peenemunde's wind tunnel requirements."

Still, however, Dornberger was not wholly won over and was worried that Wernher was merely handing out jobs for the boys.

"And I suppose . . . ," he answered wryly, "it's just a happy coincidence that the two of you are great friends and enjoy going to classical concerts together?"

The comment seemed appropriate when the colonel felt that the diminutive Dr Hermann would be more at home with a violin in hand than with a grip on the analysis of aerospace vacuum systems.

"The fact that we're good friends and love music doesn't cloud my judgment," von Braun snapped back. Bit by bit, he was finding his feet and digging in his heels. "As to that, you'll just have to trust me."

From that point on, Dornberger did and let him get on with his job. The greatest pleasure von Braun found in it was hiring some of his old Rocket Field colleagues who had been put on ice in the aircraft and gyro control section of Siemens – the conglomerate company that had given them work during the interim and was happy to do the same, during the years of war to come, for the concentration camp prisoners of Auschwitz – albeit minus the pay and privileges. The fact that the rocketeers had been paid well for their services, however, counted for nothing when von Braun strode through Siemens' door.

"Back in business together boys," he said, sporting a broad smile and waving the Peenemunde employment papers he had in hand.

No further inducement was needed and after giving only the minimum notice to Siemens, they were out of its factory grounds and back at von Braun's side.

"It's about time," one of the faithful, Klaus Riedel, said as they closed the gate behind them. "We all knew you'd come good."

Poaching draftsman/designer Otto Wiemer from the giant firm of Krupp, though, proved to be more of a problem. Von Braun extended the courtesy of asking Wiemer to meet him in Berlin and was astounded when the man threw the employment papers back in his face.

"Appalling pay and no chance of promotion," Wiemer said in response to the money and terms on offer.

Nonetheless, von Braun answered politely:

"I'm afraid the civil service doesn't pay very well. I can assure you, we're all in the same boat, but most of us do it for the love of it and can't see ourselves doing anything else."

"Well I suppose that's where we part company," Wiemer said rudely as he got up to leave, not bothering to thank von Braun for the opportunity or having the grace to say goodbye.

It took a few moments for von Braun to get over the slight and several more to face the fact, that for the first time, he had been unable to win a man over. After that, pride kicked in and he got practical by picking up the phone to hire trade school engineer Bernhard Tessmann instead.

The choice proved better, but Wiemer had put von Braun's nose out of joint and he found it hard to forget the insult. He had no idea why Wiemer disliked him, nor his reason for continuing to be a thorn in his side by speaking too freely about their missile experiments and constantly complaining to all who would listen about "von Braun's bungling of rocket development".

"You must warn him, formally in writing, about his breeching of secrecy," Dornberger advised.

Von Braun did just that, pointing out the possibility of very serious consequences which he, himself, had experienced earlier with the Gestapo. Wiemer, however, paid no heed and after a second, more serious indiscretion on his part, Dornberger ordered von Braun to alert the Abwehr, Germany's military intelligence service:

> *Wiemer is just a young idealist making frivolous remarks,* he wrote to its chief, Admiral Wilhelm Canaris. *"But unfortunately, they infringe on military secrecy. I am sure, however, that it is not out of a lack of national-mindedness, and in the hope of protecting him from the harsh consequences of Gestapo arrest, may I suggest that a milder warning from your organisation might scare him into being more prudent.*

It worked and went further to prove a point: that despite von Braun's post-war claims to the contrary, he was very familiar with Hitler's police state and was prepared to use it when necessary. The line between his actions, good and bad, however, was often blurred by sentiment.

"I don't want Oberth working with us at Peenemunde," Dornberger said, when he saw the name of von Braun's old mentor on the employment list.

Wernher stood stunned, shaken to the core at the thought of rejecting the services of such a great man.

"But we can't just cast him aside," he said in disbelief. "If it weren't for him, I'd be nothing and none of this would exist."

This was possibly true, but admire Oberth as Dornberger also did, he knew that the physicist with his theories of space would only be happy running the show and was likely to be more hindrance than help.

Whether or not he agreed, von Braun wasn't about to give up the fight.

"If you don't want him, you don't get me," he mustered up the courage to say, determined to stay loyal to the man who had forged his dreams.

He won, and for a short time felt smug about hiring his hero; but within a few weeks of Oberth's incessant interference and criticism of their A-4(V-2) plans, Wernher wished he had taken Dornberger's advice and spared himself the distress of having to put his idol out to pasture.

"We want you to investigate foreign patents that might be useful to our project," he said when he summoned Oberth to his office.

It wasn't hard for Oberth to see that he was being sidelined and the shock and sadness on his face said it all. With suppressed tears of pride stinging his eyes, he stood up and smiled his goodbye.

"But my dear boy," he then paused at the door to say. "You mustn't forget the moon and our hope of one day reaching it together."

CHAPTER
SIXTEEN

FOR THE REST OF HIS LIFE, the memory of this poignant moment would turn von Braun's body to stone, so he took no pleasure in being called 'Peenemunde's heart and soul', believing the incident robbed him of both.

Nonetheless, his natural exuberance rose to the fore, inspiring all those who worked under his dynamic leadership and benefitted from his one-on-one appeal.

"That was the big boss, Baron von Braun," chief scientist Stuhlinger informed new rocket engineer recruit Ernst Klauss, who was puzzled as to the identity of the stranger who came to chat with him on the factory floor in the middle of the night. Klauss was working overtime on a valve design, sitting alone under the dim light of his desk lamp, when another young man came through the door and wandered over to see what he was doing.

"I saw your light on and was wondering who was working so late," von Braun had said, going on to ask many more sociable questions about where Klauss came from and his family and friends.

"I didn't pay much attention," Klauss admitted to Stuhlinger. "Because he was so young, I just assumed he was someone of little account and didn't give him the time of day."

Now knowing who he was and amazed that such a man had gone out of his way to befriend him – a mere 'nobody' – Klauss felt ashamed and pledged himself to von Braun for life. For this was not a 'one-off' incident, but von Braun's code of practice. Throughout his frenetic career he never failed to familiarise himself with every member of his staff and to see to their welfare, from the most important members of his hierarchy to the lowliest of the compound's cleaners. The only time he lost his temper was when his workers were lazy and let him down.

"If you're not passionate about what you do, then *get out!*" he shouted angrily at the mechanical engineer who came unprepared to a meeting and tried to bluff his way through.

To tolerate those who gave less than their best was not on von Braun's agenda and he continued to call out each and every one of them until they were all as committed as him. For those older than him, such public reprimands were hard to take, but his very devotion to his craft incited the same in others, and it was only his youth that caused confusion. Even when visiting headquarters in Berlin, he was asked to show his ID when the top brass took him for drinks; while every now and again, older members of his staff, such as engine designer Walter Riedel, baulked at being his junior and having to address him as Doctor.

"Don't tell me what to do, Sonny Boy," Riedel said in the heat of the moment after von Braun questioned his plans; but when he called him the same in front of Dornberger, the colonel set him straight.

"Von Braun's leadership may not always be perfect, but he's a brilliant systems engineer and knows better than anyone how to fit things together. Whatever his age, his personal con-tribution to rocketry can't be paralleled and I will not have him undermined."

Dornberger was devoid of humour in such circumstances and was only critical of von Braun's gregarious tendency to laugh off insults of the like.

"Don't let them get away with it," he warned him. "I know making light of it is in your nature and makes you popular, but there are many among your staff who are jealous and will see it as a weakness to use against you."

By Christmas 1937, however, von Braun was not amused at all by the string of A-3 launch failures. For all the high-tech advantages of their new Peenemunde facility, it was a dismal result.

When construction of their new research centre finished, they had moved there in full force – the army occupying the west side of the compound, and the Luftwaffe, its east. As the army's technical advisor, von Braun had 80 people working under his direct control, which when war hit, would increase to 350 as part of the 10,000 servicing the shared army/air force base.

Having two branches of the defence forces in one place made it easy for von Braun to lend the Luftwaffe a hand with its rocket-equipped Heinkel He112 fighter plane fuselage, but he was disappointed when it refused to use him as its test pilot.

"Can't risk you being killed," was the consensus between both army and air force chiefs. "You're too important to the whole scheme."

To compensate, he was issued a Junkers Junior open-top monoplane, which he flew back and forward to his many meetings in Berlin. It optimised his time and fulfilled his need for speed, which was an obsession that did not translate too well to his driving a car.

"*Slow down!*" Arthur Rudolph pleaded on their way to an important conference as Wernher casually screeched his red Roadster around the sharp curves of the mountain pass. With hands loose on the wheel and his eyes on the map rather than the road, he was scaring his friend to death.

Still in top gear when they reached their destination, he zoomed through its gates, slammed into reverse, squeezed into a tight parking spot and jerked the car to a whiplash-stop. Rudolph took a moment to collect himself, his face white as a sheet as he pried his grip loose from the dashboard.

"See . . . we're smack on time and still alive," Wernher cajoled. With his eyes burning bright after the exhilarating ride, he was firing on all cylinders and fully revved up for the meeting.

Some said he was just flying high, but others – that he was getting way above himself.

"I have no intention of living *here,*" von Braun decreed, when he first saw his new quarters at Peenemunde.

They were perfectly adequate, but did not suit his new playboy lifestyle, so he took up residence at the island's beach resort of Zinnowitz to enjoy the water views, more glamorous atmosphere and bevy of bathing beauties; one of whom was a striking, 16-year-old so besotted with him that she lied about her age in order to call herself his girlfriend.

"Unfortunately, I'm not as committed," Wernher was quick to qualify to those who questioned the match, because he had women at his beck and call and wanted to play the field. "But I'm sure I'll remember her oh so very, very well!" he would invariably add with a wink.

The allure of wine, women and song, however, came nowhere near the excitement of his rocket science, and he coldly cast them aside when it came to business. In this case, it was the difficult business of their failed A-3 rocket tests. Apart from being discouraging, they were downright embarrassing when the Luftwaffe had already made its first successful test flight with a rocket engine fighter plane and was close to mastering its innovative, winged buzz bomb. Both achievements put the army on the back foot and it did not like it.

"Perhaps in all our zeal, we've been too ambitious," von Braun had to admit, after the sickening humiliation of their botched launches on the small, Baltic Isle of Greifswalder. There, they had test fired their A-3 rockets on December 4, 6, 8 and 11, but had failed to make them fly.

"It wasn't our fault when we were beset with difficulties," his team members said in their own defence, which to a degree was fair when rain, snow and fierce storms played havoc with their plans.

The antiquated ferry that carried them and their equipment to and from the island had been swamped by raging seas; their machinery was bogged in wet clay; and the tent that sheltered their rocket preparations collapsed on top of them from the sheer weight of heavy rain and snow. That was to say nothing of the plague of rats that, in between spreading a debilitating virus, gnawed their way through their phone cables and cut communications between firing bunkers.

No excuse, however, could get around the fact that they had a faulty gyro system. No one in their group was trained adequately in the field, so they were relying on a covert gyroscope equipment company near Berlin that specialised in as much. Their long-distance expertise had gone some way to filling the gap, but simply was not good enough.

"And so say all of us," said the delegation of dignitaries who braved the waves to witness the first A-3 launch. Bobbing in a boat offshore, they battled seasickness, huge swells and an excruciating four-hour wait when the launch was delayed due to electrical problems.

"There she goes!" one of them sighed at long last when the rocket finally took off and rose majestically into the sky. Sadly, their gasps of awe trailed off to groans when its recovery parachute suddenly deployed without purpose and was sucked into the fiery jet that reduced it to cinders in seconds.

"Well, let's hope it's not prophetic," one dignitary said as he turned away. For in honour of the Fatherland, the rocket had been dubbed Deutschland and all it had done was spin out of control and crash in a shameful ball of flame.

Needless to say, none of them returned to see the subsequent tests, and it was just as well when they proved as big a fiasco. Yet von Braun refused to be downcast and got stuck straight into investigating the problems. It meant, unfortunately, that he had to cut short his Christmas holiday at his family's country estate.

"We're sorry you can't stay longer," they all said when he kissed them goodbye.

He gave his mother a second hug and walked to his car, but when he turned to wave one last time and saw the disappointment on his nine-year-old cousin Maria's face, he doubled back to stroke his hand down her cheek.

"Don't worry, I'll see you soon," he consoled, but that was a lie when he would not lay eyes on her again until she was 16.

CHAPTER

SEVENTEEN

M OST GERMAN GENERALS were not averse to the Fuhrer's racist foreign policy and territorial expansion plans, but they were still licking their wounds from the Great War and not so keen to do battle with England and France a second time round.

Supreme Commander of the German Army, General Werner von Fritsch, was most disturbed and needed reassurance.

"Does this mean I'll have to cancel my annual leave?" he asked Hitler. Although having opened the funding floodgates for the rocketeers in his enthusiasm for the Fuhrer's military agenda, his holiday still took priority.

Such a question did not warrant an answer when Hitler's mind was on bigger things, such as taking over the world and building a new Berlin. To that end, he had been courting another extraordinary man of von Braun's ilk – architect Albert Speer – and had recently commissioned him to transform the capital city into a monumental testament to the Third Reich. Naturally, Speer was flattered by the sheer scale of the project and signed on the dotted line with no idea that he was selling his soul along with his services. It was merely an expedient after-thought that had him join the Nazi Party to further thank the Fuhrer for the favour.

As yet, Speer and von Braun were strangers, but the same calculated self-interest propelled Wernher to follow suit and sign on with the men in black.

"Nazi Party member No 5,738,692," Wernher read out loud when he was handed the official papers.

As an aristocrat, he was not used to being ranked so low on any list, but the fact that its members numbered in the millions was heartening for his homeland. And considering that he intended to limit his party participation to paying his annual dues and donning the swastika badge only when politically appropriate, he saw no reason to feel guilty. One of his higher-minded friends, however, thought otherwise and was shocked that Wernher had taken such a step.

"You surprise me," he said in thinly veiled reprimand, to which von Braun shot back brusquely:

"Devotion to Fuhrer and Fatherland has nothing to do with it. I was warned that if I didn't join the party, I'd be forced to forsake my life's work."

He made no further comment as to *who* exactly applied such pressure and, at war's end, went out of his way to make sure that all related documents were destroyed. Till the day he died, this lack of hard evidence in regard to his complicity with the Nazis pointed to his innocence and left the world no choice but to take his word for it.

It was easy enough to believe when his commitment to the cause seemed to hinge solely on his goal of getting a rocket into space. If the Reich was prepared to facilitate that dream, he was happy to follow its rules and to comply with Peenemunde's prejudicial policy: *That no one could be employed without an Aryan Certificate.*

"Which puts us at a decided disadvantage," von Braun mumbled under his breath at the prospect of knocking back the considerable brainpower of the Jewish race. However, because he was blessed with an excess of it himself, he never felt the need to openly question the order for the eight years he spent at Peenemunde.

For the great talker he was, he knew when to keep his mouth shut, and was therefore, not considered a political risk when he travelled with Colonel Dornberger to the World Expo in Paris to view all kinds of technological wonders.

"None of which come anywhere near measuring up to ours," Dornberger said smugly as he and von Braun raised their glasses in salute to the Fuhrer before taking their seats at the German embassy's banquet table.

The group of young diplomats seated around it, however, failed to lift their glasses in response. Among them was Wernher's older brother, Sigismund, who had been assigned to Paris several months before as a foreign attaché. It was he who suddenly got to his feet and with red-hot indignation turned what had begun as a festive function into a dog-eat-dog affair.

"Hitler's a loose cannon who must be stopped at all costs!" he said straight out. "His unlimited and unscrupulous foreign policies are on the brink of causing a new world conflagration."

At this astounding proclamation, the banquet hall fell deathly silent and Werhner looked at his brother in dismay, for not only had he risked his own life by publicly insulting the Fuhrer, he had put them all in peril by doing so in their presence. Yet, more surprising was that Sigismund's fellow diplomats then raised their glasses to toast his bold words, making a defiant, political stand that put a triumphant smile on Sigimund's face, but made Wernher's countenance grow grim.

Meet me outside, his eyes signalled to his brother, and without a word, they both walked out onto the balcony spoiling for a fight.

"Are you *mad!*" Wernher swung round on him to say the

instant they were out of earshot. "You're a paid envoy of the Third Reich and you're talking treason."

Like his brother, Wernher was not one of Hitler's greatest fans, but he knew which side his bread was buttered and wanted nothing to do with anything that might jeopardise his job. It was therefore worth his while to keep up his irate charade:

"Most Germans have every faith in Hitler's genius and believe he's working on their behalf with peaceful intent."

Here, he stopped, because it was hard to keep up the pretence when he saw Siggy's tongue-in-cheek reaction.

"Come now, Wern . . . isn't that a tad naïve coming from you . . . one of the big wheels in his re-militarising machine? You can't pretend you don't know what he's got in mind."

Wernher was fighting a losing battle, but with more at stake that just another world war, he was not about to surrender.

"What he has in mind is to restore Germany's pride and former glory," he justified. "A show of military might is the surest way to do it."

He was pleased with his off-the-cuff comeback, but the patronising smile on Siggy's face promptly put him in his place.

"You know, I've always admired your brilliance, Wernher," his big brother said, "but it never crossed my mind that you'd abuse it. Please take my advice and stop while you can . . . before you create a monster and make your family ashamed."

At these reprehensible words, Wernher's blood ran cold. The very thought that he would ever seek to disgrace his family was unconscionable when he had always worked tirelessly to achieve the exact opposite. As a proud man, he could not bring himself to speak and at this point believed that he would never talk to his brother again. There was nothing more to be said and their mutual silence brought an end to the one and only argument they would ever have. But it was a big one, and when they returned to the banquet hall, Wernher looked livid.

It was not the time, Dornberger thought, to fuel the fire by immediately asking for details. Afterwards, however, he pulled von Braun aside to say:

"For all our sakes, you'd better put a muzzle on your brother. Diplomatic immunity or not, he's not above the law, particularly not Hitler's and might put us all in danger."

Perhaps that was being overly dramatic von Braun thought later. After all, how often had he, himself, joked with his staff about Peenemunde being hermetically sealed against Nazi infiltration and what pleasure he and his fellow space fanatics on the base took in operating their apolitical utopia right under Hitler's nose.

That scientific sanctuary of theirs, however, was slipping away because unbeknown to von Braun, his genius was working against them. As yet, his experiments had not achieved enough to gain the Fuhrer's full focus, but the more his rockets got off the ground, the more the Nazis' attention swerved in his direction.

Whether he realised it, Peenemunde was rapidly being integrated with the Reich. To the beat of drums, the Hitler Youth regularly marched within its walls; and although out-numbered, the few Nazi Party diehards among the staff were now brazen enough to threaten their fellow workers if they dared speak out of turn. Strength, they had found, did not lie in numbers, but in the fear of brute force.

It bothered von Braun to know that his friend and key assistant Arthur Rudolph was one of them, but this moral dilemma was balanced by Klaus Riedel, with whom he was just as close, and who was taking considerable personal risk by paying out of his own pocket to smuggle Jewish friends out of the country.

"I appreciate you looking the other way," Riedel had whispered to him a few days before, but von Braun brushed his thanks aside. Not out of humility, but because he simply did not care.

When it came to politics and his two friends' opposing views on it, he preferred not to pick sides and to play it straight down the middle.

For nothing, he believed, was more important than their work and maintaining a sense of humour. Especially now when he had the more serious problem of ravenous field mice munching their way through all their electronic equipment's rubber insulation. It was just one in a string of annoyances that had to be handled.

"Give their eradication priority," he ordered Bernard Tessmann. But the young rocketeer hesitated, because only the day before, another of their in-house crises had been given top billing.

"But what about our slipping corsets?" he asked von Braun.

To the uninitiated this made no sense, but during the development of their A-4 missile, the team had invented an ingenious device that encircled the missile and suspended its main body upright. Like a woman's girdle it kept a firm, flexible grip that facilitated expansion and contraction during temperature change, but much in line with the fairer sex, it was proving temperamental.

The other engineers had wanted to spare von Braun the problem, so this was the first he had heard of it.

"Well, what about the corsets?" he flashed back in frustration.

It was out of character for him to be short-tempered, so Tessmann gathered his courage to explain.

"I'm afraid that yesterday, *Herr Doktor,* one of our missiles somehow slipped out of its corset and fell flat on its tail."

As the bearer of bad news, Tessmann expected a reprimand and was surprised when his boss responded with a roguish grin.

"Well, just be glad it didn't happen to your girlfriend!"

Von Braun always enjoyed a good joke, but the fun and games were coming to an end. Day by day, security was being ramped up on base and his failure to wear a swastika and security badge was about to land him in hot water.

"What do you *mean* you won't let me pass?" he demanded when a Nazi guard stopped him from crossing the compound.

"You aren't wearing your security badge," the soldier answered.

Von Braun threw his hands up in exasperation. There was an emergency at their launch site and he was racing to get there. He didn't have time for all this nonsense.

"But this is ridiculous!" he argued. "You *know* who I am. Just let me through."

The guard, however, had his orders and undaunted by the technical director's command and encroaching 6'2" presence, he put a restraining hand on von Braun's chest and reiterated: "You are not wearing your badge."

By laying his hand on him, he crossed the line and von Braun saw red. He slapped it away, but in response, the guard aimed his rifle at him.

At this point, the normally calm and collected von Braun was beside himself with fury and drawing an audience, all of whom were unsure as to whether they should be amused or concerned.

"I think he's going to flatten the blighter," one bystander said when he saw von Braun raise his fist.

But at that pivotal moment, the young baron realised he was causing a scene and thought better of it.

"Oh for *Christ's sake!*" he hissed as he turned to race back to his office and rummage through his desk for the black-spider badge.

When he returned flushed-faced and tight-lipped with it pinned to his lapel, the guard obligingly stood aside and saluted, but von Braun refused to return the salute, for the incident had been far more than a mere irritation. It marked the end

of his freedom and the firm control he thought he had on his
future.

CHAPTER

EIGHTEEN

WORSE OFF, however, were the Jews who had lost sight of freedom altogether, along with their right to live.

What is this appalling news we've heard about Kristellnacht? Wernher's mother, Emmy, wrote to him. *Surely these horror stories of Jews being butchered are not to be believed.*

All over the country, news of 'The Night of Broken Glass' had secured the front page of the big dailies and the local paper delivered to the von Braun country estate. To find the truth of it, one had to read between the lines – that it had not been just a bout of random violence throughout the Reich, but Propaganda Minister Goebbels' carefully orchestrated series of pogroms in which 7000 Jewish businesses, cemeteries, homes and hospitals were trashed, dozens of their faith murdered and more than 250 synagogues burned to the ground while firemen simply stood in the streets of shattered glass and watched.

Someone had to be blamed for the devastation, so to satisfy the people's bloodlust and further rally them to his cause, Hitler accused the Jews. That was preposterous, but because no one was brave enough to speak up in their defence, 30,000 of them were arrested for the crime and sent to concentration camps.

Rumours of the atrocities were flying, but because von Braun had not been a party to them, he preferred not to get involved. For a man of his intelligence, 'playing dumb' wasn't easy; nor was his attempt to pull the wool over his mother's eyes:

> *I'm sure accounts have been greatly exaggerated*, he wrote back to put her mind at ease. *I do know that many prominent Jews have fled the country and that others have been jailed because of their opposition to the government, but you must remember, Mama, that being jailed and being butchered are two very different things.*

His dismissive attitude reflected that of most Germans. So, with the good men among them doing nothing, Hitler triumphed twice – getting away with persecuting the Jews and in early 1939, marching his troops unmolested across the Czechoslovakian border to take control of the Sudetenland. The British and French had hoped to keep Hitler happy by signing the Munich Pact that sacrificed Czechoslovakia to annexation back in September, but the Fuhrer's military aggression now exposed that appeasement policy as a pipedream, and despite the dread of another world war, both England and France had no choice but to speed up their own rearmament to match the Third Reich's.

Thanks to the people at Peenemunde, Germany was a fair few steps ahead of its rivals, and with the thrill of it all, SS chief Heinrich Himmler wanted to get in on the action. Hitler, he knew, had visited Kummersdorf twice and been bored by the slow, scientific process and the fact that the promise of rockets was not immediate.

He had effectively lost interest and never bothered to travel to Peenemunde, but Himmler was shrewder. Like a trapdoor spider, he was willing to lie in wait for the explosive results. In the meantime, he was slowly absorbing Peenemunde into his SS empire and trying to lure the fabulous Dr von Braun into his web.

... oOo ...

"There's an SS-Colonel Mueller here to see you," von Braun's beautiful, young secretary, Dorette Kersten, came into his office to announce.

Bemused, if not a bit alarmed, Wernher put down his pen and stood up to shake hands with the officer in black who strode in straight after her.

"To what do I owe this pleasure?" he asked, striving to steady his voice and relieved when Mueller immediately minimised the threat factor by casually sitting down for a chat.

"This is just a friendly visit on behalf of Reichsfuhrer Himmler," he said.

The word 'friendly' used in conjunction with Himmler was a contradiction in terms, but von Braun sensibly took it at face value. It was no secret that the head of the SS was trying to inveigle his way into the Peenemunde community and that this was not the first time he had singled out its technical director for special treatment.

Von Braun would have been flattered had he not feared

the strings attached. In anticipation of them, he was lost for words and could think of nothing to do but offer the colonel a cigarette.

He took it and continued: "I'll get straight to the point, *Herr Doktor*. Reichsfuhrer Himmler thinks very highly of you and is keen to have you join his SS."

Von Braun had made that mistake before. Joining the SS horse-riding academy back in his university days had proved an embarrassment and he didn't want to repeat the exercise. Given that the colonel seemed only to be making a polite suggestion, he had no qualms about knocking back the offer.

"I'm greatly honoured by the Reichsfuhrer's kind invitation, but to be honest, I'm far too busy with my rocket work to put any time into political activity."

"My dear doctor," Mueller leant forward in his seat to say. "Signing up with the SS will cost you no time at all and for simply taking the trouble, you'll be awarded the honorary rank of lieutenant. I must impress upon you, that such a generous offer doesn't come along every day and that Himmler is most definite in his desire that you accept it."

What had started as a courtesy suddenly sounded decidedly deadly and von Braun had to think fast.

"Would you give me some time to think if over?" he asked.

There was a tense silence as Mueller stubbed out his cigarette and got up to leave.

"Of course," he then answered with a tight smile. "But for your own sake . . . don't take too long."

Von Braun gulped down hard on the implication. Now that he was playing among power-mongers, he realised the political significance of his response and the ramifications it might have on the already tenuous army and SS relations. With that in mind, he went straight to Dornberger for advice.

None of this came as a surprise to Dornberger. He had

known for some time that Himmler was after a piece of the Peenemunde pie and was out to win von Braun's allegiance. One brutal way or another he was bound to get what he wanted, so for the sake of inter-military accord, it was better to throw the Reichsfuhrer a bone while he was still prepared to beg.

"For the sake of continuing our work, I don't think you have any other choice but to give Himmler what he wants," Dornberger conceded. "I do hope, though, that our friendship and confidence in each other will continue no matter what future difficulties might arise as a result."

Two days later, Himmler was happy to see von Braun's signed application for SS membership because it proved a point and served his jealous agenda. The young baron had played right into his hands and provided him with the perfect payback. For the one thing Himmler hated more than the existence of Jews was the ever-galling existence of Reich architect Albert Speer, who had pushed him aside as Hitler's favourite.

Well two can play at that game Himmler reasoned. If the Fuhrer saw fit to keep the brilliant young Speer as his pet, then he, as head of the SS, was well within his rights to up the ante and put a leash on von Braun, who was every bit as exceptional and went one better than Speer by being a member of the aristocracy.

Unfortunately for Himmler, it was a pride in affiliation that did not work both ways. As soon as von Braun received his black uniform, he hung it at the back of his closet where it gathered dust and saw the light of day only when Himmler made formal visits to Peenemunde. On such occasions, it suffered a rigorous brushing and a serious spray of cologne to camouflage its musty smell. Somehow, though, it always worried von Braun that it fitted him to perfection.

"And brings out the colour of your eyes," his two pretty secretaries remarked.

There was no doubt it made him look dashing, but he wished that Dornberger had not snapped a photograph of him in it during one of Himmler's inspection tours. When he saw the camera slung over the colonel's shoulder, von Braun did his best to work his way to the back of the SS crowd and put himself out of focus. As hoped, the developed image of him standing in the background behind the Reichsfuhrer was blurred, but it found its way into Dornberger's photo album and survived the cull of all that might incriminate von Braun after the war. So, no matter how vigorously he disputed his SS ties in the years to come, this shot of him in SS uniform stood as fuzzy, but near-conclusive proof to the contrary.

CHAPTER

NINETEEN

IT WAS MID-AUGUST 1939 when Wernher flew himself to his parents' country estate to see out what would be their last golden summer there together. It seemed that nothing could destroy the bliss of the balmy evenings and the warmth of family chat. But during a break in their lively conversation, someone made the mistake of turning on the radio.

They were stunned, as was the rest of the world, to hear that Hitler had just signed a non-aggression pact with the Soviet Union, joining as one two world powers whose ideologies were diametrically opposed.

"Well, I suppose it's a major coup for the Fuhrer," Baron Magnus acknowledged. "At least he's made sure that Stalin won't interfere with his plans for Poland."

In theory, those plans were simply to reclaim land lost during the Great War and for that, Hitler could perhaps be applauded. But as the German people drank to his health, few of them knew his true intentions: to launch a genocidal war that would destroy the Polish state and wipe its Jewish citizens off the face of the Earth.

His forces attacked at 4.45am on September 1. No longer willing to sit back weakly and watch, England and France declared war. The decree was as good as dropping a bomb directly on Peenemunde, for from that point on, work there became frantic. Huge demands were put on von Braun and his rockets to perform. As a show of good faith, he moved from his luxurious bachelor abode on the beachfront back to his Spartan quarters on base to be on hand 24 hours a day.

"Army headquarters has given Peenemunde precedence," Colonel Dornberger assured him.

Their top priority was to protect it against its massive loss of manpower due to Hitler's military draft; and the next was to accelerate the A-4 ballistic missile so that it was relevant to the war. The army's expectations for its development were overwhelming.

"It must be finished within two years," Commander-in-Chief Walther von Brauchitsch, ordered.

That was bad enough, but then Chief of Army Ordnance, General Becker, moved that deadline forward to May 1941, and made it completely unrealistic.

"I know it's pushing the boundaries when your research and development facilities are inadequate," he explained to von Braun, "but I'm going to help out by downgrading Peenemunde's 'secrecy' code so that you can recruit technically qualified people through all military and civilian channels."

This was wonderful news and von Braun leapt at the opportunity.

"Will that include access to universities?"

Becker nodded his assent and Wernher was thrilled, because collaborating with the most eminent professors in guidance control and propulsion was a sure-fire way to speed up the program. Despite his constant concern about masterminding an instrument of mass destruction, his mind was otherwise put at ease and recruiting became fun.

"I think we can get electrical engineer Helmut Hoelzer on board if you're interested," rocket scientist Ernst Steinhoff suggested.

Having not heard of Hoelzer, von Braun was unsure of his capacity, but because Flight Captain Steinhoff was a fellow pilot and friend, he trusted his judgment.

"We trained together at the Luftwaffe's glider institute," Steinhoff continued, "and all I can say is that the man is damned good at his job."

Before employing him, however, von Braun wanted to get the measure of the man first hand, so he went to Berlin with Steinhoff to meet him.

... oOo ...

"Who's there?" Hoelzer called down from his bedroom window when he saw two men standing in the dark garden below.

It was the middle of the night and thinking that they were intruders, he shined his torch in their faces. He immediately recognised his friend, Steinhoff, squinting at the glare. But the young man standing next to him was a stranger. Admittedly, quite an impressive looking one, who was standing with his hands in his pockets and casually whistling without the slightest concern about waking the neighbours.

Steinhoff shaded his eyes from the spotlight and called back: "I want to introduce you to my friend, the baron. Come on down and we'll go for a beer."

At this late hour, it seemed insane, but no young man in his right mind would knock back the offer of a drink. There was no time to dress, so Hoelzer threw on a coat over his striped pyjamas and joined them at the corner pub.

A night out with the flamboyant Steinhoff was always enjoyable, but Hoelzer did not take to his new friend. Baron or not, this von Braun fellow seemed totally disinterested in their conversation and preferred to banter with the big-bosomed barmaids who were hanging around him like flies. It wouldn't have worried Hoelzer in the least, had the man not kept on and on with his infernal whistling.

If he keeps it up, Hoelzer was thinking, *I'm going to smack him in his face.*

He was shocked, therefore, when von Braun abruptly stopped and looked him squarely in the eyes.

"Can I ask you something, Hoelzer?" he said, his face now stone-cold and serious. "What do you do if you have a flying body and you want to keep this flying body flying in a straight line?"

Not sure whether the baron was drunk or exceptionally astute, Hoelzer did not know how to answer, but when he saw the smirk on Steinhoff's face he realised he was being taken for a ride and decided to play them at their own game.

"Well,' he said hesitantly, "it depends on the body – if you're throwing a piano off the Empire State Building or you're talking about aeroplanes. Both would require different methods, so what sort of flying body is it?"

"I can't tell you," von Braun replied to provoke him.

Hoelzer's eyes narrowed and matching brain for brain he replied: "Well then, I can't answer you."

It was a stalemate and Steinhoff was disappointed. He had hoped that his old friend, Hoelzer, would win over his new friend, von Braun, but instead they appeared to part as enemies. Hoelzer bid them a clipped 'goodnight and they watched him walk away without a word. As soon as he was out of hearing, however, von Braun turned excitedly to say: "I *like* him! Hire him as fast as possible."

It was one of the smartest moves he ever made because

Hoelzer's analog computer was to prove pivotal to the V-2's guidance and control system.

... oOo ...

For the most part, von Braun was a man of action. He knew what he wanted and the best way to get it; which was just as well when the hard reality of weaponising created a voracious need for money and resources and sparked savage in-fighting within the Peenemunde community. To avoid as much of it as possible, von Braun went out of his way to be one of the boys, never stinting at getting his hands dirty and listening intently to all that others had to say.

It's important that everyone's ideas are taken seriously, he believed, because whether they were good or not, the fact that they were having them was heartening.

It was difficult, though, for a man to be less than he was and to temper his aristocratic bearing so as not to appear a snob. Most of his staff admired him for making the effort, but no matter how hard he tried, no man could forever win friends and influence all people – especially those whose minds came near to matching his and resented being patronised.

The fine and fabulous von Braun, they were quick to point out, was far from perfect and caused friction among his fellow workers by side-stepping the system whenever he was forced to loosen his grip on the reins.

That usually happened around the area of guidance and control, which was a key part of rocket development and the field in which he was least proficient. With no theoretical or design expertise in that specific area, he could play the role of only co-ordinator, and had to rely on engine designer Walter Thiel and aerodynamics expert Rudolf Hermann to get it right. That was a 'big ask' and the reason why some at Peenemunde objected to the perception that von Braun ran the place.

"He's nothing but an opportunist who picks the brains of better men and steals the credit," mathematician Paul Schroeder said.

Braun took great exception to the scandalous comment from a member of the guidance and control team. As a result, the two of them crossed swords often. With Dr Schroeder constantly criticising his initiatives and strategically choosing to do it in public, von Braun had had enough.

"I want him gone!" he demanded of Dornberger. "The man's insults are groundless and are constantly undermining my authority."

The matter was serious and Dornberger agreed that von Braun had every reason to be angry. Of the two, Schroeder was the more dispensable, so he was gone within the week.

It was rare for someone to get under von Braun's skin, but Schroeder succeeded. Not that it changed Wernher's firm belief in free speech and open exchange of ideas, but Schroeder had crossed the line out of sheer jealousy. Considering they never liked each other, this was easy enough to accept, but von Braun was genuinely astonished when Arthur Rudolph joined the chorus of his detractors.

"Von Braun has no regard for red tape and continues to cut me out of the equation by going straight to my subordinates whenever an idea grabs him," Rudolph complained. "If Dornberger would stop nursing him along and give him more practical work to do, he'd stop sticking his nose in everyone else's business."

They would have been harsh words coming from an enemy, let alone a friend, and von Braun found them hard to forgive. Rudolph's claim that he was forever barging onto other engineers' turf and telling them what to do was most offensive.

"He does have a point," Dornberger surprised von Braun by

saying.

Fond as the colonel was of his young technical director, he often had to put a lid on von Braun's bubbling font of ideas and intolerance of them not being tended to immediately.

There were problems, Dornberger had found, when dealing with someone as exceptional as von Braun, a man who had everything at his fingertips: brains, personality and looks; the last of which caused the colonel a good deal of trouble in having to hire him a string of secretaries. One after another they fell under von Braun's spell and became inefficient, so Dornberger wound up the romantic saga by employing a middle-aged matron with a matter-of-fact manner. Well beyond batting her eyes in her boss' direction, he hoped that, at last, she could teach Wernher what he needed to know about orderly office procedures.

"Who are you?" von Braun asked when he returned from lunch to find that the blonde bombshell he hired the week before was gone. Sitting at her desk was a plain woman with a severe centre-part in her grey hair and a set of implacable brown eyes framed by horn-rimmed glasses.

"I'm Mrs Lewandowski, *Herr Doktor* . . . your new secretary," she answered through firm, thin lips. "Colonel Dornberger is keen that I should look after you."

The joke was on him and von Braun took it in good humour. A few weeks down the track, he was glad he did, because she was a blessing in disguise, relieving him of all office protocol and the constant strain of having to keep up appearances.

One way or another he was learning the ropes, and come November, most questions about his leadership ceased.

TWENTY

A FTER TWO SUCCESSFUL LAUNCHES, Peenemunde had, at last, mastered the basics of ballistic missile guidance. It would have been something to celebrate had Hitler been vaguely interested, but instead, he cut its steel quota and downgraded the program's priority in favour of his invasion of France.

"The resource is needed to shore up critical shortages on the Western Front," the Fuhrer did them the rare courtesy of explaining. But when Dornberger dared write back to argue that Peenemunde was in a serious arms race with other world powers, he received no reply, which inferred that further correspondence on the matter would be frowned upon, if not fatal.

Apart from the fear factor that invoked, the war hitting hard filled von Braun with guilt. As a space enthusiast, he had been shamefully using the previously benign threat of it to push his own agenda of shooting for the stars. Now that it was a reality, his rocket dreams were dead and Hitler was insisting that their trajectory be changed to help wipe out the rest of the world.

"It's our own fault for selling out and promising him a new wonder weapon," Dornberger said, for both he and von Braun knew that they were far from perfecting the like, and its development stretched off into the dim future. Even if they did manage to push its completion date forward, their long-range missile would not pack the punch Hitler expected, due to its trifling one-ton payload.

While Hitler had been lukewarm on the project, they were working on the premise that "what he didn't know wouldn't hurt him". But now, with his warmongering paying off and Himmler breathing down their neck, they were being subjected to much closer scrutiny and a far greater threat of gruesome reprisal if they failed.

Sure enough, their rocket program soon sustained its first war casualty – not by Hitler's hand, but it may as well have been.

The Fuhrer's financial support was feeble, despite his new demands, so Dornberger was forced to turn to his own senior officer for help. It had been some time since he had visited the head of Army Ordnance, General Becker, so he was surprised that his old friend did not seem pleased to see him.

"I only hope that I've not been mistaken in my estimation of yours and von Braun's work," Becker said gruffly in greeting without even bothering to get up from his desk; but when Dornberger baulked at his cold tone, he backed down and explained.

"Sorry Dornberger, but I've been under severe pressure from the Fuhrer about shortfalls in munitions supply and he's just publicly humiliated me by promoting that rabid little autobahn builder Dr Fritz Todt to out-rank me as Armaments and Munitions Minister. With him in charge, you can be sure all rocketry will be put on the back-burner."

Such defeatist talk was disturbing, especially coming from the man all rocketeers revered as their godfather. Becker was the very backbone of their operation – the eternal optimist whose remarkable insight had launched the army into their program. But now, the immense strain was showing in his face, and Dornberger tried to dredge up the right words to console him. Sadly, nothing seemed adequate:

"You've done your best, I'm sure," was all he could come up with before he saluted and left the general's office, feeling very uneasy.

Nothing, however, prepared him and von Braun for the shock of finding out that Becker put a gun to his head minutes after he had walked out the door.

A shadow fell over Peenemunde, both in mourning of his death and the fact that Hitler did not. His formal note of condolence barely mentioned Becker's name, while its cold-blooded postscript got straight back to business:

> *I refuse to approve mass production of long range missiles until they can actually fly.*

Point-blank as it was, the comment was fair enough coming from a man who hailed from the WWI trenches. There, in the blood-soaked mud, he saw the stark reality of war and could only comprehend the value of vast quantities of regular weapons. In fact, given Hitler's innate wariness of their project, Dornberger and von Braun often wondered why the money kept coming in to fund it. Albeit in dribs and drabs during the initial stages of the war, the dam burst in 1941 and it started flooding in thanks to the Luftwaffe's devastating miscalculation of its might.

After the formal declaration of war, there had been little to no action on the military front and Hitler was bored. To get the ball rolling, he launched his Blitzkrieg and scored a lightning-fast victory that knocked France out of the war before it really began.

"England's next," he warned.

It's people, however, had different ideas and demonstrated them during the Battle of Britain; a monumental moment in history that changed the course of the war and the direction of von Braun's life. Suddenly Hitler turned to him with new found enthusiasm.

"I want that new wonder weapon of yours and I want it now!" he demanded in a flurry of disillusion over the Luftwaffe's failure to destroy the RAF's spitfires and sterling spirit during their dogfights over London.

Instantly, the A-4, soon to be renamed the V-2, was restored to top priority. Yet, despite being given this vital boost, its development dragged on because it was such a massive project; one which was perhaps overly ambitious and unwieldy because its concept, mathematical calculations and complicated systems integration were all going on in von Braun's brain rather than being formulated on paper.

That mind of his constantly functioned at fever-pitch, swirling with facts and figures to fulfill the Fuhrer's mandate, while stubbornly sustaining the statistics to keep his spaceflight hopes alive. It helped that the few fellow workers who had followed him from his old rocket group to Peenemunde, were just as keen to cling to the dream.

"I've been wondering whether we should add wings to the missile," one of them suggested.

Von Braun's eyes lit up at the idea.

"Why not?" he answered excitedly. "Even if they do little to extend its range, they'll make it look more like a spaceship."

At times, he was like a boy with a new toy, but this particular game he was playing was deadly serious and with Becker gone and Todt not interested, he needed the support of someone phenomenal. It was just fortunate that Hitler felt the same way and quickly slotted architect Speer into the equation.

TWENTY-ONE

MUCH *TOO* QUICKLY to everyone's way of thinking, but Hitler did not care. To capitalise on Speer's extraordinary efficiency, he shuffled him into a military role, making room for him by disposing of Armaments Minister Todt via means far more brutal than those used to push General Becker into committing suicide. When Todt's plane mysteriously went down and Speer, who was supposed to be on it, suddenly was not, a collective gasp of dismay rose from the Reich's ranks.

"I can't blame them for thinking the worst," Speer was first to admit, because he too was suffering from shock. "But I swear it's not how it happened."

As far as Speer knew, he was telling the truth, for Hitler's unswerving devotion to him included sparing him any involvement in his dirty work. Yes, Hitler knew that Todt's plane was sabotaged and for that reason was horrified when Todt offered Speer a seat on it at the last minute. It was a kind gesture for which Speer was grateful because Hitler was running him ragged with his architectural project and wanted him back in Berlin as soon as possible.

Why, Speer then wondered, did the Fuhrer keep him up talking into the early hours of the morning at his Wolf's Lair headquarters in East Prussia so that he'd miss the 6am flight? When Speer was finally allowed to go to bed, he dropped onto it too exhausted to get undressed and way too tired to get up in time to catch the plane.

He woke with a start, however, at the roar of its engines. Leaping from his bed, he looked out the window to watch it take off; and seconds later, to see it explode in a rolling red ball of flame as it plummeted to earth.

Todt's burnt body was still smouldering when Hitler offered Speer his job. It was in appalling taste, but knowing what happened to people who displeased their Fuhrer, Speer thought it safer to accept it and endure the scathing looks of his peers; all of them silently saying what they thought of him, but none brave enough to say it out loud whenever Hitler was around.

Todt's suspicious death would always raise eyebrows, but it was the best thing that ever happened to von Braun and his team. Speer was now Armaments Minister and a man after his own heart – young, dynamic and with a shrewd eye on the future; not to mention, a degree as an accomplished mathematician in his own right, which predisposed him to their program. Contrary to Hitler's lacklustre attitude towards it, Speer was thrilled by their operations and never missed an opportunity to visit the seaside headquarters.

"For me, this project of yours has a strange fascination," he admitted to von Braun over drinks. "It's like the planning of a miracle, which is exactly what the Reich needs."

Free, for a short time, from Hitler's incessant demands, the pressure was off and Speer settled back in his fire-side chair, comfortable in the company of men of his kind and thoroughly enjoying being part of their apolitical, scientific circle. They were the 'people of tomorrow' and if he had his way, he would have happily thrown in his lot with them.

Unfortunately, that would never happen, because, like

von Braun, he'd had a meteoric rise to power to control a gigantic project; the likes of which was the opportunity of a lifetime that left him indebted to Hitler for life with no chance of escape. He only wished he could warn von Braun not to make the same mistake. Yet, he could see it was already too late, for the expression on the young baron's face was the same as his own reflected each morning in the mirror. It was the face of a man obsessed with an unrelenting passion and near-unreachable goal for which he would sacrifice everything.

Such introspection, however, was wasted on von Braun who, unlike Speer at this moment, wasn't worried about his moral compass going awry. In the early post-war years, it was to be the distinguishing factor between them, but during these halcyon days, their aim was precisely the same: to ensure that German genius reigned supreme and showed the way through the modern age.

It was a pity, at this pivotal point in rocketry, that Operation Barbarossa got in the way and diverted Speer's and Hitler's attention. It was Speer's job to provide all armaments and munitions for the invasion of Russia, and convinced of his army's fast victory there, Hitler took a chunk of the operation's funding away to give to the Luftwaffe and navy for a second attack on England. Peenemunde, as a result, was left strapped for cash and on low priority.

Their V-2's first test flights were dismal failures, and although Dornberger and von Braun secured permission to brief Hitler on their progress at Wolf's Lair, that meeting, too, fell flat.

"No luck," they reported back to their Peenemunde colleagues after the Fuhrer refused to finance their 46-foot tall missile with 50,000 pounds of thrust and a range of 300 kilometres. "Apparently he dreamed last night that our rocket wouldn't work and wasn't prepared to discuss it further until our V-2 staged at least one successful flight."

It was fair enough, given their poor results, but Dornberger and von Braun were disappointed and beginning to get on each other's nerves.

"He'd have to be the *one person* in the world you haven't won over with your copious charms," Dornberger said in part jest to quash his irrational annoyance with von Braun for failing to dazzle the Fuhrer.

"Well, *maybe* you shouldn't have prematurely promised him the V-2's mass production," von Braun flashed back, with no intention of shouldering the blame.

It was the first time they had fought and although they knew it was fruitless, frustration made them keep it up.

"We'd have a better chance of achieving it," Dornberger swung round on him to say, "if you and my other top men didn't take yourselves off on business trips for days on end, leaving our test launches in the hands of junior staff."

"I'm not doing it for the heck of it!" von Braun answered, feeling well within his rights to be angry when his frantic flying from one firm to another across the length and breadth of the country was to secure a working rapport with Germany's industrial giants and thus, a constant supply of tools for their V-2 production.

In his heart, Dornberger understood, but after a series of test stand explosions at the hands of unsupervised employees, three of their non-flight V-2s had been destroyed and he was fed up. He ended the argument by issuing an order:

"I want you, Thiel and Riedel present at Peenemunde at all times and I have no sympathy, any longer, for your complaints about our rocket development being pushed too fast because of orders from above."

Von Braun opened his mouth to protest, but Dornberger hadn't finished.

"And another thing . . . I've had it up to here with your gentlemanly dealings with the Air Ministry. I'm sick of you dividing your time and expertise between the two of us. You're army, von Braun . . . *army* . . . *remember that!* All meetings in regard to the Luftwaffe's plans for rocket interceptors and anti-aircraft missiles must cease. As of now, you concentrate your efforts solely on the development of our V-2."

CHAPTER

TWENTY-TWO

THAT WAS HARD FOR VON BRAUN TO DO when problems also arose on the family front. The two telegrams he received from his father in quick succession pulled the rug from under him:

> REGRET TO SAY YOUR UNCLES FRITZ AND
> SIEGFRIED KILLED IN ACTION IN HOLLAND STOP

He was still recovering from that blow when a second telegram was delivered to his door:

> TRAGIC NEWS STOP WE NOW MOURN ALSO
> THE LOSS OF YOUR COUSIN YOUNG FRITZ
> KILLED IN ACTION LAST WEEK STOP

Suddenly, the war was very real and raw; the only good news being that their deaths made Baron Magnus heir to the ancestral von Braun estate of Neucken – a rambling, rural mansion with plenty of room to wander and commune with his forebears' ghosts.

His relatives died true to their noble knight's heritage, but there was nothing noble about the feelings their deaths stirred in Wernher. As he recited the Lord's Prayer over their empty coffins, his heart hardened at the thought of their unrecognisable bodies scattered far afield. Until this emotive moment, he had remained remote from the war Germany started, but now it had become personal and there were rumblings of revenge in his soul. Gone was his guilt over a weapon of mass destruction and the worry of being the man destined to create it.

It was contrary to his resilient nature to stay bitter, but war went resolutely on and hit home again when his brother Siggy decided to cross swords with one of the Fuhrer's most dangerous henchmen – head of Hitler Youth Baldur von Schirach, who at war's end was fated to spend 20 years behind bars for crimes against humanity and who had threatened Siggy with far worse for having recklessly voiced his anti-Nazi views.

"You're lucky to be alive," Wernher reprimanded his brother, much relieved when Siggy's sudden transfer as an envoy to Africa finally put an end to his loose lips causing trouble.

There, Siggy would sit out the bulk of the war in a British internment camp before an exchange of prisoners saw him spend the rest of it on diplomatic duty at the Vatican in Rome. All of this was made easier for him having met and married Hildegard Margis before he left for Ethiopia. As to her credentials for marrying into their noble family, neither his mother nor father dared ask after they had deemed the woman to whom he was previously engaged unsuitable and raised all hell in their eldest son. From that point on, they vowed never to interfere with their sons' romances again. But they found it very hard to keep silent over Wernher's surprise selection of a wife: a physical education teacher from Berlin.

"He can't be serious," Emmy could not help but say to her husband across the breakfast table.

The baron flapped open his newspaper to hide the grimace on his own face.

"Say nothing . . . say *absolutely* nothing," he answered. "We're not setting foot on that hostile territory again."

The bride-to-be was 26-year-old Dorothee Brill, a dark-haired beauty with a robust constitution, wrap-round white smile and a complete absence of aristocratic distinction. Every weekend, Wernher was flying to Berlin to see her in his army-issue Messerschmitt and returning to Peenemunde each Monday looking decidedly happier. The relationship seemed serious and with his playboy days apparently over his staff were pleased to see him settle down.

His mother, however, was not, and despite her husband's warning, decided to tell her son that she did not like her. Wernher took exception, annoyed that the woman he whisked home on the weekend to introduce to them had made such a bad impression. Usually he and his mother saw eye to eye, but this time he was angry enough to defy her.

"We've decided on a spring wedding," he announced.

That was that as far as the family was concerned, but it wasn't so simple to get permission from the SS. Due to the Reich's ethnic cleansing policy, all marriage applications had to be processed through Himmler's Race and Settlement Office to avoid the possibility of contaminating their pure Aryan race with Jewish blood.

To help the process along, Wernher took advantage of his honorary rank in the SS by identifying himself, on Peenemunde stationery, as SS captain Dr Wernher von Braun, and sending his application direct to Himmler.

> *As a result of my fiancé losing both her parents in the last bombing raid over Berlin,* he wrote, *I would like to accelerate our marriage and am most grateful to you, Sir, for permitting me to address you personally in regard to the matter.*

He signed off with a confident Heil Hitler and a postscript that read: *A hereditary pass for my fiancée is enclosed.*

Here, he made two strategic mistakes: the first was that his letter found its way into the Reich's impeccable record-keeping network to survive the war and serve as rare evidence of his SS involvement; and second: that it was sent too fast – a sure sign that he had not taken the time to delve more deeply into Dorothee's true ancestry.

For Himmler, warning bells rang as soon as he saw her address. She was living in an uptown unit in an area predominantly populated by Jews.

Wernher's parents were surprised when they did not receive an invitation to the wedding, but more astonished still to find out that it never went ahead. Dorothee's name was not mentioned ever again and for the sake of his career, von Braun was instructed to wipe her memory from existence.

Whether from fear or simply having second thoughts about making a lifetime commitment, von Braun's undying love for her did not linger long and he soon reverted to his old womanising ways. On his next business trip to Paris, he had a passionate affair with a French girl that put her life in peril as a German collaborator after the war and risked Wernher's happy marriage to another, when in 1963, the pretty Parisian contacted him again in America.

> *When I saw you interviewed on television, my heart leapt with joy to know you were still alive,* she was to write in a letter addressed to NASA. *For twenty years, not a day's gone by without you being in my secret thoughts. When you didn't rescue me from prison after Germany's surrender I supposed you were dead, but thank God you are not and that I was spared execution because I didn't divulge your real name or tell them how important you were.*

The fact that she suffered so much for their enduring love made him ashamed, for she, in return, never crossed his mind. Certainly, he had not meant to put her in harm's way when, at the time, the prospect of Germany actually *losing* the war was unthinkable. In post-war USA, however, it was all a dream of a love long lost showing unsettling signs of turning into a nightmare, its nuisance factor strongly outweighing nostalgia. He knew he should make amends.

And I will, one day, he told himself, but her letter was soon buried under a pile of bills on his desk and there was no record that he ever wrote back.

TWENTY-THREE

THE RAF'S OFFENSIVE AGAINST GERMANY meant that Peenemunde was vulnerable to attack. Its safe seclusion from the war was over and von Braun was worried. Quite apart from the havoc it could cause to the compound, it threatened the life of his younger brother, Magnus, who had recently come to work with them as a chemical engineer. It was nice for Wernher to have him around, but it was just one more responsibility to add to the rest.

Fortunately, Magnus was not among the casualties after the first British bombs dropped, but the pressure was stepping up at Peenemunde. Within days, Himmler took control of the rocket program as a preliminary to putting all autonomous armament plants under his auspices.

"I intend to use concentration camp workers for our weapons production and I need you to sign off on it," he informed Armaments Minister Speer.

Speer hesitated. For moral reasons, it went against the grain, as did Himmler as a human being, so he was happy to hinder him whenever possible. A tense silence passed between them, but Himmler stood his ground with his cold, pale face and neat round glasses.

"Whatever your personal dislike of me," he said to break the stalemate, "the Fuhrer would be most displeased to see it impact on the welfare of the Reich."

It was a threat, pure and simple, and although Speer was sure that between the two of them it was he who had Hitler's support, Himmler had made a valid point. Wartime shortages of conventional labour left them no option but to make use of prisoners. So, he signed his name to Himmler's plan and gave him free rein to do his worst.

What did it matter? Speer reasoned, when he himself paid no mind to the nuts and bolts of the Nazi's genocide machine. Remote from it in his Berlin office, he focused instead on not seeing reality.

However, by the end of 1942, even Himmler, who enjoyed watching the worst of it first hand, had to admit that it was not working as well as he had hoped. The prisoners lacked enthusiasm for their job and were dying in droves. Piles of their emaciated corpses were clogging up the system and Himmler became concerned about their appalling conditions. For business, rather than humanitarian reasons, he issued a new order to all his SS plant supervisors:

"Every one of our manufacturing plants has become grossly inefficient. The mortality rate must be reduced to optimise output, so feed the labourers just enough to keep them on their feet."

Peenemunde was not exempt from the directive. Both its east army and west Luftwaffe facilities were taking advantage of what free labour was on offer. Like Speer, von Braun knew it was happening, but chose to separate himself from the stench of the suffering and the moral dilemma it posed. Having played no part in deciding to use slave labour, he felt content in exempting himself from accountability.

Try as he did, however, to distance himself from the atrocities, his good friend Arthur Rudolph kept him well informed of them. As factory liaison officer and a committed Nazi, Rudolph was in the thick of it and took some relish in speaking of the hardships being inflicted on the slaves, while often wondering why the ever verbose von Braun never had anything to say on the subject.

It was a risky business for Wernher to sit on the fence when passion for his craft and the patriotism on which it relied were forever urging him to take a fatal leap to its dark side. Yet, he clung tight to his non-committal perch and claims of scientific immunity, because he was smart enough to know that one day his life might depend on it. As long as he kept his mouth shut about Peenemunde's slave labour, the facility, in his mind's eye, remained neutral territory, excused from the horrors of the Third Reich.

It took some talent for him and Speer to live in their fantasy world of bearing no responsibility for wrongdoing while being the brains behind its technical implementation. On this point, they were akin. Keen to keep up his support of von Braun's program, Speer headed up the military delegation invited to view his next V-2 test launch.

He was sorry that he did because it nearly killed him.

... oOo ...

"Astounding!" Speer exclaimed when the four-storey-high rocket slowly rose from its launch pad and appeared to balance, for a brief moment, on its own jet of flame. When it then vanished with a thunderous roar into the low-lying clouds, he was awestruck.

"It's a technical miracle," he turned excitedly to say to von Braun, "completely defying the law of gravity."

Thus encouraged, von Braun began to discuss the distance the projectile would travel, and for 30 seconds it did before they heard a horrendous bang. It was followed by an eerie second of silence and then the whistling of rapid acceleration warning that the missile was heading back to Earth . . . and fast. For a split second, they all stood frozen to the spot, before someone had the sense to scream out: *"Run!"*

With no time to do it, von Braun pushed Speer, face-first, to the ground, flung himself down beside him and braced for impact. Fortunately, the missile landed far enough away to keep them intact, but left them with a disconcerting, ear-ringing deafness for the rest of the day. The near-death experience should have been enough to scare Speer off, but despite the fear and failure of the launch, he was still thrilled by the possibilities and continued to champion their cause.

"I don't think Hitler believes that you'll ever achieve your missile's guidance and control," he confided to von Braun. "But *I* think you will and I'm prepared to back you financially until you do."

Such confidence in von Braun was due more to Speer's feeling of camaraderie than commonsense. In truth, he was beginning to come around to Hitler's defeatist way of thinking in regard to the whole rocket program. Yet, despite their tepid attitude towards it, Speer convinced the Fuhrer to push on.

"Hitler liked the look of you from the start and is willing to give you the benefit of the doubt," Speer explained.

Von Braun was genuinely surprised. "But he never looked once in my direction when he visited Kummersdorf."

To this, Speer gave a sardonic smile and said: "Never make

the mistake of underestimating the man. He's got eyes in the back of his head and never misses a beat."

Speer would have been the first to tell him that the Fuhrer's favour was a wonderful thing that made all things possible, but that daring to disappoint him would end in despair. Now both he and von Braun walked that fine line, so there was a sigh of relief all round when Peenemunde engineer Helmut Hoelzer's analog computer radically changed the equation and made a mass-produced guidance system possible.

> *The bird picked up speed and passed the dreaded 'sonic barrier' without a problem,* von Braun wrote in his report to Speer, taking due note that this time, the Armaments Minister was happy to learn of its success from a safe distance. *The nose of the rocket broke soon after, but having flown a great deal longer than any of our prior tests, it appears we're on the right track.*

Speer knew what hopes the young inventor was placing on this experiment and felt a brotherly pride in his success. For von Braun and his team, this was not just the development of a weapon, but a giant step into the future of technology.

CHAPTER

TWENTY-FOUR

HOT ON THE HEELS OF THE SUCCESS came Hitler's greatest failure — the Battle of Stalingrad. He underestimated Russia's resilience as much as he did the potential of von Braun's rockets. Despite the ballistic missiles' growing success, and more likely because of it, the Air Ministry was taking advantage of Hitler's vulnerability to talk the army's V-2 project down and stir up the Fuhrer's doubts about it.

"Only because they have their own agenda," Dornberger was quick to point out. "Goering's gang will say and do anything to beat us to the punch with their V-1 buzz-bomb."

Code named Cherry Stone, the Luftwaffe was perilously close to completing what the English would come to know as the dreaded 'doodlebug'. Although both Speer and von Braun advocated that the two projects should be complementary rather than competitive, it continued to be a source of healthy rivalry between the two forces.

To make sure that the army stayed a step ahead with its V-2, Dornberger sent out a memo to all staff:

They all rallied to the cause and on October 3, 1942, their rocket flew 80 kilometres and approached airless space. The East Peenemunde people were jubilant. With champagne glasses held aloft, they danced and drank till dawn, while von Braun literally wept with joy into his beer before making a slurred speech:

"This is a watershed moment," he said, "the day that our V-2 became the first man-made object to touch the edge of space. Now we all know what it is to reach for the stars."

In his inebriated state, he could swear that those stars were all twinkling in the eyes of his staff, but just one look at the dark, deadpan anger in Dornberger's made him sober up fast. He was only grateful that his boss had the decency to reprimand him in private.

"This is the last time I'll tell you," Dornberger said. "Our rockets are to be manufactured for no other purpose but weaponry. You know how much I share your dreams, but now that Germany's starting to struggle for survival, they must be put aside with no more talk of space travel. Stalingrad's been a fiasco and if we infuriate Hitler any further, he'll clamp down on our project altogether and probably transfer us all to the Russian front."

Fortunately, their recent launch success came at a good time. As the world's first ballistic missile, their V-2 heralded a new international arms race and Hitler sniffed another shot at success. He had been patient for a long time, waiting for the wonder weapon Peenemunde promised and now he insisted that they come up with the goods.

"I want 5000 of them for a mass attack," he demanded, after receiving his last depressing report from Stalingrad.

For want of an outlet for his rage, he was lashing out in all directions and grasping at straws with no concept of the perplexity of missile manufacture. The sheer enormity of their intricate production and deployment would render the V-2 near useless. At the absurdity of the command, tempers flared all round.

"Hitler has a few suggestions of his own in regard to our rocket's warhead," Dornberger snarled as he threw the Fuhrer's blueprints on the conference table.

Von Braun lifted an eyebrow at the unintelligible scrawl, but when he opened his lips to speak Dornberger immediately shut him down, his raised hand and serious expression stopping Wernher from saying something sarcastic.

"Our Fuhrer has also ordered that bunkers be built on the Channel coast for V-2 deployment."

Von Braun wasn't averse to that idea, but as a tried and true artillery man, Dornberger was dead against it.

"They'd be a disaster," he stated. "The only way our missiles will be effective is with mobile launch pads. Static positioning will make us sitting ducks."

For other very valid reasons, von Braun did not agree, which put him at loggerheads with the colonel for a second time. Neither of them would budge, but von Braun won the day because he backed Hitler's idea, and that was that.

When, in the future, Dornberger's theory proved right, von Braun was quicker to apologise than the colonel was to forgive.

"Next time, stick to your own field of expertise," Dornberger would say. "You leave the business of war to me and I'll leave the scientific tinkering to you."

As for now, the next V-2 test flight had just taken off and accustomed to it never hitting its mark, Dornberger and von Braun were standing at the centre of its projected target still arguing over the subject.

"*Watch out!*" they suddenly heard rocket designer Bernhard Tessmann call out.

They looked up, and seeing the missile hurtling towards them, ran for their lives, both making a spritely leap over the nearby sandbag barrier to take cover. At the big bang, they sat dumbstruck in the dust, their open-mouthed shock at having survived turning to laughter and a congratulatory slap on the back when they realised that for the first time, their rocket landed smack on target.

It was hazards like these that stopped Hitler from ever personally visiting Peenemunde, but in his stead, Himmler came often, not flinching at being present during their next string of launch failures, because he was determined to make his presence felt now that Speer was trying to muscle in on the V-2 project and take it over.

After meeting Dornberger in Berlin to discuss the building of bunkers, road mobile units and production, Speer had moved in his own men. One of whom was Gerhard Degenkolb, a mechanical engineer who had succeeded in speeding up the production of locomotives by discarding components that were not absolutely necessary. With Germany's war fronts faltering and the call for locomotives reduced, Speer switched Degenkolb's talents to rockets and appointed him head of the special committee for the V-2. It was an unexpected move that relegated von Braun to another role.

"Head of final acceptance committee," Dornberger informed him. "You'll be responsible for specifying the requirements and test procedures for all components and for stopping inadequately manufactured parts reaching the assembly line."

Thinking that he and Speer were friends, von Braun took a moment to digest what he saw as a demotion, but after being assured that it was not, he got back to business, much of which was now focused on his fiery confrontations with Degenkolb.

"In this business you can't afford to put quantity over quality," von Braun argued vigorously.

"If we've got to produce 900 rockets a month, you'll have to get up to speed, von Braun," Degenkolb yelled back. "We've no time for fastidious experimentation any longer. It's on the assembly line and out!"

Von Braun upped the volume of his voice to match the man's. "We're not talking about canned food here, Degenkolb. Just one wrong move with that fix-em-quick assembly line of yours and you'll blow us all to smithereens."

They were never going to see eye to eye, so Degenkolb took his complaints to Speer.

"If you want to achieve optimum production, you're going to have to stop that smug scientist friend of yours interfering with our new industrial methods."

The problem was that the V-2 was von Braun's baby and he saw every vehicle as a handcrafted experiment subject to endless improvement; each missile receiving eleventh-hour amendments to better its performance at the hands of brilliant craftsmen.

Speer explained as much to Degenkolb, but he wasn't interested.

"Well, with the Fuhrer agitating over their mass production, you know as well as I do that we haven't got that luxury."

That was true and as Germany's foremost efficiency expert, Speer knew that he had to talk von Braun out of his meticulous, old scientific ways and train him into their new conveyor-belt culture.

TWENTY-FIVE

VAST FORMATIONS OF RAF and American bombers had begun daytime raids over Germany. In July 1943 Hamburg was flattened, leaving 80,000 dead, and after a devastating sixth-month siege, Hitler had to accept that Stalingrad was lost.

You are expected to fall on your sword, he made clear to the commander of the failed Russian campaign, General Friedrich Paulus, by promptly promoting him to Field Marshal. Just in case that was too subtle, the note that accompanied the fifth star for his epaulette, spelt it out:

Never in history has a German of this rank dishonoured himself by surrendering to the enemy.

"Well, there's always a first time," Paulus said when he refused to fire the pistol put at his disposal. After the horrendous suffering and pointless slaughter of his entire Sixth Army in the sub-zero Soviet war zone, he had completely lost faith in the Fuhrer and was no longer prepared to sacrifice his life for the sake of the Reich.

Cowardice had nothing to do with it. He needed more courage to defy Hitler than to fire the fatal shot into his brain; and the fact that he dared do it sent a dangerous message to the German military hierarchy: to break ranks and disobey the Fuhrer was possible.

Most of the Wehrmacht 'old school' knew that the war was effectively over and that Hitler was growing madder by the moment. The men of honour among his staff could clearly see him feverishly clinging to his dream and were questioning their blind obedience to what they now knew was a nightmare.

Unfortunately, there were still deluded diehards such as Propaganda Minister Joseph Goebbels, who refused to see the light and called for 'total war'. With that proclamation came his promise of a new wonder weapon that would turn the tide.

"Insanity!" von Braun said when Degenkolb moved their December deadline forward to September to make good on that promise. It was a staggering expectation, but realising that his life was on the line if he did not perform, von Braun said no more and obeyed.

"I think it's do-able," Arthur Rudolph said to spur him on.

Having recently returned from an inspection tour of the Heinkel aircraft plant, Rudolph had seen the company's splendid exploitation of SS prisoners and was full of renewed hope for the similar injection of manpower they needed. At his prompting, Peenemunde followed suit and when Goering, Himmler and Grand Admiral Donitz came to visit the compound, they were impressed by the fresh supply of men working hard on Hitler's behalf.

"Albeit looking bedraggled and a little unwilling," Donitz commented, when he saw one of them in rags being bludgeoned senseless by an SS guard.

At the flash of concern on Donitz's face, Colonel Dornberger had to think fast.

"You must remember that they are all condemned men – thieves and murderers to whom we've offered the leniency of hard labour rather than a death sentence."

Donitz, as an intelligent man, found the explanation barely believable, but its tenuous grasp on morality sufficed to clear his conscience. He hesitated for a few seconds to let the excuse sink in and then went happily on his way, content in the knowledge that they were merely being cruel to be kind.

A newly arrived electrical engineer, however, did not see it that way when he came in the compound gates as the Grand Admiral was driving out. He was instantly confronted and appalled at the suffering of the concentration camp workers.

"It's not just a case of able-bodied prisoners doing useful work," he protested to his colleagues over lunch. "It's brutal, political persecution."

He said it loud enough for von Braun to hear as he walked past the engineers' dining table. He stopped to make a comment but thought better of it and moved on. Slave labour had nothing directly to do with him and he did not want to get involved now that he was preoccupied with his V-2s fast-tracked production. These were strange times and his staff noticed a change in him – that the usually talkative, quick-to-joke young baron had grown decidedly silent and grim-mouthed; not proud of what he saw around him nor of himself for making no stand against it while it served his purpose.

The upside was that both he and Dornberger were rewarded for their compliance to the Nazi system by being promoted. Dornberger was made brigadier general by the Fuhrer, while von Braun's rise up the ranks came courtesy of Himmler. The SS Reichsfuhrer made a special trip to Peenemunde to present him with his silver oak-leaf epaulettes, because he knew that von Braun was also a favourite of the Armaments Minister and that such a personal gesture would get him one up on Speer.

So, it was back to the wardrobe and the brisk use of the clothes brush when von Braun was told that Himmler was on his way. Rigged out in full SS military regalia, he looked most impressive when he thrust out his arm in salute. By the end of the day, formality turned to the familiarity of a fireside chat with a select group of officers in the baronial Hearth Room of Peenemunde's officers' mess.

"Reichsfuhrer, what are we really fighting for?" von Braun felt at ease enough to ask.

The blunt comment coming out of the blue had Dornberger sit bolt upright in his armchair, ready to explain it away. Himmler, however, appeared to like the fact that Peenemunde's technical director had been forthright, and he responded in kind with his full-blown, racist plans for the brutal subjugation of Europe.

Von Braun listened intently without blinking an eye, and encouraged by what seemed to be his avid interest, Himmler returned the favour by not flinching the next day when he witnessed their V-2 test flight veer crazily across the sky before diving into the Luftwaffe's Peenemunde West airfield, blasting a crater 100 feet wide and destroying three of their planes.

Used to the rivalry between their east and west facilities, Dornberger's instinct was to shout out a triumphant *"Bullseye!"* But this was a serious mistake on their part and he braced himself, instead, for Himmler's reprimand. When it came, it was baffling.

"Goering won't be happy," was all he said, devoid of emotion, before he left the compound without saying another word.

Von Braun watched as his black sedan rounded the corner and drove away.

"Well that's done it," he said. All the good work he'd done, including having to sit through the man's mind-numbing diatribe on Nazi ethics had gone up in smoke.

He and Dornberger were astounded, therefore, when they received a phone call from Speer early the next morning:

"Himmler's reported back favourably on your work," he said. "The Fuhrer wants you both here today to give a presentation."

'Here' was Hitler's Wolf's Lair headquarters; and 'today' meant that they had only a few hours to prepare and get there. Flying was the only option, but with no time to come up with anything better, they had to rely on a colour film of one of their successful V-2 test launches. Being a last resort, they had no idea that it would come closer to hitting the mark than if Hitler saw the real thing. The truth was that the Fuhrer loved going to the movies, and short of having a box of popcorn on his lap, he settled down to enjoy the show.

When the guard at the door had initially stood to attention and announced: *"The Fuhrer!"* von Braun was shocked to see his transformation. Accompanied by Speer and Generals Keitel and Jodl, Hitler walked into the darkened room swathed in a cape hanging heavily on his hunched shoulders, the dilated pupils of his once electric-blue eyes burning black against his pallid face. He seemed to have aged 30 years overnight, but trying not to let his dismay show, von Braun stood straight and tall on stage, waiting for his cue to begin.

The film started rolling and in strong, dynamic style, he took them all by storm, narrating the silent movie with the aplomb of a professional. When, for the first time, Hitler saw the majestic spectacle of the great rocket rising from its launch pad to soar into the stratosphere, he let out a gasp of awe. And Speer, who was more in control for having seen it before, smiled – proud of von Braun's immense achievement and for selling it to the Fuhrer so convincingly.

"So, we made it after all!" von Braun finished with flair as Dornberger joined him on stage to share in the hearty round of applause.

"How did it feel speaking in front of such great men?" Dornberger whispered, as they both clicked their heels and gave a curt bow.

"Easy," von Braun tilted his head to whisper back. "I just imagined them all in their underwear."

"I like that young man," Hitler was saying at the same time to Speer. "He lectured without a trace of timidity or boyish enthusiasm."

"Young, but brilliant," Speer replied, and taking the opportunity to outdo Himmler in his patronage of von Braun, continued on to say: "Age is no barrier for genius and if it were up to me, I would, here and now, award him the title of professor."

Such an impromptu promotion shooting von Braun to the top of his field was not within Speer's power, but it was well within Hitler's, and taking the idea on board as if it were his own, he got up awkwardly from his chair to shake Wernher's hand.

"Congratulations Professor," he said, " . . . on your wonderful success."

Von Braun stood stock-still, momentarily struck dumb by the honour Hitler had only twice before bestowed on Speer and Willy Messerschmitt.

"Thank you, *Mein Fuhrer,*" he gathered his wits to say as he felt Hitler's grip on his hand grow painfully tight.

"But remember," Hitler continued. "I'm after total annihilation, von Braun. Don't let me down."

TWENTY-SIX

"**I** WANT TO HIT LONDON WITH OUR V-2s in October," Hitler told Speer. "We'll need 20,000 of them built by then and I'm putting you in overall control of the program to make sure it all happens."

Speer knew better than to argue, but he could clearly see von Braun's jaw-dropping reaction when he passed on the preposterous order. Pre-empting his valid objections, Speer raised a restraining hand:

"No need to say a word," he said. "Just do your best."

Von Braun never did anything but, so months of intensive work followed. Now that Hitler had given him the green light, he was under relentless pressure from the Armaments Ministry and the SS, added to which were the Luftwaffe's demands for an anti-aircraft missile to counter the Allies' massive bombing offensive. High ranking Nazis were daily interfering with his project, which was not only annoying, but meant that he could no longer claim exemption from their crimes by being safely cocooned within the more traditional Army Ordnance network. Before he knew it, he had become an essential cog in the Nazi machine and was working tirelessly in support of its madmen and murderers.

It was hard to say how it had all happened. All he knew was that his meteoric promotion to professor thrilled him and he had no doubt as to who made it possible.

"I owe this to you, I'm sure," he had said to Speer on the night of his Wolf's Lair presentation, and Speer did not deny it.

"Congratulations to the youngest professor in the Reich," he answered, before introducing von Braun to one of Berlin's top economists, Hans Kerhl.

"That rocket of yours is phenomenal," Kerhl complimented him.

"You just wait," von Braun replied, riding high on all the praise. "Someday soon, one of my rockets will reach the moon."

Kerhl smiled and gave him a congratulatory pat on the back before going home to his wife and saying in head-shaking disbelief: "At headquarters today, I meant a real lunatic."

Considering the Nazi ranks were full of them, standing out as worthy of the label was quite an insult. Von Braun, however, came nowhere near being crazy. It was, in fact, the sanest thing he had ever said, for in the midst of his excitement and what should have been his undying gratitude towards Hitler and his Reich, he remained detached from both, loyal only to his own ambition. In the eyes of history and the blame for war crimes to come, his comment spoke volumes for his innocence, showcasing his one-track mind aimed solely in the direction of space.

The truth was that he felt like a fraud. His disillusionment with the war had long since set in and he knew all along, that contrary to Hitler's hopes, his missile could never reverse its catastrophic course. At this stage, he was exploiting the system for his own ends and it was simply a question of whether he survived the war to achieve them. He was working 20 hours a day, seven days a week, barely able to snatch a moment's sleep while having to tolerate Hitler's neurotic outbursts whenever his unrealistic deadlines were not met. What admiration he'd had for the Fuhrer was quickly fading to a strange feeling of ill-ease whenever he was in his hypnotic presence.

"If I were a more religious man, I'd find it worrying," he confided to his younger brother, Magnus, over a late supper. "Hitler's always been a law unto himself, but it seems to me, these days, that he doesn't think himself answerable to even a higher power."

It was a rash comment made in the heat of the moment, because it had been a boiling hot summer day and tempers were flaring at the impossibility of meeting the Fuhrer's demands. Magnus, too, was feeling the strain, but still somewhat under Hitler's spell, he was not in the mood to mollify his big brother.

"Not everyone believes in God," he snapped back with that touch of Nazi fanaticism Wernher was now finding disturbing.

"No, but to actively embrace the opposite is a concern," he said, swilling down his brandy before further arguing the point. But all ideas of doing that were suddenly cut short by the sound of Peenemunde's air raid siren.

As its unfamiliar wail wound to a crescendo they looked at each other in dismay, for an instant not sure what to do because up until now the compound had largely avoided air attacks due to its masquerade as a mere experimental air base. Word had not reached them that an RAF reconnaissance plane photo had shown tall, upright objects resembling rockets on their facility and that they were now the Allies' prime target.

Wernher had saved Magnus' life once before by arranging his transfer from the high-risk Luftwaffe ranks to a safe assignment at Peenemunde, but ironically, here they now were on the frontline under far more imminent threat of death.

They moved fast, flinging open the door to see that the artificial fog system had already been activated and the compound was enshrouded in mist. A coral-coloured moon shone through its haze and within minutes the sky was dotted with little red and green lights.

"Christmas trees!" Magnus said in alarm, recognising the RAF's target-marking flares.

The same dazzling display had appeared in the sky before the blanket bombing of Hamburg, and the resulting firestorm that nearly destroyed the city had sent a wave of panic across the Reich. Now, at Peenemunde, flak fire had begun and there was no time left to think.

"We'd better get to the bunker," Wernher shouted through the syncopated thunder of their anti-aircraft guns.

Not a minute too soon, for the second they were inside its claustrophobic confines, the enemy bombs and incendiaries began to rain down. Six hundred Lancaster, Halifax and Stirling heavy bombers emptied their 1800-ton payload on the compound, one of which hit close, shaking loose a layer of sandbags and dirt that knocked them off their feet.

As they came to their senses, the shelter door flew wide open and there stood Dornberger, half dressed in army jacket and pyjamas, with his face caked in blood.

He was fit to drop, but as he teetered, von Braun leapt to his feet to break his fall.

"Where are you hit?" he yelled through Dornberger's half faint as he searched frantically for some sign of an entry wound.

"Just aftershock," Dornberger surfaced from his swirling semi-consciousness to stammer. "Not my blood."

God only knew whose blood it was when their Peenemunde housing settlement was coming under such heavy fire. The RAF had made it their first target, hoping to kill off the centre's engineering leadership. One look at the conflagration beyond the bunker said they were doing a fine job. It was a miracle

Dornberger survived, but they could only wonder at how many of their colleagues out there in the dark had not. With the air raid now at its worst it was too soon to find out. But blind as they were to their friends' fate through the smoke and fire, the Allies were blinder still in the black night trying to pinpoint such a small target and the bulk of their bombs missed the mark.

"The stupid bastards have killed their own," one of the surviving engineers stumbled into the bunker to announce after the first wave of attack was over. "Most of their bombs hit the forced labour camp and everyone there's dead . . . must be at least 600."

"What about the women's quarters?" Dorberger was now stable enough to ask.

"Gone!" the engineer confirmed. "All their houses are on fire and everyone in them must be burnt to a crisp."

Before they had time to mourn their loss, the second wave of bombing began, this time striking at the production factories, before a third wave targeted the development works. They could feel the shock waves of the intense bombardment through the ground and in anticipation of the devastation awaiting them outside, their initial fear changed to fury. As the earth rumbled beneath their feet, they sat in jaw-clenched silence waiting out the raid, until at last the roar of RAF engines faded into the distance.

"Do you hear that?" Wernher asked Magnus when all fell quiet.

"I don't hear anything."

"Exactly . . . looks like we're good to go," he said as he shouldered open the shelter door near blocked by flaming debris.

All outside was burning brilliant orange and at the sight of the flames devouring their buildings, Dornberger was devastated.

"Oh my beautiful Peenemunde!" he exclaimed in an uncharacteristic outburst of emotion, but as a hardened military man, it quickly changed to commonsense.

"You've got to get to Building 4!" he ordered von Braun with urgency. "And no matter what, salvage as much as you can."

That was easier said than done when their Building 4 Development Headquarters was at the centre of the conflagration. Not prepared to play the coward, however, von Braun didn't hesitate and plunged into the inferno, barely able to see or breathe with his eyes and lungs stinging from the smoke and the scalding heat pressing him to pass out.

Dashing from one small pocket of fire-free earth to the next, he managed to reach the building, only to find that half of it was already in cinders and that flames were raging on the roof of the one wing left standing. Fortunately, it was the one that housed the most important of Peenemunde's top-secret documents. With only minutes to act, he braced himself to fight his way through the blaze but was suddenly stopped by the touch of a hand on his shoulder.

"What in the *hell* are you doing here?" he said in total disbelief when he swung round to see his secretary, Dorette Kersten, standing behind him.

He hadn't known she was following him and he was furious, for now he was responsible for her life as well as his own and would have admonished her further had her soot-stained face and anxious blue eyes not looked so beguiling in the fire's glow.

"You can't do it all yourself," she lifted her chin defiantly to answer, in their deathly predicament, daring to stand up to her superior. "You'll need help."

In the midst of the inferno, there was no turning back and no point arguing, so he grabbed her hand and they ran together into the headquarters' hallway. As yet, it was not ablaze, but with all electricity down, they could navigate the black corridor only with their backs pressed flush to the one remaining wall as they sidled down its length to the sound of the fire's encroaching roar and crackle.

"One . . . two . . . three," von Braun counted to himself as he felt his way past each office aperture and then: *"Yes . . .* this is it!" he said out loud, when he finally felt the door to the room containing the all-important safe they were after.

The area was fast filling with smoke and with no time to work out its combination, an emergency-induced shot of adrenaline gave him the strength to smash out the timber casement window. Between the two of them, they painstakingly pushed the hot metal box across the floor and toppled its lead-like weight off the edge of the burning building to the ground below where a group of SS soldiers had gathered to help carry it away.

"I never thought the day would come when I'd be pleased to see them!" von Braun said sarcastically to his secretary's surprise. But before he had time to better monitor his words, the floor beneath their feet began to burn through their shoes and the dense smoke started to asphyxiate them.

The only way out was back the way they came, but at twice the speed. Hand in hand, they ran the gauntlet, moving fast down the long, dark corridor, before blindly negotiating the stairs. When memory failed them as to their exact number, they tripped over the last few and fell heavily on their knees. Robbed of the luxury of worrying about being hurt, von Braun scrambled to his feet, dragged his secretary back up on to hers and pulled her the last few yards out the front door to burst free from the flames.

He and his beautiful accomplice felt a surge of elation at having played out the adventure, but the grisly task of searching for human survivors was far more gruelling. Fortunately, there were more survivors than they expected emerging from the sizzling ashes, because most of the slit trenches and shelters that had been built for such a contingency stood up to the challenge. Sadly, however, one of them sustained a direct hit and did not.

"It's Thiel," von Braun said when he found his friend, Walter – Peenemunde's chief of rocket design – dead in the rubble.

It took him a while to identify him because Thiel's corpse, along with the bodies of his entire family, was dismembered and burnt almost beyond recognition. No one would have blamed von Braun if he had broken down in grief, but instead, he was gripped by a gut-wrenching rage. The war had just got way too up close and personal, and whether or not his V-2 could turn its tide, he was glad now that it was capable of wreaking a suitable revenge.

TWENTY-SEVEN

ONE THING WAS SURE: their rocket manufacture could no longer remain as exposed. So, to work in conjunction with what remained of Peenemunde, the order was given to build an operations centre underground.

"Speer's ministry will pay the bills," Hitler informed Himmler, "but you will have overall control of the new Mittlewerk facility near Nordhausen."

Himmler was jubilant. Taking charge of this subterranean central works, dubbed Dora by its labourers, not only enhanced his private empire, but came as a real slap in the face for Speer, with whom he'd had an on-going power struggle heading up the missile program. Fortunately for the Fuhrer, the difficulty of choosing between them was lessened by Speer having recently let him down.

"Speer couldn't stop the series of hits on his scattered missile sites after the Peenemunde raid," Hitler explained to Himmler, disappointed that his Armaments Minister had failed to perform with his usual peak efficiency.

Speer had been unwell lately with a nervous collapse due to serious work overload, so to spare his favourite further strain,

Hitler turned to Himmler, who was at his best inflicting excessive workloads on others.

Half of the 60,000 concentration camp prisoners herded through Dora's dark tunnels were destined to die. Their part in the V-2 and V-1 'buzz bomb' production process was to slave 18 hours a day in the 90-degree humidity, crawling like animals through the unventilated caverns with little food, no water for washing and only a few drops more to drink. Deprived of sunlight, fresh air and any form of sanitation, they dropped like flies, while the piles of their emaciated carcasses and the constant flow of raw sewerage attracted vermin far worse. In the absence of toilets, barrels with single-plank seats were provided for relief and the guards' ongoing amusement. Those more bored among them, regularly pulling the plank midway through a prisoner's bout of diarrhoea to see him fall, full body, into the tank of foul excrement.

"How are we meant to survive under such conditions?" one recently arrived prisoner asked an old-timer who had miraculously lasted more than two months at Dora.

"We're not," he answered. "If hunger and disease don't kill us, then the relentless brutality of the guards will."

With the war not going their way, Germany had nothing to lose and there were no holds barred. For them, it was a race against time, and with so many atrocities having already been committed in the name of the Third Reich, one more at Dora would hardly make a difference. Von Braun's V-2 was their last shot at turning the tide and to that end all was sacrificed. It was now a case of quantity over quality, so with half the slaves at Dora expected to expire, the SS insured themselves against risk by bringing in twice the number they needed. The sheer scale of the scheme, together with the swarming subterranean masses made it an unwieldy project that required ruthless efficiency.

"And I've got just the man for the job," Himmler announced when he made SS Brigadefuhrer Hans Kammler the facility's commandant.

Kammler had all the right credentials. He held a degree in civil engineering and as the Chief of SS Construction, had distinguished himself by building the gas chambers at Auschwitz. He was a Nazi of the worst kind, whose sociopathic tendencies and boundless grasp on brutality guaranteed optimum production. Experience had taught him that what was not achieved by honest toil and sweat was better extracted by cruelty and mass murder.

"Himmler's most effective henchmen . . . the workers' fate is sealed," Speer sneered, still smarting over the SS Reichsfuhrer's triumph, but more so alarmed by what he saw when he made his first inspection tour of Dora. It was supposed to be a straight production site for submarines, aircraft and armaments, but it looked more like Hell.

"Well, *you're* financing it," Kammler said in cold-blooded response when Speer complained about the inhumane treatment of the prisoners. Far from showing Speer the respect due a superior, Kammler felt safe enough under the protection of Himmler's wing to add snidely: "I will, of course, be more than happy to register your objections with the SS Reichsfuhrer."

The animosity between Speer and Himmler was no secret; nor was Himmler's capacity to stoop to the lowest level to rid himself of anyone who rubbed him the wrong way. He had already attempted to kill Speer when he had been ill in hospital. While he hovered at death's door, Himmler tried to help open it prematurely by conspiring with Speer's physician to inject a fatal dose of morphine.

No one but Speer's nearest and dearest knew of Himmler's intent to murder, and had Speer's wife not demanded a second doctor's opinion at the last minute, he would have been dead.

The whole experience had shaken him. Lying helpless in bed, Speer's position of power within the Reich counted for nothing and he found out that he was expendable. He should have reported the incident to Hitler, but unsure as to which way the man might swing, he decided instead to steer clear of ruffling any more fanatics' feathers.

"But have you seen what goes on there?" he could not help but ask von Braun when they next met.

Speer hoped that comparing notes might help, because since witnessing the atrocities within Dora's depths, he had felt sick to his stomach. Appalled by the brutality and haunted by that one prisoner, all skin and bones, who had looked him straight in the eye and silently cursed him to damnation. Now seeing that destination as a distinct possibility, Speer had tried to make some sort of amends by ordering the immediate construction of outdoor labourers' quarters to at least give prisoners the benefit of breathing fresh air. But by the look of them, it was too little too late.

"Not as yet, but I'll be at Dora next week," von Braun answered, snapping Speer out of his guilt trip – one of many he had been taking since being sure that Germany had lost the war and in his dread of the consequences to come.

"Tread carefully," he cautioned von Braun. "You and I walk the same path and the cost of our careers is about to fall due."

His words of warning left von Braun none the wiser until he went to Dora the following Monday. There, in his supervisory role, he was responsible for monitoring prisoners' expertise and was waiting with pen and clipboard in hand to welcome the fresh crew of 1200 inmates newly arrived from Buchenwald.

"Hardly *fresh!*" he said to the overseer, shocked by their state of deterioration. "Most of them can barely walk, let alone work."

At the look of dismay on von Braun's face, the man shrugged. "You get used to it."

And von Braun did, learning very quickly to turn a blind eye; while in between his frequent business trips back to Peenemunde and Berlin, he limited himself to his work in Dora's laboratory. Safe within its sterile surrounds, he tuned out to the nightmare going on beyond, exempting himself from the moral decisions needed to prevent the prisoners' suffering. It was the sensible thing to do when earlier he had made the same mistake as Speer in reprimanding one of the SS guards for his savage conduct. As technical director of the facility, the last thing he expected was for that guard to spit at his feet.

"Mind your own business von Braun," he said crudely, "If you want to side with the swine, we can easily fit you up for one of their uniforms."

Such flagrant insubordination should have been punished, but they both knew that at Dora decency was dead. While the soldier brazenly capitalised on a free reign of evil, von Braun's gut instinct was to back away, as much from a feeling of foreboding as from his error in having tackled the wrong person. If he wanted to make an official protest, he would have to approach a more senior member of the SS and be smarter about what he said.

"The prisoners' bad health is hampering my V-2 production," he put pragmatically to the higher-ranking lieutenant on duty. "The fact that they're unskilled and disloyal makes it hard enough, but your men's constant abuse of them in their weakened state renders their work even more inferior and inflicts higher failure rates."

He made his point with a cold dispassion to which the SS could relate. The result was that they behaved themselves for a few days and for that, the prisoners who saw through von Braun's ruse, were grateful.

One of them, in particular, caught his eye. Frenchman Charles Sadron, who as a professor of physics had been arrested for his activities in the Resistance. He was dirty, dishevelled and near skeletal, but even his sallow face and sunken eyes could not hide his hallmark of intelligence.

"You are a professor?" von Braun approached him to ask, having recognised one of his own and gone out of his way to look up the prisoner's records.

Sadron nodded but refused to lift his gaze or to open his lips to any of his oppressors. It was hard to do when von Braun's tone seemed kind.

"I'm sorry for all you are suffering," he said. "I'd like to see you more safe and comfortable working in my laboratory."

At this, Sadron could not help but look up and meet von Braun's eye. It was against the grain to like what he saw in the young German's face. It showed integrity and for a heady moment, he was tempted to say 'yes' to spare himself further pain. Yet, clinging tight to his courage and fighting the fear of imminent death, he slowly shook his head.

"Thank you, *Herr Direktor*," he decided to do von Braun the courtesy of answering. "But I will not desert my friends, nor be drawn into the disgrace of assisting your Nazi war machine."

Von Braun could have taken exception and ordered the man's death all the sooner, but instead, he gave a curt nod of acknowledgement and retreated, humbled by Sadron's bravery and his own mounting sense of shame. For despite his genuine concern for the prisoners' welfare and Speer's warning, he knew in his heart that he would always give his work precedence.

TWENTY-EIGHT

H E COULD HARDLY BLAME HIS FRIEND Arthur Rudolph for feeling the same when he was transferred to Mittlewerk as production director – a middle management role that gave Rudolph a modicum of power to exercise in whichever way he chose. It was good for von Braun to have a friend with whom he could discuss Dora's moral dilemma, but he fast found out that Rudolph was not the suitable confidant. His adherence to the Reich's ways had not diminished and although he was too clever to openly advocate brutality, he did nothing to stop his deputy beating and kicking the inmates.

"Perhaps you could speak to your deputy about it," von Braun took advantage of their friendship to suggest, but that friendship was all that kept Rudolph's temper in check.

"And perhaps you shouldn't interfere and just concentrate on your *own* baby," he shot back sharply, referencing von Braun's pet name for his V-2.

Obviously, the subject was not up for debate, and content that he had at least tried to do the right thing, von Braun took Rudolph's advice and got on with his job. It was time he did, because other troubles were brewing at the facility. The difficulty of building missiles in between tripping over dead bodies in Dora's half-dug tunnels was taking its toll, not only on the inmates suffering atrocities, but on their Teutonic taskmasters from whom Hitler was expecting miracles.

"There were meant to be 200 rockets finished by December!" Rudolph ranted at engineer Albin Sawatzki, who had been sent from Speer's department to speed up the production process.

He had failed abysmally, forcing only four through to completion by Christmas 1943, and Rudolph had to drag him from his New Year's celebration to sign off on them. Sawatzki must have been drunk when he did it, for all four missiles were so faulty that they had to be sent straight back for repair. Such sub-standard craftsmanship stemming from Germans seemed odd and Rudolph smelled a rat.

"Sabotage!" he put to von Braun. "I'm convinced of it."

It stood to reason that the prisoners would try to throw a spanner in the works, but the prospect opened up a whole new can of worms. Sabotage demanded the death penalty and implementing it would involve von Braun in what could later be construed as a war crime. Like Speer, he knew the war was winding down and that soon they would be held accountable.

His V-2 was the Reich's last hoorah, but knowing it would not be enough to sway the outcome in their favour, he was already looking to greener pastures. Without war getting in the way, he could finally concentrate on what really mattered: flying his rockets to the moon. It was now just a matter of surviving until Germany's capitulation and choosing to whom he would surrender himself and his expertise.

After the shameful way the Reich had treated Russia, the east would be a 'no-go' zone, and given that his V-2 would soon target England, he guessed he wouldn't be wanted there either. America, however, was far enough away for its mainland to have not borne the brunt of any bombing and probably would not hold as big a grudge. As the land of liberty, intent on leading the world in all endeavours, it was bound to be more expedient in forgiving any enemy from whom it might profit.

War had fast-tracked technology and made von Braun a valuable commodity. Already America had embraced Einstein and the stream of German-Jewish scientists who had fled to the safety of its shores. Surely, von Braun reasoned, with space being the next frontier on the world's agenda, he and his knowledge would be welcomed with open arms.

Such sensible, forward-thinking smacked of treason, but von Braun was still a true patriot. Hailing from Germany's ancient order of knights, it was a matter of honour that he keep fighting for the Fatherland until if fell and treaties were signed. By then, he had no doubt that Hitler would have brought the nation to its knees and if he survived, he and his dreams would have to follow the money trail without being burdened by the blame for the Holocaust. To that end, he started tying up all loose ends that linked him to Nazism by systematically destroying all documentation that might implicate him in more than merely doing his duty.

During the post-war crime trials to come, this conspicuous lack of written records in regard to him would appear peculiar when von Braun was a writer by nature; one who could not help but express his emotions and knowledge on paper. As a child, he churned out one space fantasy novel after another. As a student, he composed a series of scholarly submissions. And after the war he was to become a prolific author of popular books and articles. That such an exuberant man of words failed to pick up a pen throughout the entire course of the war was highly suspicious. Yet, with no hard evidence to indict him, he was to escape with a clean slate, cleared of all crime.

"I can honestly say that I never witnessed an act of sabotage nor ever received an oral or written report in regard to a proven case of it," he was to testify to a US court.

It would be a carefully worded statement to back up his claim of innocence and one which was to be vigorously debated by an eyewitness.

"Together with his entourage of German scientists, Professor Wernher von Braun saw everything that went on at Dora, but never once protested against it," a survivor from the facility would say from the witness box. "On his frequent visits to the underground factory, he walked its corridors and regularly passed its piles of dead bodies without batting an eye. He may not have actually witnessed an act of sabotage or received a formal report of it, but I vividly remember him watching the prisoners' execution."

It was hard to establish the facts when the witness in question had suffered horrendous persecution and had his own axe to grind. Fair or not, payback for him was sweet and appropriate for any German.

"Yes, I saw what I saw, but it was war and most soldiers saw worse," von Braun would argue back. "But how could this man possibly know whether or not I protested against it, when he was not privy to my comings and goings and certainly not to my consultations behind closed doors?"

By then, too much time had elapsed to vouch for the truth either way, and although an element of doubt would forever taint the court's verdict, the gavel slammed down in von Braun's favour, for he was far too valuable an asset to lose.

TWENTY-NINE

IN 1944, however, von Braun's V-2 production team was up against more fundamental problems than sabotage. Their manufacturing network – a coalition between Peenemunde, the Mittelwerk factory and a multitude of industrial contractors – was getting its wires crossed. Most of the parts provided were unreliable, and being designed to the individual makers' specifications, rarely matched the missiles' assembly points. Add to this the many failed launches and rockets that broke up on re-entry and it was fast becoming a political powder keg.

"They're blaming us!" Dornberger stormed into von Braun's office to say.

He threw the two memos he had received from the Armaments Ministry and SS headquarters down on the desk and jabbed his finger at the words both had repeated:

> *You are to be held accountable for your false claim*
> *that your V-2 development was near completion.*

The rot had set in and thus started the last year of WWII – the most difficult and dangerous of von Braun's life.

He gulped down hard when he was ordered to Himmler's headquarters in Hochwald. The first time he was summoned there, a year or so before, he had been unsure as to whether the SS Reichsfuhrer would hang a medal or noose around his neck. This time he guessed it more likely to be the latter and had to gather his courage to go.

To his surprise, Himmler was all politeness and looked no more intimidating than a country school teacher. Yet, unconvinced by his calm facade, von Braun stayed on his guard.

As mild-mannered a villain as ever cut a throat, he couldn't help but think when Himmler forewent the formality of throwing a salute and walked over to warmly shake his hand.

"I trust you realise, von Braun, that your V-2 has ceased to be an engineer's toy and that we are all eagerly awaiting it," he said straight out, before adding more sympathetically: "I can well imagine the pitiful position you're in . . . a frustrated inventor enmeshed in army bureaucracy. You know that the Fuhrer's door is always open to me and if you put yourself entirely in my hands, I'll be better placed than the clumsy army machine to beat the problems you're encountering."

At this moment, with his tone so conciliatory, Himmler seemed a far cry from the horrible man wading knee-deep in blood that he was said to be. Nonetheless, von Braun had to surreptitiously wipe his hand dry on his trousers once free of the man's clammy grasp.

"Thank you, sir," he answered, "but Major General Dornberger is the best chief I could hope to have. The truth is that it's technical trouble and not red tape that's holding things up."

Himmler remained expressionless at both the rebuff and the verbal acknowledgement of Dornberger's recent promotion, so von Braun embellished.

"My V-2, you see, is much like a small flower that needs sunshine, fertile soil and a good gardener's tending. To pour a big jet of liquid manure on that flower to make it grow faster would more likely kill it."

It was a pretty analogy which Himmler appeared to take on board. After some more small talk, he smiled and said goodbye.

For von Braun, it had been imperative to knock back his offer because it meant a closer association with Dora's Commandant Kammler. That was unthinkable, so he was pleased to have pulled off the interview without causing offence. But a month later he found out that he *had*, because Himmler hit back. Like a beast lying in wait for its prey, he pounced on von Braun's 32nd birthday.

At two o'clock in the morning, von Braun was jerked from a deep sleep by the sound of thumping at his door. Disoriented, he fumbled for his alarm clock and checking the ungodly hour, swore as he stumbled out of bed.

"You are to accompany us to Stettin Police Headquarters," one of the two black-clad Gestapo agents said when he angrily flung open the door. "You are needed there to make an important witness statement."

"*Now . . . in the middle of the night!*" von Braun protested. "Why in the hell did you wake me for that?"

He knew that the Gestapo worked in mysterious ways, but while at first outraged by their midnight intrusion, his firm jaw dropped in shock when they cited their orders.

"You're arresting me?" he said in disbelief.

"No, Herr Professor . . . just taking you into protective custody."

The thin distinction calmed von Braun down to an extent, so he dressed quickly and followed them to the car waiting downstairs.

"Move over and make room for three more," the driver instructed him when he got into the back seat.

"Who?" von Braun threw back belligerently.

He had to wait for the answer until the black sedan pulled up in front of his brother Magnus' flat, before making two more stops to collect Klaus Riedel and Dornberger's liaison man, Helmut Grottrup. It was alarming, to say the least, when the four of them were put in a holding cell at police headquarters, but von Braun was determined to make light of it.

"Good! At least it'll give me a chance to sleep."

He always fought fear with humour, but those closest to him knew that the more worried he was, the more he joked. Yet, in this instance, all four men were merely bewildered, none of them having a clue as to what they had done wrong until dawn broke and they were taken to the interrogation chamber.

"You are here on the charge of treason," the Gestapo agent sitting at the desk informed them.

He took a moment to readjust his glasses so that he could read them the specific allegations:

"On the night of March 2 this year, at a party held at Zinnowitz, you were overheard making seditious comments in regard to the war . . . that it was sure to turn out badly, so your primary aim should be to create a spaceship."

The four men looked at each other in dismay. It had been a casual, social affair and having drunk too much, none of them had any recollection of their conversation.

"But this is ludicrous," von Braun then responded. "If impolitic things were said under such inebriated circumstances, they certainly were not to be taken seriously."

His objection was ignored and the interrogator turned his attention to Riedel.

"And you, Herr Riedel, were heard making the treasonous assertion *that the V-2 was no murder weapon*."

It would have been laughable had they not been acutely aware of the consequences. Any comments about losing the war or not using their rocket as a weapon were seen as defeatism and punishable by arrest, detention in a concentration camp and/or execution.

Himmler! von Braun hissed under his breath, realising what a fool he had been in assuming the SS Reichsfuhrer had taken his rebuff on the chin. Now, because of his stupid mistake, not only he, but his brother and close friends had to pay.

Himmler, however, was staying out of the picture and letting his minions do his dirty work. If there were to be any political fallout from the scientists' arrests, he wanted to distance himself from culpability and any resulting delays to the V-2's production. Nonetheless, with von Braun having so flippantly dismissed his offer of help, he wasn't about to let him off scot-free. The fear factor so far inflicted on the young scientist was going a long way to salve Himmler's wound. But he had to content himself with that, for straight after the four men's preliminary interrogation, General Dornberger's phone rang with the news of their arrest and a command with which he too had to comply:

"You are to report to Field Marshal Wilhelm Keitel immediately," he was instructed by a voice over the crackling wire.

One did not question such an order, but to make the meeting on time meant a long trip to Hitler's Berghof mountain-top retreat near Berchtesgaden. Delayed by icy roads and snow, it took Dornberger a full day to get there.

"The charges are so serious," Keitel explained to him within minutes of his late arrival, "that your men are likely to lose their lives. How people in their position can indulge in such dangerous talk is beyond my comprehension."

Dornberger immediately leapt to their defence: "They're just scientists, not concerned with military ethics. So they've foolishly spoken out of school, but you can't be serious about getting rid of them. They're absolutely essential to our program. Von Braun's my best man. His whole soul, energy and indefatigable efforts are devoted to the V-2. To arrest him for its sabotage is farcical!"

Aware he was getting nowhere with Keitel, Dornberger took a moment to collect himself before he lashed out again:

"I demand to speak directly to Himmler."

"He doesn't want to see you," Keitel said with a weak shrug. "You'll have to take it up with General Kaltenbrunner at SS headquarters back in Berlin."

He knew he was being given the run-around, and by the time Dornberger drove back to the capital, he was in a white-hot rage. It didn't help when Kaltenbrunner was not available and he was shown, instead, into the office of the head of Gestapo, Heinrich Mueller. Barging in the door, he went straight on the attack.

"I see no difference between the SS and Gestapo, nor between being arrested or taken into protective custody. Either way, you have my best men behind bars and will be held personally responsible for stalling our V-2 production."

That was a sizeable threat to have hanging over his head, yet Mueller remained unmoved.

"I'd advise you, Dornberger, to say no more," he calmly replied, tapping his finger on the fat file the Gestapo had also compiled on *him*. "You see, we can readily produce double the evidence against you for doing the same."

What evidence? Dornberger was left to wonder but backed away because he knew the Gestapo was expert at manufacturing lies punishable by death.

With their meeting a stalemate, the four men were left to stew for a further few days in prison, baffled by their jailers' bizarre system of surveillance. One day, denying them food and water, while the next, allowing von Braun to receive friends, flowers and champagne to celebrate his birthday. As soon as he ate his cake, however, two SS officers came to read out the formal charges against him:

"You are accused of sabotaging rocket development by diverting it into spaceflight; of planning to fly to England with all your V-2 plans; of maintaining your pilot's licence for that purpose; and of making complaints about the inhumanity at our concentration camps."

"All charges, bar one, are false," von Braun competently fired back, though he was truly unnerved. "You are correct about my complaints in regard to the concentration camps because although I love and fight for my country, I don't approve of superfluous savagery. As a German citizen, I believe it's my right to voice a personal opinion without it constituting treason."

It was well said and its ring of truth made the SS officers defer the matter.

Although he had won the first round, von Braun was left disconcerted and for the first time in his life, questioning his courage. At the following interrogation, he could feel his legs shaking beneath him and with his confidence at its lowest ebb, his face suddenly lit up with relief when the door swung wide open and Dornberger strode in looking illustrious in his general's uniform. Without saying a word, he went directly to the chief interrogator's desk and thumped a document down in front of him. The fact that it was signed by Fuhrer headquarters meant that the show was over and, on the spot, the four men were granted a three-month conditional release.

"How did you pull it off?" von Braun asked, when with a bottle of fine brandy in hand, Dornberger came to collect them from their cell.

"Not easily, I can assure you. I had to fight tooth and nail before I finally got help from the Abwehr. Fortunately for us, a few of its officers aren't exactly enamoured of the SS."

Dornberger believed he deserved full credit for freeing them and had no idea that a far more powerful hand behind the scenes had pushed the buttons – that during a rest cure in the Italian Alps, Armaments Minister Speer had heard of the situation and personally intervened on von Braun's behalf to secure all four men's release.

When Speer returned to full-time work and found Hitler still grumbling about his interference, he had some explaining to do.

"Trust me, *mein Fuhrer*," he said. "I know the men well enough to be sure of their innocence and patriotism. I'm convinced they had no concept of the trouble they were causing by speaking so freely of their rocket dreams. They're just hot-blooded young men blinded by passion for their science."

Still not convinced, Hitler stared hard at Speer, his glazed eyes seeming to sear straight through to his soul in search of the root of Speer's desire to play von Braun's protector. Sensing as much, Speer took a big gamble. He threw caution to the wind and laughed out loud.

"Oh, let's get this all in proportion, sir . . . the young men were drunk at the time and were actually trying to work out ways for their rocket to deliver *mail* across the Atlantic after we win the war!"

When put that way it did seem funny and Hitler's lips quivered in response. Not enough to break into a smile, but because Speer never failed to put him in a good mood, he was prepared to come up with a compromise.

"Well, as long as von Braun's indispensable to you," he said, ever willing to give Speer his all, "he's exempt from any punishment, but it's on your head if it has serious consequences."

Von Braun had no idea that it was Speer who shielded him from harm and how grateful he should be. All he knew was that he now actively hated Hitler and everything for which he stood. The whole incident was surreal and had stripped him of his last shreds of attachment to the Nazi regime. As a scientist, essential to its plans, he had never before suffered its full force, but now felt as if the truth had slugged him over the head.

From here on in, I'll have to keep my mouth shut and play the game, he told himself, having at last made sense of Speer's past words of warning.

As for Speer, his allegiance too was wavering. If he wanted to survive the war, he had to camouflage that fact by making a show of his total commitment to the Reich. Rather than hide from its frightening reality, he became very vocal in his demands; like any good warrior, knowing that attack was his best form of defence.

"To achieve optimum performance in the area of rocketry assigned to me, I want complete freedom of action with a clear delineation of jurisdiction," he stated to temporarily break the hold Himmler had over operations. "Otherwise I quit."

He knew that Hitler would never have that, so for the time being, he and von Braun were safe.

CHAPTER

THIRTY

IT WAS D-DAY. As the Allies landed in Normandy to invade Hitler's Europe, Germany launched its first V-1 buzz bomb. Of the ten thousand to be fired at London, 80 percent would miss their mark, but those that didn't were destined to destroy more than a million homes and to kill 10,000 British people.

They were payback for the British air raids battering Berlin, and Germany was using them to spare itself the high cost of flying heavy bombers across the Channel and to instil terror through psychological warfare. Night and day, their 'Doodlebugs', as England dubbed them, appeared over London; the sound of their flight punctuated by an ominous few seconds silence as they hovered over their target before plummeting to impact with a high-pitched whistle.

The instant death and destruction they wrought had those Londoners lucky enough to survive living every hour on alert, forever racing for the protection of bomb shelters and sorting through the resultant rubble for what was left of their possessions and dead relatives. At the around-the-clock torture, nerves were frayed and tempers flared; none more so than Prime

Minister Churchill's, who vented his rage in a general memo:

> *If the bombardment has a devastating effect on London's centres of government and labour, I am prepared to consider drenching the enemy in poison gas to stop all work at their flying bomb bases. I do not see why we should always have the disadvantage of acting like gentlemen while they take constant advantage of being the cad.*

Diplomacy was dead due to the ferocity of German attacks, and Churchill was sure that his words echoed the sentiments of the English people when their expectation was of worse to come.

As to that, von Braun was working like a demon, fine-tuning his V-2's explosive encore for the British theatre of war. It had become a matter of pride – not for him but for the army, which had sponsored his rocket from the start in competition with the Luftwaffe's V-1. The V-2 was aspiring to be better, but it cost twice as much and the buzz bomb was already up and running, causing the devastation it promised.

"But the benefit of von Braun's long-range V-2 is its versatility," Speer explained to pacify the Fuhrer. "It can be fired from a ship or any street without the need for a prepared launch site."

Speer continued to champion von Braun's cause, even though he knew, as did the young scientist, that its effect on the war would be minimal. There was still the danger that the projectiles would not take off straight and that their steering was unreliable. Given also that the ever-stoic English were standing up to the challenge of the V-1, there was every chance that they would endure the threat of the V-2. The reality was that the missile had missed its market, aiming for a technology too advanced for its time.

"It'll come into its own during future conflicts," Speer assured von Braun on the quiet.

He nodded in acknowledgement, grateful to the Armaments Minister for knowing the truth and strategically keeping it from Hitler.

A great deal, at this point, was being kept from the Fuhrer, including the secret plans for an assassination attempt on his life. It failed and Speer was horrified to find himself implicated, when having survived the bomb blast at his Wolf's Lair head-quarters, Hitler was shown the list of conspirators. Although only his right hand would continue to shake as a result of the explosion, seeing Speer's name pencilled in at the bottom of that list broke his heart.

Von Braun and the rest of the Reich had to wonder why Speer escaped being strung up with piano wire as were other men with far less evidence against them. Yet, although the strength of Hitler's attachment to Speer spared him the steel noose, their relationship was now tainted with suspicion and was never quite the same.

"We'll both be walking on eggshells until Germany's surrender," Speer told von Braun. "Under no circumstances must either of us be tempted to tell Hitler the truth of the V-2."

On that score, Speer had little concern, because he was sure, that like him, von Braun was quietly working for his own ends: planning the continuation of that work after the war while shrewdly extricating himself from post-war punishment for the Reich's atrocities. There was light at the end of the tunnel, Speer believed, for both he and von Braun were 'must have' commodities for whom the enemy would be prepared to overlook a few inconsistencies.

After his years of phenomenal success, it did not cross Speer's mind that he might have overestimated his own worth; that his hereto much sought-after talents would be largely redundant after the war, with the victors no longer needing the inside running on how the losing side functioned. What information he could give them would be enough to spare him the death penalty, but not a 20-year stint at Spandau Prison; whereas von Braun, with his exciting grip on future technology, was far more valuable and well worth them side-stepping morality.

Perhaps von Braun was astute enough to see this, but with Hitler's purge after the failed assassination attempt in full swing, his mind was elsewhere and on the brink of being frantic after hearing that his brother Siggy's mother-in-law had been arrested for her contacts with a communist resistor. Nothing had been proved against her, but within days she was found dead in her cell with cuts and bruises inconsistent with her so-called suicide. It was all getting much too close for comfort.

"Are you all right?" Wernher rang through urgently to ask Siggy, breathing a sigh of relief when his big brother, sounding hale and hearty at the other end of the line, laughed off his concern.

Nothing, however, about the situation was funny. With the SS rounding up and executing all suspected of treason, Wernher was worried that Siggy would be called to account for his many anti-Nazi sentiments voiced in public. As brave as it was to do, Wernher always thought it wiser to keep his mouth shut. Albeit feeling ashamed that other men of his class, like coup conspirator Count von Stauffenberg, had the guts to make a stand against Hitler and die for it, Werhner's own sense of self-preservation was stronger and all he wanted was to whisk himself and his family away to safety.

Fortunately, the only fallout from the post-coup cull to affect him was Hitler's loss of faith in his top staff. Consequently, Himmler, who he continued to trust implicitly, was given *carte blanche* over their V-2 project and much else. With his new-found power, he and his side-kick, Dora's Commandant Kammler, promptly pushed General Dornberger from power and took control of all V-2 mobile launch units.

"But you *can't* leave us in the lurch...not at this critical point!" von Braun rushed to Dornberger's office to say, when to save face, the general applied for a transfer. "Can't you just focus on the big picture and put your pride aside. For all our sakes, please stick with us . . . even if that means offering that bastard Kammler your help."

That was impossible for a dignified man like Dornberger to do. With Kammler now reigning supreme over the long-range rocket program and Speer's influence waning, there was no longer a place for him.

Everything was on a downhill slide, including a third, devastating attack by American bombers on Peenemunde that destroyed its test stands and left fifty more of its people dead. Calmly stepping over their corpses in the compound came close to numbing what was left of von Braun's sensitivity, but when he was informed that his dear old friend Klaus Riedel had been killed in a car accident, he was utterly shaken. It was all he could do to read the police report:

> *Car careened into a tree and burst into flame*
> *as a result of driver falling asleep at the wheel.*

For that, von Braun blamed himself, because the man was exhausted from working all hours at his side. Riedel had been with him from the start – from their star-struck veneration of Hermann Oberth and the wishful beginnings of the Spaceflight Society, through to Riedel's role as head of the test laboratory at Peenemunde and their mutual imprisonment at Stettin. Now he was gone, along with his share of their dreams.

At this sad reality, something in von Braun snapped and there followed a few days of savage behaviour on his part for which he believed God would never forgive him.

No one else would have found out had three of Dora's labourers not survived to testify against him in the post-war courts where they explained, in detail, his short-term streak of cruelty:

"Von Braun slapped me hard across the face for accidentally stepping on a fragile component inside a missile's tail section," one of them was to report from the witness box, before a second man swore on the Bible and said something far worse:

"When I began my shift, I noticed that my chronometer was missing, but I found it a little later under another console. It was obviously just a stupid shot at sabotage by someone on the prior night shift, but because anything of the like got the death penalty, I told the SS supervisor that it'd just been dropped there by mistake. He immediately started shouting *Sabotage!* and von Braun, who was walking through the facility with his entourage at the time, stopped and without listening to my explanation, ordered the SS guard to give me 25 lashes. He then judged them not sufficiently hard and ordered them struck more severely. *'And as the good for nothing you are, you deserve more,'* he then said when my back was ripped raw."

"You don't understand," von Braun would say in his own defence to the American judge. "It was a case of the lesser of two evils. Had I not satisfied the SS by making a point of punishing him severely, they would have hanged him on the spot."

The third witness was to vouch for that:

"One day . . . ," he would recount, " . . . we were suddenly ordered to stop work to watch the hanging of six saboteurs from metal hoists. There was a group of Germans standing some distance away, some of them SS, some civilians. *'Who is that?'* I asked my fellow prisoner when I saw one of them sway unsteadily on his feet at the sight of the execution and he answered: *'That's von Braun'.*"

So, the court was to establish time and place, but his motive would remain debatable. In September 1944, however, his bout of bad temper was replaced by depression when the first of his ballistic missiles was successfully launched at London.

"Why look so glum?" a colleague asked as he handed him a celebratory glass of champagne. But von Braun refrained from drinking it.

"I wanted my rockets to travel to the moon and Mars, not to hit our own planet," he answered, feeling now only contempt for himself for having briefly replaced reason with reprisal. "I hoped the war would be over before they could be used to kill people."

"You've nothing to feel guilty about," his companion flashed back with contempt. "Not when they've killed so many of ours."

That was true, but von Braun was torn. Because he and his brothers had been spared the trauma of the battlefields and had many fond memories of their visits to London, he felt less vindictive towards the enemy than most Germans. To know that the ancient city was being destroyed by his own hand made it the blackest day of the war. It was too late, however, for regrets and he had to get practical.

Yes, I love London, he told himself in justification, *but I love Berlin more and the English have been bombing the hell out of it. Now it's our turn.*

The first V-2 hit Chiswick at 6.43pm and the next impacted on Epping seconds later. All told, his missiles would claim the lives of nearly 3000 men, women and children and injure an additional 6000. Add to this the many more who died in its manufacture and he had created something of which Commandant Kammler said he should be immensely proud.

He wasn't, but it was too late to turn back. By December,

Hitler was making his last losing gamble on The Battle of the Bulge and demands on von Braun became ridiculous. He had five different projects on the go at one time, none of them fully researched or with the necessary manpower to complete. Along with his continued efforts on the V-2, he was working on the Wasserfall anti-aircraft guided missile, while still at conceptual stage was the A-10 booster, the A-11 multistage missile and the long-range A-10 rocket with the winged A-9 mounted atop. It was all too much for one man, but given that they were all being designed with future spaceflight in mind, von Braun was working on them like a fury, because time was running out.

News that Soviet tanks were only a hundred kilometres away spread panic throughout Peenemunde. Hordes of starving refugees were trudging westward across the island warning of Soviet retribution and telling tales of rape, plunder and murder. US and British forces had advanced into western and southern sectors and with bombing intensifying, communications were down, supplies were not getting through and von Braun was at his desk struggling to come to terms with his 10 conflicting orders.

"Well what am I supposed to do?" he said in exasperation to his deputy, Eberhard Rees. "Five of them are threatening death by firing squad if we evacuate Peenemunde and the other five say we'll be shot if we don't!"

If it were only up to him, he knew exactly what he would do, having already packed his bags for America. It was not as easy as that, though, when he was responsible for the rest of his Peenemunde crew. So he gathered his six most trusted of them together to discuss the situation in secret:

"Germany has lost the war," he stated as a matter of fact, although it had not as yet been made official. "If we are to keep our extraordinary team together with a view to future accomplishments in space we must decide to which country we run."

Although all six scientists were onside, his direct remarks took them aback. For most of them, far more was at stake than simply furthering their careers. They had families and properties in Germany to protect, so while they digested the idea, von Braun made his own plans clear.

"My vote's for America," he said, "because there lies the money and motivation. And let's face it . . . in my rather young lifetime, our country has lost two world wars. Next time round, I want to be on the winning side."

PART THREE

OPERATION PAPERCLIP

CHAPTER

THIRTY-ONE

THE ENEMY WAS ENCAMPED half a kilometre away and von Braun was excited. He and a few of his Peenemunde scientific team had been holding out in a ski-resort on the German-Austrian border for weeks waiting for the American troops to arrive so that they could negotiate a surrender.

"*I'd* better go," Magnus said when it was decided that one of them should cycle down the hill from their hotel to begin preliminary talks. "I speak better English than the rest of you and I'm definitely the most expendable."

Right on both counts, Magnus had an audacity that matched his older brother's and was eager to confront the enemy with the news of their whereabouts. They were hot property and every branch of the Allied forces was scouring Germany to find them. Although the war was over, it was dangerous to present oneself alone in the open when the odd, angry shot was still being fired.

He stripped off his German uniform for the last time, put on civilian clothes, and tying a white handkerchief to his bike's handlebars, pedalled down the hill towards the Advanced

Antitank Patrol Unit of the 44th Infantry, US Army Third Armoured Division.

When the soldier on outpost duty saw him coming, he took aim with his rifle, but Magnus rode on, not putting on his brakes until just a few inches shy of the prospective shooter.

"We want to see Ike," he said highhandedly.

The soldier snorted in contempt, because this brash, young German turning up out of the blue was referring to none other than their Supreme Allied Commander, General Dwight D. Eisenhower.

"And when I say 'we'," Magnus continued imperiously, "I mean, my brother, Baron Wernher von Braun, Major General Walter Dornberger and their fellow V-2 scientists who are waiting at the hotel up there on the hill."

Dumbstruck by the man's effrontery and the enormity of his claim, the soldier stood speechless, but then rallied to say:

"You're *nuts!* Just like the rest of your mad race."

Having had his say, he ordered Magnus to raise his hands over his head and nudged him on his way to the command tent with the butt of his rifle.

The intelligence officer's response to Magnus' claim was just as blunt but slightly more receptive, because with everyone competing for the spoils of war and the V-2's elusive inventors taking top billing, he knew he would be a fool to discount it.

"Show me!" he demanded.

Magnus waved the *'all clear'* in the direction of the mountain-top hotel, signalling for a small band of men to spill from its front door and walk down the winding track towards them.

The officer watched with a shrewd eye, hoping to be convinced, but something didn't sit right, when having reached the bottom of the slope, a convivial young man with a winning smile and a broken arm bandaged in plaster, stepped forward to introduce himself as Dr Wernher von Braun. Having envisaged an older, bespectacled academic the officer found it hard to believe that this man, barely in his 30s, was the much-lauded inventor of the V-2. What's more, far from being reticent about making contact with the enemy, he was chatting to them as if they were old friends and instantly winning them over with his excited talk of rockets and space.

"You don't seem the least bit afraid," the officer commented contemptuously.

Von Braun came back with a sudden, cold assurance: "Why should I be?" he said. "We have the V-2 and you want it. It would serve no purpose for you to treat us badly."

His clipped, Germanic tone was more in keeping with what the officer had expected. Somehow it added to his credulity, and given that this so-called scientist seemed so happy and at home in the enemy's company, the officer dismissed what had been his initial instinct – to smash the man's teeth in – and instead, offered von Braun and his team, eggs and bacon for breakfast.

"What happened to your arm?" he asked, helping von Braun to pour his coffee, because his arm cast made it difficult.

"Car accident four weeks ago," he answered. "Damn thing veered off the road and rolled three times into a ditch."

He left out the part that it happened during his escape from Peenemunde and that he was at the wheel driving at twice his usual souped-up speed.

... oOo ...

To surrender themselves and their rocket secrets to the Americans had meant heading south to meet up with their advancing forces. The only problem was that with the war near lost, the SS had the same idea and had given them two options: that they either use von Braun's team as a bargaining chip to secure freedom for war criminals such as Commandant Kammler, or that they deny the enemy the rocket team's expertise altogether by killing them.

Neither option appealed to the scientists, so they secretly planned to head off on their own with von Braun taking advantage of his SS uniform to smooth the way. Apart from von Braun's zeal to sell himself to America, things were getting too hot to handle at home. Allied bombs were falling without a break and Kammler had effectively stripped him of power by appointing a new Nazi scientist, Alfred Buch, to oversee all secret weapons in the Harz Mountains.

"Don't trust von Braun," Kammler immediately warned him. "We suspect he might be in touch with the Allies and is certainly more interested in rocketry for personal reasons than for the Reich."

Kammler had got it only half right, because as yet, von Braun's being in touch with the Allies was merely a plan, not a reality. Since his Gestapo arrest, however, Kammler had been keeping close tabs on him, confidant that he knew what von Braun had in mind.

'Leave him to me," Buch replied, going straight to von Braun's office to ply him with hard-hitting questions.

After an hour of being bullied into compliance, von Braun had walked from the meeting looking as white as a sheet – and sure that it was time to go.

Hitler had ordered that all at Peenemunde stay and fight to the death, but the SS were in control and favoured evacuation. Not soon enough to von Braun's way of thinking, when everything was rapidly deteriorating around them. The Nazis, with their backs to the wall, were spitting venom and lashing out with unprecedented savagery. In the rush to remove all evidence of their atrocities before the Russians arrived, they were making a clean sweep of the concentration camps, culling what was left of their emaciated inmates by the quickest means possible. For the disposal of the last 1500 they locked them in a barn and burnt them alive.

Those flames destroyed what was left of the veil obstructing von Braun's clear view of the Reich. Now he could see that it represented unprecedented evil. But with his loyalty in question, he knew it was imperative to play along with it a little longer to make good his escape and avoid becoming one of its victims.

Having promised Buch that he would play his part in the general SS Peenemunde exodus, he was ordered to run the length and breadth of Germany to stash excess V-2 parts and top-secret files. At the same time, he raced to tie up loose ends of his own, the most important of which was to fly home and ensure that his parents and von Quistorp cousins were safe.

"You must come with me," he begged "The Russians are only 30 kilometres to the east."

"We're not leaving our home," his parents answered emphatically.

Fortunately, his aunt and uncle, along with his lovely 17-year-old cousin Maria had made more sensible plans.

"We're escaping to our estate near the Dutch border," his uncle told him.

With only a day to do it, they had to move fast, so Wernher helped by securing them space on one of the ships carrying equipment to the Baltic port of Luebeck. In their haste, they had to leave most of their possessions behind.

"What does it matter?" Wernher said to hurry them along. "They're not as valuable as your lives."

They were lives that were of supreme importance to him, having grown in significance with each of his many visits to their estate. There, he had watched golden-haired Maria mature into a remarkably beautiful young woman who was as much devoted to him as he was to her. They were first cousins, of course, which by modern standards seemed wrong, but centuries of German blue-bloods had their blessing.

When he saw her safely on board, there wasn't much time to say goodbye and even less to speak of love, but on such a subject little needed to be said.

"Be safe and for God's sake, do whatever you have to do to stay alive," he warned as he turned to go. But the look of terror in her eyes at his alarming words made him stop ... and on impulse, pull her into a passionate embrace.

"Don't be scared. I'll be back, I promise," he whispered. "Wait for me."

It was a promise he wasn't sure he could keep when in April 1945 the news was all bad. Within a week he'd had his car accident and was lying flat on his back in hospital, wondering which way he would die ... whether he would be blown apart by the Allied bombs raining down, or shot by the SS to prevent his capture.

That was certainly the impression he got when he overhead Himmler's hushed conversation with Kammler in the hospital corridor:

"Every Allied power will want von Braun," the SS Reichsfuhrer said in a tone suggesting that something should be done to stop it happening. "Churchill's already campaigning by calling him 'The War Wizard' in his radio broadcasts."

Those broadcasts were now nothing but doom and gloom.

On April 2 the announcement was made of US President Roosevelt's death, along with the news that the Allies had liberated Buchenwald and Belsen concentration camps.

"Let's just be grateful that radio isn't a visual medium," the English announcer added on seeing the grim photographs pinned to his brief.

The newspapers, however, ran with them on the 28th featuring a front-page picture of Italian dictator Mussolini after his execution – shot and hanging upside down to be spat on and stoned by his own. A happier bulletin followed soon after: *The Fuhrer and Eva Braun are wed,* but the very next day, rumour had it that they were dead.

Whether it was all for good or bad depended entirely on how one looked at it. For General Dornberger, it was a clear-cut case of expediency.

"It's time to put our baby rocket in the right hands," he said to von Braun.

... oOo ...

"When Berlin fell to the Soviets on May 2," von Braun said to wind up his account to the US officer, "I and over 100 of my team chose to flee to the relative safety of your American front. Many of us were separated in the process, but I'm sure all can be rounded up if necessary."

Now close to convinced that he had the 'real deal' in his possession, the officer wiped the bacon grease from his lips and put his napkin down on the table.

"Well," he said in his thick Southern drawl. "If we haven't caught the biggest scientist of the Third Reich, we've certainly caught the biggest liar!"

THIRTY-TWO

THE US AUTHORITIES NOW HAD A PROBLEM. To bring Nazi scientists back home would not go down well with the American people. While they debated keeping it under wraps, their troops tore apart what remained of Dora's V-2s for transportation and testing in the US. Hard work made lighter with the help of the facility's few surviving prisoners who knew the ropes and were still strong enough to struggle to their feet.

Meanwhile, von Braun was filling out his US application form for German scientific personnel. He quickly provided his name and address, but hesitated over Question 2:

> *Have you any implications in war crimes or other*
> *Nazi activities?*

His hand hovered over the options before ticking the 'yes' box. Next to it, he wrote:

> *Joined SS (under pressure) in 1941. Rank reached: Major.*

He was smart enough not to lie, but the words: 'under pressure' and the reference to his Gestapo arrest further down the page were to shield him, for the rest of his life, from accusations of Nazi complicity.

The space provided for final comments was optional, but he used it to best advantage:

> *I always was and still am a German,* he penned with a pride in his heritage he would never hide. *However, I consider Germany dead as a nation. Its only hope is to co-operate with Western allies to act as a bulwark against eastern hordes and as a beachhead for British and American forces in the coming struggle.*

Such anti-communist sentiments, manufactured for the occasion, were to serve him well. For the time being, though, it was a waiting game with him and his team under intense interrogation. Difficult as it was for them to reveal information, it was harder still not to be in receipt of it.

The collapse of the Reich cut communication with their families and von Braun was worried sick about his parents. What news that arrived via passing travellers told only of horrendous Soviet revenge and the huge section of Germany to be handed over to Poland. As a result, 12 million of his fellow countrymen would be expelled from the east and thousands would die, ironically reversing Germany's role from culprit to victim.

It hardly seemed that the war was over when the Allies were prepping for the cold one to come. America had already taken the lead by pilfering the bulk of rocket paraphernalia before the British and Russians even arrived.

Stalin was furious.

"This is absolutely intolerable!" he bellowed at his top staff. "*We* defeated the Nazi armies. *We* occupied Berlin and Peenemunde, but the blasted Americans got the rocket engineers!"

He worked fast to remedy the situation, rounding up as many German V-2 engineers and technicians he could find still wandering astray, along with the abandoned trainloads of von Braun's missile equipment. Within days, both men and machines were spirited away to the USSR for research and development.

"Don't worry," von Braun assured his US interrogators. "You've got all the brains of our outfit. Russia's just grabbed its general hands."

That was good to know, but von Braun was merely throwing them a bone to distract their attention from the elephant in the room. It was time he came clean.

"So where did you stash the mother lode?" US Colonel Holger Toftoy asked outright.

As Chief of the Army Ordnance Technical Intelligence in Europe, Toftoy was in charge of getting 'everything to do with rockets' safely to America. He had been busy in Paris directing operations when the urgent dispatch arrived from Germany:

> *One of the greatest scientific and technical treasures*
> *in history is now securely in American hands.*

That was code for: "We've got von Braun!", so he dropped everything and flew straight to Germany to talk to the man face to face. They had a lot to discuss, with one matter taking priority.

Somewhere out there in German soil, von Braun and fellow rocket experts Dieter Huzel and Bernhard Tessmann had buried the V-2 research archives and were holding out on where to dig. To extract such crucial information, the Nazis would have used torture, but Toftoy just called a spade a spade.

"Put it this way," he said. "No co-operation . . . no free ticket to America."

Dornberger, von Braun and their team mulled it over, grateful that Toftoy let them do it in peace when other US troops had bashed out Walther Riedel's teeth trying to extract the same information. It was dangerous to throw away their trump card, but they knew it would be only a matter of time before someone talked under duress, and that to speak now might help them negotiate the best deal.

"Before we give you what you're after, we have one request," von Braun said to get those negotiations underway. "We're greatly concerned about our families and I, in particular, about my parents, Baron Magnus and Baroness Emily von Braun. All their family estates were lost due to the war and they're stuck, without money or refuge in a Soviet-controlled zone. If you can get them and all my associates' families to safety, we'll give you what you want."

Spurred on, Tolstoy quickly arranged for some of those more accessible families to be transported to a disused military barracks in the lower Bavarian city of Landshut where women and children would be housed and fed while their husbands worked in America.

For Baron Magnus and his wife, however, it had to be a 'cloak and dagger' affair. Under the watchful eye of trigger-happy Soviet soldiers, the two aging aristocrats had to make a run for it in the dead of night, before being smuggled aboard a rusty, cattle train that rattled them on their way to Berlin, then further south down the tracks to Landshut.

"Thank you," von Braun wrote in a letter to Toftoy's staff officer Major Jim Hamill, who had been ordered to see them to safety.

That done, it was time for the missile men to fulfill their side of the bargain.

"Alright Colonel," von Braun said on the team's behalf. "The archives are stowed in the iron ore pit Georg-Friedrich in Doernten."

Toftoy slapped his knees in triumph, stood up, and went straight to the phone to order the archive's retrieval – 14 tons of it in all. Yet, true to his word, he stopped as he picked up the receiver.

"In the meantime, gentlemen," he said to Dornberger and von Braun, "you're to make a list of the rest of the team you wish to take with you to America, so that we can start tracking them down as soon as possible."

... oOo ...

"500 of them . . . those Krauts have gotta be kidding!"

The US Army was appalled by the number of German scientists and secretaries deemed imperative. It was preposterous enough to stall proceedings, but von Braun managed to talk one of his interrogators – US scientist Richard Porter – into seeking out as many of his old colleagues as possible in the ever-optimistic hope that the Pentagon would eventually give in.

"We found your man Rudolf Hermann and his aerodynamics group on the outskirts of Berlin near dead from starvation," Porter let von Braun know. "We whisked them and their 'wind tunnel' out of what's soon to be the Soviet sector in the nick of time. Your missile guidance specialist, Wilhelm Angele, was working as a farm hand near Hanover for nothing but food and water."

And so the stories rolled in as Toftoy whittled down their list to 200. It was hard going with von Braun constantly breathing down his neck with his string of objections, so Toftoy was relieved when he received Porter's urgent cable:

> *Time running out on Nordhausen search before Russians arrive. Request that von Braun be flown here to help.*

The browbeaten Toftoy was happy to get him off his back. Within an hour von Braun was on an army plane; and as soon as it landed, transferred to one of its canvas-covered trucks in which he was sit for weeks, scouring Germany for his people.

The bad news was that the Joint Chiefs of Staff in Washington were prepared to approve the intake of only100 of them in what they called Operation Overcast. With these slashed numbers came stiff stipulations:

a) Those who come to America will be under only a six-month contract: *To assist in shortening the Japanese war and to aid in post-war military research.*

b) Any alleged war criminals discovered after arrival will immediately be sent back to Europe for trial.

In the months to come, their treatment of their own American public was not to be much better. A formal announcement that some German scientists and engineers would be brought to the US was to be followed by a complete clampdown on any further information.

A hopeful von Braun had mustered way more than a hundred of his staff at the town of Witzenhausen, crowding 80 families into an abandoned schoolhouse. There, in its draughty corridors, they were living hand to mouth with next to no food and even less chance of making the final cut for America. It was fortunate, then, that von Braun and only half of them were adamant about going there. The rest needed persuasion because better options were available.

"The Soviets are offering higher wages and promising that we can stay in Germany to do our work," Helmut Grottrup put forward as his argument.

The fact that he did not want to go with von Braun was disappointing when they had shared so much together, not in the least of which was their terrifying Gestapo arrest.

"Well I'm going," the youngest member of their team, Walter Wiesman, flashed back. "There's nothing left for us here in Germany and America offers us a new life."

"But who's to say that the Americans won't just bleed us dry and send us straight back here?" rocket engineer Konrad Dannenberg countered, making a valid point because the Soviets did just that to those of von Braun's crew who opted to go east.

In most instances, however, it was simply the fear of the unknown that made many of them decide to stay and take their chances on war-ravaged, home soil in which, due to thirst and starvation, some would soon be buried. Von Braun supposed it was a sad form of natural selection, but before giving up on those who did not share his vision of the future, he tried once more.

"There's no need to be afraid for your wives and children," he told those who were scared of savage retribution if they set foot on US shores. "I'm sure that the Americans will treat us well."

When Colonel Toftoy arrived and saw the wretched conditions under which they were living, he backed up von Braun's claim.

"I'll order food and milk for the children immediately," he said, but it still was not enough to sway the majority.

Either way, Toftoy had a tough job ahead sorting his way through the names of those who wished to come. With them all needing background checks and security screening, their papers were scattered all over his office, making von Braun laugh when he walked through the door.

"Not funny," Toftoy looked up with rubber stamp in hand to say. "How about putting some of that German efficiency of yours to good use and help me organise this lot."

Von Braun calmly scanned the papers and photographs carpeting the floor, before picking up and collating three of them.

"Why don't you just put a paperclip on those you've okayed?" he said, as he reached for one lying on Toftoy's desk and slid it on the top left-hand corner of Bernhard Tessmann's file. "It's not rocket science."

Too tired to smile at his quip, Toftoy shrugged in compliance and between them, they had them all signed and sealed in an hour, with127 files neatly stacked in a pile.

Toftoy shook his head and reiterated: "We've only been given the go ahead for 100."

Here was where von Braun drew the line, having already lowered his expectations from his initial 500.

"It's 127 or I don't go."

He meant business, so somehow those extra 27 slipped through the system, as did the name of the whole operation. No longer known as Operation Overcast, it was renamed Operation Paperclip, thanks to von Braun having temporarily switched his bright ideas from projectiles to the proper use of stationery.

All would have been done and dusted had Britain not wanted its fair share of post-war intellectual reparations with a view to a little operation of its own called Backfire.

"We think it only appropriate that America lends us a few of the German rocketeers to school us in V-2 handling and launching," said the British head of Missile Projects, Sir Alwyn Crow, making thinly veiled reference to the fact that their ally had done them in the eye. "We will need the services of scientists von Braun, Axster, Steinhoff and Rees for one week.

America agreed for the sake of international relations, immediately dispatching the four scientists requested, with a small bonus besides: Major General Walter Dornberger.

He, however, was not welcome and was immediately shipped off to a British internment camp with other high-ranking German generals standing trial for war crimes and indiscriminate bombing of civilians. With the infamous Kammler missing, presumed dead, Dornberger was their chosen scapegoat.

"That's not fair," von Braun protested. "Without Dornberger our group would have amounted to nothing and if you imprison him, we will refuse . . . "

Dornberger cut him off mid-sentence to issue his final order.

"You must go ahead as planned," he commanded as he was handcuffed, "They have to do what they have do. When the truth comes out, I'll try to join you in America."

Von Braun and his three colleagues watched as he was led away, saluting when Dornberger – the father of their rocket program – turned one last time to silently mouth the word 'goodbye'.

It was enough to embitter them from the start of their English stay and von Braun fully expected to be treated just as badly. As soon as he set foot in Sir Alwyn's office, however, he was welcomed with a smile and a happy few hours of shoptalk.

A comfortable detention centre near Wimbledon served as his billet from where he was picked up by an RAF driver each day to be delivered safely to the British Supply Ministry. All in all, the chauffeurs were friendly chaps, bar one who thought to call him to account by stopping in front of a building which one of his V-2s had destroyed.

The Englishman pulled on the brakes and said nothing, sure that the sight of it and the sudden, loud silence between them would instil some semblance of guilt, but von Braun would have none of it when much worse had been inflicted on Berlin. Far from feeling sorry, he remained frigidly technical, trying to work out the precise way in which his V-2 impacted the six-storey building, while wondering what had become of the German undercover agents who used to radio damage reports back to base.

They were damned good at their job he was thinking, while the driver watched him in the rear vision mirror for any signs of remorse. *They'd have reports back to us about each V-2's effectiveness within only an hour of them being launched.*

Such efficiency had been engineered by Armaments Minister Speer, whose expertise had not been courted by the enemy, as supposed, and who was, at this very moment, awaiting trial for war crimes in Nuremberg. Shocked by the fact that his friend was sure to be executed, von Braun was relieved to learn later that Speer's genuine sense of guilt spared him the noose.

Oddly enough, this was the one thing he and Speer did not have in common. For despite their similar finesse and remarkable workings of the mind, 'regret' had rarely crossed von Braun's and as yet, he had barely burdened himself with any sense of shame.

Why should I? he reasoned, when on August 6, 1945, America dropped the atomic bomb on Hiroshima.

THIRTY-THREE

KARMA PAID HIM OUT for being so cold-hearted. "It's hepatitis," the doctor diagnosed when von Braun fell desperately ill.

Although he had contracted the illness during his broken arm treatment, its symptoms did not manifest until he and his advance team of six other US-bound rocket experts landed at Fort Strong in Boston Harbour.

Apart from having lost a lot of weight, he had felt well when the seven of them were first flown by military transport to Versailles. And certainly, he was in fine form when the day before that, at Witzenhausen, he climbed into a jeep with his associates, Eberhard Rees and engineer Maxe Neubert, to be driven as far as the French border.

"Well, take a good look at Germany boys," he said when they crossed the Saar River. "We won't see it for a long time to come."

That seemed a strange thing to say when they were only under a six-month contract in the United States. It was the first clue von Braun gave that he intended to stay there for the rest of his life and was in the process of pulling the wool over his old enemy's eyes; starting with him entertaining his companions on the drive with a series of anti-American jokes told in German to exclude their US driver. A Lieutenant Morris Sipser, who as a young intelligence officer of Jewish descent, kept his mouth firmly shut and his eyes on the road.

It was not until he pulled up at the US airfield that he opened his lips to speak.

"You know, I thought you Krauts were meant to be clever," he turned to say in fluent German. "Didn't it occur to you that I might speak your language and be able to understand everything you said?"

Well, no it didn't, von Braun thought, when the general consensus among Germans was that Americans were brash and not too bright. For an awkward moment, he stood with his luggage in hand doing a mental re-wind of all his unguarded remarks. He was well and truly caught out, but it was too late to take any of them back. So he didn't bother when there was little chance that the lieutenant would overlook them and no hope, whatsoever, that he would ever see beyond the Holocaust.

None of it augured well for his fresh start in the New World and later, von Braun put his *faux pas* down to the fact that he was hatching hepatitis. By the time he had reached Boston Harbour to begin US processing, he was jaundiced, suffering chronic fatigue and nausea and was wondering how he would survive with only the minimal treatment on offer.

He was still weak at the knees when Major Jim Hamill escorted the seven of them by rail to Baltimore. As the soldier who had seen his parents to safety, von Braun was predisposed to liking him, but was surprised by what Hamill said when their train pulled into the station.

"Here's where we go our separate ways. Von Braun, you'll continue on with me to Washington and the rest of you will get off here and be taken to the Aberdeen Proving Grounds to get started on sorting out that 14 tons of your research material we've stored there."

Hamill, as a native of New York, had earned a physics degree before entering the army. As one of Toftoy's staff officers, he was assigned as their boss for the next few years, so the six scientists did what they were told, while von Braun went with him to the Pentagon.

He may as well have still been in SS uniform for the stir his appearance caused in its corridors. A deafening hush fell over them as their footsteps echoed on the polished concrete floor. Men of the military stepped aside to let him pass – *not*, it seemed to von Braun, as a mark of respect, but to distance themselves from evil, while the secretaries, unlike their German counterparts fawning over him back home, watched him walk past in cold-eyed silence, their red lips pursed in reproof.

"Don't take it to heart," Hamill said with some sympathy, seeing the proud tilt of von Braun's chin as the sole representative of his once great, but beaten, nation. "It'll take a little time for everyone to get used to the idea of opening their doors to the enemy.'

"It doesn't concern me in the least," von Braun snapped back with a crisp bravado to which Hamill might have taken exception had he not got used to the ingrained arrogance of von Braun's baronial background and years of believing he belonged to the Master Race.

Oddly enough, Hamill no longer thought of him as his foe, but as a potential friend – a man, forthright and gregarious, who was forever willing to talk on any subject, at any level. Yet, far from being daunted by his formidable brainpower, Hamill could not help but smile at the look of guileless wonderment on von Braun's face when he was told that their final destination was El Paso, Texas.

"The Wild West!" he responded with bright-eyed excitement at the recall of the westerns he read and revelled in as a boy.

"Well actually, Fort Bliss," Hamill qualified. "It's our closest army base to White Sands Proving Ground in New Mexico where you'll be doing much of your work."

Hamill had been there before and was less excited. He was a city-slicker and nothing about its dry desolation appealed. As their train sped south, the very thought of the vast stretch of desert awaiting made him thirsty.

"I'm just going back to the next carriage to get us some water," he said, which was strictly against his orders when he had been told to stick to von Braun like glue.

The presence of the Peenemunde crew in the USA was still classified information and, for the time being, needed to stay that way.

Surely leaving him alone for two minutes won't hurt, Hamill reasoned, but when he returned with glasses of water in hand, he was horrified to see von Braun avidly chatting to a stranger – a Texas businessman, whose cigar was puffing smoke nowhere near as thick as von Braun's German accent. It was a dead giveaway and Hamill panicked.

"What was that all about?" he asked anxiously after the man, with his prosperous paunch and pinstripe suit, thankfully got off at the next stop. There was much back-slapping and hand-shaking going on between them and Hamill was worried ... worried enough for von Braun to have some fun.

"Well, I'll tell you," he answered, as he nodded a final farewell to the businessman still waving from the platform.

"When Mr Keeler out there asked about my accent, I told him I was from Switzerland. He wanted to know my line of work and I said the steel trade. And would you believe it? He was in the same business and knew it like the back of his hand."

Hamill winced, dreading that von Braun had spilled the

beans. Yet far from doing that, he was enjoying every minute of drawing out the suspense, teasing Hamill every inch of the way with his talk of ball-bearings and blast furnaces.

"But the best part . . . ," he said, before putting Hamill out of his misery, "was that the man actually *thanked* me when he said goodbye."

"*What?*" Hamill bounced back in dismay, making it hard for von Braun to continue with a straight face.

"Yes . . . America, he said, owed the Swiss big time and that if it hadn't been for our help, the damned Germans might have won the war."

It was 'score one' for von Braun, but the smile fell from his face when they reached their destination. By the look of it, it was not to be a case of fulfilling a Cowboys and Indians fantasy, but a long, hot, five years of living and working in the wasteland where the V-2 trove had been dumped in wait for its creator.

"So much for the New World," von Braun mumbled, making no attempt to hide his disappointment. Given America's big-time talk and ready access to cash, he had envisioned premises flashier than Peenemunde, but had got nothing but cactus and coyotes.

"Well what did you expect?" Hamill replied, "That the roads would be paved with gold?"

"Not exactly, but I hadn't counted on there being no roads at all!"

For here he was in the middle of nowhere. Stuck in a desert prison from which there was no escape, bar dying of tedium.

"This is where they tested the atomic bomb," Hamill said to inject some life into the scenario.

The dust, however, had settled on that explosive few seconds of excitement and with the bomb already dropped to force Japan's surrender, the German scientists' prime reason for being here no longer existed. Still, they were being stashed away in the sand and isolation to stop any other countries getting their hands on them before a new purpose for them was found.

Von Braun could have told them that that purpose was the moon, but in the post-war pandemonium when every country was busy licking its wounds, the prospect of something requiring yet more moral fibre and money was out of the question. So, in every respect, von Braun felt lousy. Sick with disappointment and his disease, he supposed his welcome could not get any worse.

... oOo ...

"I don't like him being here," the commanding officer of Fort Bliss said to Hamill as soon as they arrived. He refused to shake von Braun's hand and looked at him with undisguised disdain. "I was wounded in both wars and have no intention of playing host to any Nazi."

"That's not for you to decide," Hamill countered sharply, before suddenly having to wrap a supporting arm around von Braun to stop him collapsing. He was as sick as a dog, soaked in sweat and his temperature was raging.

"Didn't you get the War Department's dispatch?" Hamill continued angrily as, without the commanding officer's help, he managed to awkwardly manoeuvre von Braun into a chair.

That dispatch, Hamill could now see was scrunched up in the officer's waste bin and retrieving it, he read it out aloud:

> *The Secretary of War has approved a project whereby certain outstanding German scientists and technicians are being brought to this country to ensure that we take full advantage of those significant developments deemed vital to our national security.*

"Here, sir . . . ," Hamill then said, thumping the communiqué down on the commander's desk, "is one such outstanding German scientist who needs to get to hospital. I suggest that you see to it immediately."

Von Braun was relieved, at first, that he did, but his stay in the Fort's infirmary was to last a very long and depressing eight weeks. There, among nothing but wounded US soldiers, he was without companions and had been warned not to reveal his identity. He could hardly, however, hide his heavy accent.

"Hey *Dutchy* . . . do you want to play a bit of poker?" a soldier who took pity on him asked one evening – Holland being his best bet as to which allied nation von Braun belonged, because the one-in-a-million chance that they were sharing their ward with a German was unthinkable.

Von Braun chipped in for a few hands, but threw each one for fear of causing offence or drawing unwanted attention. Still woozy and not completely well, he was swamped by the sense of the unfamiliar. Everything seemed so strange, so very surreal, and feeling alone without friends or Fatherland, he suddenly had an alarming compulsion to cry.

"If you'll excuse me, gentlemen," he said in a hurry before seeking the privacy of the dimly lit courtyard outside. There, in his wheelchair, he took a few moments to feel sorry for himself before the sound of a familiar voice made his spirits soar.

"What . . . still not on your feet von Braun?"

He looked up with a jolt that turned to joy when he saw his second in command, Eberhard Rees, and Major Hamill walking towards him.

"Well what took you so long!" he leapt up with a surge of his old strength to say, only sorry that he had to limit himself to a handshake when his every instinct was to wrap his arms around the man.

"They finally let me join you here," Rees happily explained, "and the others are on their way."

The good news took a moment to sink in before von Braun looked up at the moon and let out a sigh of indescribable relief: "So," he said, "let's get this show on the road."

THIRTY-FOUR

UNFORTUNATELY, IT WASN'T THAT SIMPLE. Their six-month contract dragged out to a year, but still their presence in New Mexico was kept a secret from the American people, while their sub-standard quarters at White Sands and Fort Bliss felt more like leper colonies than centres of technical excellence. Although the war was over, they were ostensibly POWs sweating it out in the back of beyond as quasi captive consultants to the US military.

"I suppose we should be glad of it," von Braun said when 125 employees from the General Electric Corporation came to work with them.

It certainly showed that America was serious about moving things along and staying at the forefront of missile development, but just like the Reich, their minds were set on advances in weaponry, and the small band of German rocketeers realised they were back to square one, having to fight to keep their space aspirations alive. Being outnumbered by the influx of US engineers and technicians didn't help, but the balance was soon set right.

"*That's* better!" von Braun said, when at long last his

hundred-strong contingent of Peenemunde colleagues, who had been delayed by red tape, finally turned up.

It was hard to contain his excitement when their bus drove into the compound. The dust in its wake settled and after a moment of breathless anticipation, its concertina doors opened to disgorge the first of its foreign passengers. They stepped out tentatively, shielding their eyes from the blazing sun and with them looking the worse for wear, von Braun's mouth straightened before lifting into a radiant smile when he caught sight of his brother Magnus among them.

The intensity of joy at their reunion validated Wernher's business decision back in Germany to make his brother head engineer of gyroscope mass production at the Mittelwerk facility. He'd had to override all rumours of nepotism to do it, but had he not, Magnus wouldn't have been important enough for America to save and would most likely be dead.

The US vetting system, however, appeared to be full of holes. Despite its wheels grinding exceedingly slow, it had failed to pick up the fact that nearly half of the Peenemunde imports had been members of the Nazi Party, 21 of whom also belonged to the SA, while two were affiliated with the infamous SS. Add von Braun's membership to its ranks and that made three worthy of being kept under close surveillance. Those most suspicious constituted the lesser proportion of the team, but it was enough to forever brand them all as *the Nazi scientists*, and for von Braun to realise that US authorities had actively turned a blind eye to achieve their own ends.

It was wonderful for the rocketeers to be together again, but their team was soon stripped of two – V-2 combustion chamber engineer Hans Lindenberg, who died of diabetes within days, and another member of their group who was sent straight back to Germany because he developed schizophrenia.

"Probably from the shock of seeing this God-forsaken place,"

Wernher said scathingly to Magnus. "It gave me one hell of a turn, I can tell you, and it's been damned hard adjusting after we were so pampered at Peenemunde."

That, Magnus soon found out for himself. Money was near non-existent, as were the appropriate facilities. All White Sands' launching equipment and rocket parts had been pilfered from Germany and arrived in shoddy condition. With nothing but the most rudimentary of tools available, not much could be done to repair them, given the basic wooden workshops at their disposal under which their engineers had to crawl to run their own cabling.

"Watch out for snakes!" von Braun cautioned when one of his men volunteered for sub-floor wiring duty.

His warning was unnecessary given the drama of the previous day, when wriggling his way between gravel and timber joists, another of their engineers came face to face with a rattlesnake. The deadly western diamondback was half coiled with its head reared for attack, and from sheer shock he struck out at it with his torch. It lashed back, sinking its venomous fangs into his hand. Hearing him scream, his team pulled him out from under. Other than knowing it could kill him, they hadn't a clue what to do and could not have been more grateful to the group of US soldiers with the hometown advantage, who raced to their rescue.

"*No!*" one of them said, slapping von Braun's hand out of the way as he tried to apply a tight tourniquet. "Just a light, constricting band above and below the bite and keep him calm. There's anti-venom back at the Fort Bliss. We'll have to get him there fast."

With no concern as to country or creed, Americans and Germans drove there together on a shared mission to save a man's life.

"What a farce this whole war's been," von Braun said when

the emergency was over and he shook each soldier's hand in thanks. "When it comes down to it, we're all one."

It was a defining moment that helped his team settle in. But letting bygones be bygones did not stop them being bored.

"It's just not good enough," von Braun complained to Hamill. "We're treated like criminals. We can't go anywhere without a military escort, all our mail is censored and our living conditions are primitive in those torturous hothouses you call barracks."

"Like the ones at Auschwitz you mean?" Hamill countered caustically to put him in his place.

To this, von Braun had no comeback. What had happened during the war was inexcusable and it would be a long time before Germans could speak up in their country's defence. To be fair, most of their US guards treated them well, but snide comments of the like flowed thick and fast from those soldiers among them who had seen the worst of the war and were still not convinced that von Braun had not had a hand in its atrocities. For him, therefore, it was a case of the less said the better when words spoken in haste or anger could well incriminate him.

There was no alternative but to play along, so he stopped fighting the inevitable and threw himself into it, forsaking his old country's tried and true to embrace the different ways of the new. It was hard to do when he had been so proud of the honorary title Hitler had given him. Even now, his colleagues still referred to him as *Herr Professor*, but considering the source, he now found it embarrassing.

"Just call me Wernher," he told his German team. "From here on in, I work under Hamill with the no-nonsense title of Project Director."

"What's more," he continued with a fresh enthusiasm, "Although, at this point, we're only here on a month-to-month basis, I urge you all to teach yourselves English. I know that mine could stand some improvement."

The improvement he put in place turned out to be debatable. With him and his team tutoring themselves from American GI slang and the *Zorro* movies playing in El Paso, they developed a dialect of their own, their German accents tainted with a Texas twang and the odd expletive which would forever mark them as the Peenemunde Paperclippers and, in the future, make all the dignitaries von Braun lectured in Washington laugh.

If nothing else, their self-schooling helped pass the time and excruciating tedium. They were confined to base with the US government paying them a pittance, a third of which was sent to their families in Germany, while another third went in taxes.

Von Braun's proficiency on the piano meant they could entertain themselves with evenings of song. But without women or the occasional sip of wine, the young men ran amok.

They reverted to boarding school boys, cutting loose with water bomb and pillow battles between barracks – a series of midnight forays during which von Braun temporarily dispensed with his super-human IQ, to act the Neanderthal.

"This won't do!" Hamill rebuked them when he saw the result. "The place is a disaster zone."

He looked the other way, however, when on random nights, some of the missile men slipped past the guards to take strolls in the desert under the stars. There, to once again lift their minds to loftier levels and contemplate the universe.

"Let them be," Hamill instructed his men. "Just keep an eye on them from a distance. After all, where can they run?"

Nowhere, the Germans found out, beyond their Sunday-school-like excursions, when with packed lunches in hand, they were shuttled by bus to the more distant desert and mountains to broaden their horizons. Sadly, the scenery there was just as drab and merely added to their depression.

"But it's only a trickle," Tessmann said despondently when they pulled up on the banks of the *Rio Grande*.

The river's very name had promised the spectacular, and with their high-flying lives having been reduced to daily humdrum, they had been counting on it to stir their spirits. Like all else in this desolate part of the world, however, it too had dwindled to nothing and lost all its zest.

They were fed up – sick to death of sitting twiddling their thumbs when their families back home were in dire need of them.

"I'm formally requesting that your Army Intelligence launches a special mission to get our families out," von Braun put to Hamill. But with the war still raw and no German being in a position to make demands, it came to nothing.

Finally, their fretting was allayed when they were given their first real assignment.

As well as training the American GE employees in V-2 assembly, von Braun was to instigate the Comet supersonic ramjet project. Thrilled to have his mind working again at full capacity, he promptly churned out 40 pages of calculations for ramjet motors, before having to put his pen down in frustration. He had never worked with their type of propulsion system and without any aerodynamicists on his team he was stumped.

When he admitted as much, Hamill was not only unhappy, but downright furious that the navy had beaten them to the punch.

"We've been left out of the loop," he said as a surge of hot rage had him loosen his tie. "They've shipped nine members of your Kochel wind tunnel team, plus most of Peenemunde's relevant parts, straight to Wright Field Aeronautics Base in Ohio. Their chief . . . your old friend Rudolf Hermann is with them."

At this devastating news, von Braun picked up that dormant pen of his and hurled it at the wall.

"Well, that's that," he said as its ink splattered to the floor. "*He* was the man we needed."

It left von Braun no choice but to send any questions he had by mail to his old associates: Hermann at Wright Field, as well as Ernst Steinhoff and Walther Riedel, who were still sorting their way through the Reich's research papers at Aberdeen Proving Grounds.

"Now all I have to do is wait two weeks for their answers to wend their way back to me via your shithouse army system," von Braun complained to Hamill, his sentence punctuated with an expletive, as were all his conversations now that he had mastered his GI-style English.

Both of them were bad tempered, but with nothing to be done to improve their situation, Hamill tried to see its bright side:

"In the meantime, von Braun, you've got some very good men working with you."

"Yes," he scoffed, not in the mood to be cajoled, "now that there are more Germans among them."

Hamill was used to von Braun's patriotic swagger, but with shreds of their former enemy status still alive, his American sensibilities kicked in. The world may well have laid down its weapons, but he still enjoyed crossing swords with words.

"To the victor go the spoils," he said with a shrug, temporarily sacrificing their friendship to flex his US muscle.

Yet despite being one of the vanquished, von Braun flashed back: "You're just lucky you got the richest haul."

Hamill's eyes narrowed, weighing up whether it was worth going one better.

"You're an arrogant son of a bitch." he said, unable to resist.

And with no intention of denying it, von Braun threw him a broad smile.

CHAPTER

THIRTY-FIVE

VON BRAUN SOMEHOW always got away with it. His whopping ego never grated as did that of his baby brother Magnus. Although clever like the rest of his family, the youngest of the three von Braun boys lacked the charm to pull it off, while his strict adherence to the privileges of his aristocratic rank made him obnoxious.

"He wouldn't be so bad if he'd just stop rubbing his good breeding in our faces," his fellow rocketeers were prepared to concede.

But his US guards found everything about him galling.

"He's a pretentious little snob whose high-handed indiscretions make him a worse threat to security than half a dozen discredited SS generals," one of them said after Magnus' blue-blood instincts had him slap an American soldier across the face for issuing an order to which he objected. It should have got him shot, but instructions from above were to treat all German scientists with kid gloves.

His own family was not so delicate.

You must do something to curb your brother's rash behaviour, his father, Baron Magnus, wrote to Wernher from Germany.

His letter came in response to one Wernher sent him six weeks before in which he briefly mentioned his concerns about Magnus, before discussing matters much more important. His first V-2 had been launched successfully from White Sands and with the promise of 70 more to come over the next five years, he was bursting with pride over Germany's superior ingenuity, while singing America's praises for having the foresight to embrace it.

I'm hoping you can join us here as soon as possible, he had written to his parents. *I'm genuinely excited about our prospects in America and want to assure you that it doesn't feel like unfamiliar territory with so many Germans already settled here.*

Nevertheless, he knew it would be a huge step for his parents to take. As diehard members of the nobility, they would loathe deserting their country to become dependent on their sons.

I only wish I could share your enthusiasm, Baron Magnus went on to write in his reply, *but your dear Mama is in bad health from malnutrition and is not fit to travel. We are existing in a strange homeless limbo, with the Russian victory having put an end to the eastern European aristocracy and our entire landowning class. All is lost . . . my two dear sisters have been killed and our estate, with its centuries-old library and lands, is no more.*

Poverty, however, won out over pride and left the baron no choice, so he made one final ruling as the head of the von Braun household: that young Magnus break off the scandalous engagement he made before quitting Germany; one that threatened to link them to the lower classes and a woman not yet divorced from her first husband.

Wernher dreaded passing on the message, but Magnus seemed unperturbed.

"It's absurd," he said, "that as grown men, we're being told what to do."

Truth be known, Magnus was glad of the excuse to break free from a commitment he long since regretted. He was ashamed, in fact, that his passing passion for a pair of pretty hazel eyes had seen him inflict such a piece of poor taste on his family. The drama of war's end and his daring departure to foreign shores had impelled him to propose, but given that time and distance had not made his heart grow fonder, he was now perfectly happy to dispense with his fiancé at his father's command.

That boy seems ever to be the source of our concern, the baron had scribbled in his postscript to Wernher. *He'll always take whatever he wants at any cost, so make sure you keep a tight rein on him.*

It seemed Wernher did nothing but. Wherever Magnus went, trouble followed and he never ceased having to watch his back. First, pulling him into the rocket business to save him from the Front; then, putting his name on the short list for America ahead of others who were more deserving. Brotherly love made him glad that he did, but now rumours were rife that Magnus had illegally smuggled in a hoard of platinum from Germany. Frankly, Wernher did not want to know, but the truth was hard to ignore when all at Fort Bliss were laying bets on how he did it.

"He had it cast as a set of mechanic's tools," someone suggested.

Another, that he had brought in the undeclared metal in

basic bars. Either way, everyone was sure that he had sold it to an El Paso jeweller.

It was never substantiated, but it did seem strange that he was the first at Fort Bliss to buy a spanking new car, while his older brother and boss on a higher salary, could only afford a second hand model much later.

"If it weren't for our respect for you Wernher we'd give him a swift kick up the ass," one of his German colleagues commented in his colourful new US lingo.

Despite that feeling being unanimous, Magnus stayed safe under his brother's protection, albeit feeling the sting of sibling rivalry that constantly had him come off second best. For having forbidden Magnus' marriage to one German girl, their parents could not have been more thrilled when Wernher confessed his love for another.

> *I intend to propose to my cousin Maria,* he wrote in
> his next letter to Germany, *and would be grateful,*
> *father, if you would formally approach her on my behalf.*

The baron never moved faster and within hours secured 18-year-old Maria's answer.

"It never crossed my mind that I would marry anyone else," she replied when he offered his son's hand in marriage. First, apologising for Wernher being some years her senior and then for the fact that in America, marriage between first cousins might raise a few eyebrows.

Among the German elite, it was a centuries-old practice, and seeing nothing wrong with it, they could only rejoice. Wernher's joy was so intense that it sparked an epiphany – the acknowledgement that such all-encompassing love came from God. It was a revelation so profound that he saw their coming together as divinely inspired and his reason for finding religion.

My darling little Dresden doll, he wrote to her, putting a pet name to her delicate, china-like beauty. *The Texas sun has never shined so bright, yet it is just a weak lamp compared to the warmth of your devotion. You have been mine since I held you in my arms at your christening and I will love you until the day I die.*

He had lost a great deal in leaving Germany – his title, his lands, his inheritance. To salvage something of his past, he was determined to at least marry within his old aristocratic ranks. Maria was his guarantee, his compensation – a gracious remnant of what had once been. Taking her with him to live a new life in a new world would render it a dignity and perpetuate all that was once fine from the Fatherland.

The whole family would be together again to thrive and prosper, bar his older brother Siggy, who had left his wife and children safe in Vatican City to return and help out in Germany. It was mistake, for as soon as he set foot on its soil, he was thrown into a US prison as a former Reich official. When he was released a few months later, he went straight to Landshut to see to his parents' welfare.

"I'm thinking of relocating my family to Australia," he told them.

"But why, when you can come with the rest of us to America?" his mother questioned, not understanding that after Siggy's stint in jail, he was a little less inclined towards the USA and wanted to keep his options open.

At least he's alive and well and will most likely join us in America later, Wernher wrote to console his parents, before tackling all he'd planned on paper in person.

"I need permission to return to Germany," he requested of Hamill on one of their working trips to New York. "My parents are ill and because they and my fiancé aren't yet classed as my dependents, they can't get travel passes. I'll have to go home to see to it all and marry Maria so that I can bring all three of them back with me."

It was a lot to ask, but recognising von Braun's strategic importance to America, Hamill used the emergency clause in their Paperclip contract to make it happen.

"You will be under constant military custody during your entire stay in Europe," he stipulated. "We can't risk the Soviets making a grab for you."

Von Braun held up his hands in mock surrender:

"That's fine by me," he replied, just as keen as Hamill that he should stay clear of Russia.

So began his whirlwind romance. Shipped with his American minders to Bremerhaven, he went by rail to Landshut, on the way bartering three cartons of cigarettes for flowers to give Maria. With beautiful blooms in hand and US escorts at his side, he stepped onto the Landshut platform to revel in his joyous reunion with his wife-to-be and parents, who he had not seen in two years.

They hoped their wedding would be a private affair, but to hold back the crowd, the local Lutheran church had to be cordoned off with a ring of American MPs and Bavarian police, as did their honeymoon apartment.

"Just pretend we're not here," one of the US soldiers said. "If you want anything, we'll be in your kitchen."

"Perhaps we should wait till we're on board ship," Wernher suggested when neither the comment nor the apartment's paper-thin walls were conducive to any form of romantic rollicking.

Yet, that too did not work when only female passengers were offered cabins and Maria had to bunk down with her mother-in-law rather than her new husband.

If Wernher weren't so frustrated, he would have been amused.

"Well, see you at Fort Bliss," he said, having to force a smile as he stroked his hand down her porcelain pink cheek.

Unfortunately for the newly-arrived von Brauns, Fort Bliss did not live up to its name, only offering one small apartment to house all four of them for months until separate accommodation could be prepared.

"This is intolerable!" Baron Magnus exclaimed, as his tired eyes scanned its very small surrounds. With a sigh of desperation, he sat down heavily on the one available chair and put his head in his hands.

"There's not even the most basic appliance, let alone a servant to use it," he complained, suddenly finding it impossible to come to terms with all they had lost.

He was worn out, but angrier with himself for having survived the unspeakable horrors of war, only to be brought undone by the superficial. It was a different time and different place and he doubted he would ever adjust to having and being nothing.

Wernher had never seen an open display of affection between his parents, but he watched now as his mother, Emmy, rushed to wrap a loving arm around her husband.

"Never mind, my dear," she whispered as if consoling one of her children. "It's really not so bad when you consider that our German cities are in ruins, millions of our countrymen are destitute and our former leaders are awaiting execution for war crimes. At least here we're safe until things get better."

It certainly started to shape up that way. The rocketeers' contracts were extended to five years, their salaries were increased and their families began arriving from Germany after the US government formally unveiled its Project Paperclip and informed the public of the scientists' presence at Fort Bliss. All would have augured well had it not sparked a savage backlash.

When the headline: ***115 TOP GERMAN V-2 EXPERTS AT EL PASO*** hit the national dailies, religious spokesmen from around the country, sent a telegram to President Truman:

The Germans' former eminence as Nazi Party members and supporters raises the issue of their fitness to become American citizens or hold key positions in American industrial, scientific and educational institutions.

Following suit, the liberals and Jewish groups sent a far more forthright letter to the press:

We protest at the employment of these so-called Nazi scientists on the grounds that they are carriers of race hatred and alien ideology – minions of a monster, who have been morally and criminally compromised by their work for the Third Reich.

Strong words coming from such a source were not surprising, but when American scientists, formerly fellow Germans, spoke out against them, von Braun and his team were shocked. Among them was the illustrious Albert Einstein and Oppenheimer's colleague on the Manhattan Project, Hans Bethe.

We want no part of the V-2 booty. The fact that these men were directly linked with a regime whose infamy included the most brutal persecution of free science must fill every citizen, and in particular, every scientist, with deep apprehension. We advise that they be sent directly back to where they came from as soon as their work is done.

Meanwhile, in the House of Representatives, a politician put more pep into the protest.

I have never thought that we were so poor mentally in this country that we have to import those Nazi killers to help us prepare for the defence of our nation.

Most of the military agreed. Von Braun was a prime security risk, but due to the peculiar absence of any documentation to implicate him in anything worse, the moral issue of America wrongly providing him with a haven was lessened. In all good faith, therefore, their priority turned to the Cold War and America's business needs, both of which stood to benefit from the input of superior German technology.

The war crime trials at Dachau were over and their findings were now classified. They had seen Mittelwerk's General Director, Arthur Rudolph questioned; its Planning Director, Albin Sawatzski dying mysteriously in a US jail, and thanks to the help of the US Army, von Braun avoiding in-person testimony altogether. The rest of the Peenemunders kept their mouths shut. When the gavel came down for the final time, the US military put all files under lock and key because the prospective worth of the defendants' knowledge topped all other considerations.

Von Braun was in Washington while much of it went on, and as he and Hamill walked from the Pentagon they were beset by a swarm of scoop-scavenging journalists with flashing cameras.

"Just barge your way through and make no comment," Hamill said as he started shouldering his way through the crowd.

Von Braun followed close behind resisting the repeated call of his name and the mockery of shouted *Sieg Heil* salutes. But just before breaking free from the mob, a reporter caught hold of his arm.

"*Herr Doktor*, do you have any response to what the American people have to say?"

Von Braun stopped, and rejecting Hamill's advice, turned to answer:

"It's a free country . . . thank God!"

CHAPTER

THIRTY-SIX

THE RED SCARE soon made the Paperclip protests and past Nazis old news. It posed a more imminent danger and although a full-scale communist invasion was not yet on the cards, the US Armed Forces were bracing for the possibility while waging an in-house war of their own.

"Our home grown Viking missile can double the V-2's altitude and is half the weight of that Nazi dinosaur," the navy boasted to counter the air force's rush of interest in von Braun's Fort Bliss project.

Since the war, the American military budget had been slashed and the aviation industry was fighting to survive. Looking to exploit German technology, the president of North American Aviation was already fraternising with the missile men at Fort Bliss with the intention of using their V-2 as his model for the production of rocket engines at his soon-to-be Rocketdyne division near Los Angeles.

This came as a major boon to von Braun. For some time everything had been peaceful, if not deadly dull at Fort Bliss with no research facilities nor talk of advanced rocketry or space exploration.

"Our minds are being wasted," his team complained. "Now it's not space, but *time* that's the problem. None of us are getting any younger and if we don't act soon, it'll be too late."

They had no choice, however, but to sit out the frustrating three-year hiatus.

"My *wandering in the wilderness years*," von Braun would later call them, during which he stayed dedicated to family and his new-found religion. Unfortunately, along with it came a new sense of shame that had him roaming the desert each night to speak one-on-one to God in the hope of securing forgiveness for sins forever to remain a secret between them. Yet, every time he looked up at his star-studded confessional, his mind would instead start crunching numbers to plot a path to the moon.

His first step in that direction was to consolidate his footing on Earth by becoming an American citizen.

"I'm afraid there's a hitch," Hamill said when von Braun applied to begin the long naturalisation process. "Because you and your team came here as army employees, you're technically illegal immigrants. To start your five-year citizenship waiting period, you'll have to physically re-enter the country according to the rules."

Von Braun looked at him aghast: "You've got to be joking . . . and how exactly do you propose I do that?"

It seemed a sensible question, so he was surprised by the silly answer:

"You'll have to walk across the Rio Grande Bridge over there into Mexico and as soon as you get to Juarez, turn around and catch a streetcar straight back onto US soil. It's no more than two blocks, so the fare will only cost you five cents."

Swearing at the absurdity, von Braun rolled up his shirt sleeves and strode towards the bridge, half an hour later leaping off the streetcar at its Texas stop, with a smile stretching from ear to ear.

"Well that's the best nickel *I* ever spent," he said, slapping Hamill on the back. "Feels good to be legal."

At least it would have if his now lawful application for citizenship didn't trigger a 10-year FBI investigation into fresh allegations of war crimes and the accusation that he had withheld information about vital documents in Germany that his brother Siggy had supposedly buried in a tin under a tree.

"Well what was in it?" the bureau demanded.

Von Braun looked distrait: "Just personal things . . . a manuscript of my father's memoirs and other bits of family memorabilia."

"And perhaps further directions to other stashes?" his interrogator interjected.

To this pointed accusation, von Braun said nothing, his silence infuriating the man enough to have him recommend that he be sent straight back to Germany to face court.

"Well *that's* not going to happen!" Colonel Toftoy and Major Hamill agreed, both adamant that they could not risk von Braun floating around Europe ripe for the USSR's picking.

The controversy made young Mrs von Braun distraught.

"But what will I do if they send you back?" she cried with her hands cupping her eight-month pregnant belly.

"They won't," Wernher said, sure of his strategic importance. "My American captors are my greatest protectors. They're more scared of the Reds that any of my possible Nazi links."

He was right and the allegations soon melted away. The FBI turned its attention to easier investigations and put the issue of von Braun's immigration on the backburner.

The reprieve left him free to enjoy the birth of his first of three children – a baby girl they named Iris, who like her younger sister and brother to come, came into the world as a perfect example of the Aryan race: bright, blonde, blue-eyed . . .

"And just as beautiful as her mother," Wernher would always say.

Hot, dry Fort Bliss, however, was hardly the place for their upbringing, so he was thrilled when Toftoy took him to see what was to be their new, sweet home in Alabama.

"It's just like Germany," Wernher reported back excitedly to Maria after having scouted out their future home town of Huntsville. "Everything there is so green, with glorious mountains all around. You can smell fresh mown hay . . . and the trees . . . at long last, the trees! At Bliss, we have to drive 200 miles to see five of them together."

"It sounds wonderful," she replied, catching his contagious joy, "But I don't understand what's brought it all about."

It was simple – the Soviets. For some time Toftoy had been pushing for the development of a missile with nuclear capabilities and new facilities in which to build it, but his proposal had been vetoed by the Pentagon.

Events in 1949 changed all that. The Cold War officially began, the Iron Curtain came down over Europe, Mao Zedong established the People's Republic of China, war clouds gathered over Korea, and the Soviet Union tested an atomic bomb. Suddenly, the Pentagon was all over Toftoy's idea.

"How soon can your German rocketeers come up with a 200-mile, nuclear-capable missile and other longer-range ballistic weapons?" they quizzed him. "And how large a facility will they need?"

Within days, Toftoy was on his way to North Alabama to check out the old WWII army post on the outskirts of Huntsville in Madison County – the Redstone Arsenal that was soon to become the new Army Ordnance Rocket Centre with a corps of several hundred US engineers and scientists and 115 German rocket specialists. As yet, no one knew that those 115 carried in their briefcases the blueprints for the US space program.

... oOo ...

Huntsville seemed an unlikely place for such a pivotal point in history. All it could boast was a population of 15,000 and being the watercress capital of the world.

"*Hicksville*, Alabama" was the Germans' more appropriate estimation of it – an insular backwater that incited a cool reception on both sides; its residents just as keen to turn up their noses at their Teutonic invaders as were the German intruders to cringe at being cut off from civilisation. Not in a position to complain, however, the newcomers kept their objections to themselves, but the town council was very vocal about its:

"Tennessee's been handed 7000 work opportunities and *we're* getting stuck with a hundred Krauts," the council said after Huntsville had recently lost its bid to host America's profitable new Air Force Wind Tunnel facility.

During the war the town had boomed with a workforce of 14,000 making poisonous gas and artillery shells at the Redstone Arsenal, but peace had brought close to 100 percent unemployment. The wind tunnel's 7000 jobs would have made the world of difference. Yet, despite their disappointment of instead having the less lucrative rocket facility dumped in their backyard, Huntsville was remarkably tolerant, bar a small faction determined to hold a grudge.

"I wouldn't if I were you," Wernher warned, when he pulled up at a Huntsville service station en route to their new home and Maria got out of the car to use its restroom.

The need was pressing, so she was annoyed when her husband stopped her.

Without saying a word, he pointed to the sign, written in aggressive red paint that the station owner had hung on the petrol pump:

GERMANS NOT WELCOME!

The look on Maria's face must have said it all, for a passerby stopped to say:

"He has to be forgiven for that, my dear. The last time we saw Germans they were shooting at us and one of them killed his son."

It was a horrible way to start, but as the early years of the 50s rolled on, the von Brauns were happy, on the whole, in Huntsville. They were all together with three generations in one place: Wernher, with his wife and children, his parents and brother Magnus; all of them doing their level best to assimilate. Baroness Emmy was teaching English to the other rocket scientists' wives, and his father was doing all he could to fit in. With his walrus-moustache and gold-handled cane, he cut a fine figure as he strolled down the main street each day, stopping to chat with everyone he passed.

"For my part," Maria explained, in her want to hasten the befriending process, "I've given out our private phone number to everyone in town. I want them to feel that we're always accessible."

It was a kind gesture that wasn't so wise.

"Could I get a ticket to the moon?" a prank caller rang in the middle of the night to say.

The next day, the von Brauns got an unlisted number.

While not wanting to be quite so familiar with the townsfolk, Wernher was going out of his way to do the social rounds, attending dinner parties and joining local organisations. He was hunting and fishing with the business and political men in the area, acting as president of the local astronomical society, while instigating the Huntsville Symphony Orchestra in which he and a dozen of his German scientific team regularly performed. To this he added regular talks to community clubs about space exploration, brightening up their boring small-town existence by showing slides of proposed space shuttles and men walking on the moon. He forgot, in his zeal, that many among them were still vehemently anti-Nazi and resented being pushed beyond their safe boundaries by the enemy.

One of these worked in the local hardware store. A middle-aged man in bowtie and striped suspenders, who as a show of contempt, put a black comb to his upper lip and thrust out a Nazi salute in answer to von Braun's request for a set of spanners.

Another was a farmer who stood up during von Braun's address to the Huntsville Country Association to shout: "The day a man lands on the moon, I'll fly a bale of cotton to Washington with wings strapped on my back!"

The fact that he was applauded was hard to take, but von Braun had the sense to join in the joke. It was impossible to laugh, however, when others he would have thought more educated, called him crazy:

"That man's insane! He belongs in a mental asylum, not a university," the bank manager said after von Braun's address to the Chamber of Commerce. There, he discussed the concept of weightlessness in space and the impact of gravitational pull, which the money man's limited mind had obviously failed to grasp.

He did, however, approve von Braun's home builder's loan. With it, his three-bedroom bungalow was built, during which process he was insulted, again, by one of the workmen:

"I sure ain't gonna paint the house of that Nazi nut who wants to go to the moon."

Even though von Braun expected as much after the war, he fought hard not to be offended. But when, as a result, he started doubting himself and his wisdom in having made the massive move to America, he toughened up and fell back on his ever-winning way of tacking trouble with humour.

It was a hot, humid day when he gave a speech at the Women's Church Society. Having stopped to share sandwiches and tea, he thought he had won the brood of Bible-bashers over, but his kind participation and titillating good looks merely stirred their concern.

"He's a godless man," one woman commented to another as they watched him walk away. "I'm worried about his soul, so I shall send him a letter."

Von Braun laughed out loud when he read it:

> *For your own sake, dear sir, I beseech you to forget all this irreverent talk of space and simply stay home and watch TV as the Lord intended.*

He wrote back:

Dear Madam,

> *You are familiar, no doubt, with Genesis and the story of Jacob's ladder. The angels are ascending and descending it, as are we. If the good Lord does not want us to go up and down His creation, all he need do is tip the ladder over!*

CHAPTER

THIRTY-SEVEN

THE GOOD NEWS WAS that Dornberger had arrived in America. After a few years of English imprisonment, he had been released and under the auspices of the US Air Force, was now working as an executive for Bell Aircraft Corporation in Buffalo. He immediately tried to lure von Braun over to Bell in the belief that their air force studies would soon lead to a manned space plane.

"You know how much I'd love to be in on it," von Braun responded after a few restless nights of indecision, "but I'm committed to the army and feel personally responsible for our Redstone Project. I'm afraid it has to be 'no', but I can't tell you how good it is to have you back on the scene."

The edge came off von Braun's elation, however, when Dornberger promptly pilfered other key members of his Redstone staff for which he had no intention of apologising.

"What was the first thing I taught you?" he said sharply when von Braun tried to take him to task. "That there are no friends in business."

It was a lesson von Braun rarely had to put into practice. Being hardline did not come as naturally to him as did his flair for public relations. As the quintessential marketing man, he knew the power of advertising and how to use it:

Congratulations, you are a technical salesman without equal, a British rocketeer wrote to say when von Braun published a series of spectacularly illustrated articles in *Collier's* magazine to sell the concept of space to the American people. The articles impacted on the market with a wow-factor that overnight positioned von Braun as the king of print media promotion.

"We don't like it," Walther Riedel and several others from his Peenemunde team protested. "It's nothing but cheap commercialism that prostitutes our serious science."

There was truth in that, but von Braun knew that the only way to further their serious science was to win over the public, creating an audience so vast and strong that the government would be forced to fund their cause. He had an uphill battle, however, when there was an element within his own group who always worked against him. Guided missile expert Adolf Thiel was the worst of the dissenters in his dislike of von Braun's flamboyant way of spreading the word.

"*And* of the fact . . . ," Thiel added, "that you're considered our technical superior purely because of your pretty face and gift of the gab."

That went both ways. Von Braun was every bit as offended to think that his success was based solely on his physical appeal; that he was being written off as a lesser mind by those who refused to believe he could be blessed with both. It was an insidious, in-house jealousy that had gone on for years, and having had enough, he slammed his fist down hard on the conference table.

"We can dream about the moon and rockets until hell freezes over!" he said. "Unless everyone out there understands it and the man who pays the bills is behind it . . . no dice. So, you just worry about the damn sanctity of science and I'll talk to the people."

Unfortunately, media coverage was not always kind – one day labelling him a space visionary, and the next, a crackpot. Like most of America, the science editor of *Time* magazine could not make up his mind:

> *Von Braun is more than a mere technician. He is a prophet and something of a mystic who is viewed by his peers with a mixture of suspicion and admiration. When he speaks to the public of his confident plan to travel into space, people say he is preaching to the birds, but no one can deny his strong following of small boys buying spacesuits in toyshops and the trail of space dust left sprinkled in teenage enthusiasts' eyes. He is the Pied Piper of Space, leading our children on a crusade to sure disappointment.*

Von Braun's rebuttal in the next issue was short and profound:

> *Enthusiasm and faith are the key ingredients of every great project. Prophets have always been laughed at, deplored and opposed, but some have proved to be following the true course of history.*

As to that, Redstone Arsenal was well on its way to being an American replica of Nazi Peenemunde, with von Braun as the civilian director of the army's Guided Missile Development Division. Under the auspices of Brigadier General Toftoy his Redstone missile was being run through a series of test flights, some of them successful, some not.

"Well why did that one explode?" Toftoy asked irritably, pressed as he was to match the Soviets rocket program stride for stride.

The Cold War was pepping up and with the Russians having a hydrogen bomb and being close to perfecting a ballistic missile that could accurately hurl nuclear warheads at any continent, the US was at a decided disadvantage.

"I don't know," von Braun answered honestly.

He was as disappointed as Toftoy with the failure, but more so by the fact that just like Nazi Germany, the never-ending demand for weapons was shoving his dreams of space aside.

It was all very depressing, as was his parents' sudden decision to return to Germany.

"But you can't go," he argued when his father broke the news. "What's left for you there?"

"Nothing but the comfort of the familiar," Baron Magnus answered. "When we die, we wish to rest in home soil."

In typical Germanic fashion, his reasoning was by way of the most morose, but pre-empting Wernher's objections, the baron had also seen to the practicalities.

"You mustn't worry about us," he continued, "My pre-Hitler years of public service have entitled me to a government pension. It should be enough to see us both out."

All this talk of death was unsettling, but it was reality, and when Wernher waved them off from the wharf, he knew he would probably never see them again.

"I hope you won't miss me as much," Magnus said soon after. 'I'm moving on from Huntsville to work at the Chrysler Corporation in Detroit. Their missile division has offered me a job with a wage I can't refuse."

Wernher was shocked, stung like a little boy at the desertion of a brother who no longer wanted to play the game.

Seeing his disappointment, Magnus said in consolation: "Surely you must have expected as much? You know as well as I do that it's time I stepped out from under your shadow."

For a while, Wernher felt quite alone with his family all going their separate ways, the chance of Siggy ever coming to America having been dashed when he decided to enter the diplomatic service of the Federal Republic of Germany. It would not be until 1968, when he became Permanent Representative at the United Nations in New York, that he and Wernher would see each other again – a short three-year stint of family get-togethers before Siggy returned to Germany to take on the role of Secretary of State.

There was nothing for it but for von Braun to focus all his attention on work. With more and more missiles being fired from Redstone, he struck out to better their dependability and to tighten the sloppy technical workmanship that was holding both him and his rockets back.

"At some point, I'm hoping our missile performance will make our targets more dangerous than our launch areas!" he snapped sarcastically, rousing a nervous laugh from those in the boardroom, before he strode from it in blood-boiling frustration.

It came as some relief that the missile became more reliable by the mid-50s, but the endless refining of its design was driving von Braun mad.

"It's not as if we're flogging a dead horse," Arthur Rudolph argued in the rocket's defence.

Yet it seemed that way and von Braun was fed up. To end any further dispute, he put his hand on Rudolph's shoulder.

"Art," he said, "You remind me of the fellow who married a virgin and kept telling her how good it was going to be once he got it perfected."

The debate was done and a deep freeze on their rocket design went into effect while von Braun put his mind to different use.

... oOo ...

"We'll just have to face the fact that we don't understand it,"
US Army general James Gavin said to the other members of
their technical group in Washington.

They had been doing their best to evaluate the Soviets'
new missile program through covert photography, but the
Pentagon experts were at a loss to comprehend it.

"We could always get von Braun up here to look at the pictures."
Gavin suggested, but his idea was slapped down.

"There's not a chance of that. He hasn't got the special security
clearance," his superiors said, still smarting from the war.

Gavin threw his hands up in desperation: "For God's sake,
the past is past and we're running on empty here. All we need
is the guts to admit it."

"That's enough!" he was reprimanded, but he refused to
give up.

"So, while the Pentagon sits back protecting its pride, the
Soviets are making mercurial progress and walking all over us."

Something in that sentence hit a nerve and the Pentagon
placed a call to Huntsville.

"We were wondering, Dr von Braun, if you could give us
some help."

Von Braun moved like lightning, boarding a plane within
the hour to be in Washington that same day.

"It's very simple," he said as soon as he was shown the
photographs.

Calmly and with complete confidence, he went on to describe
the entire system down to its plumbing, its propellant and where
it was stored; filling them in on how the missile was fuelled,
while providing a comprehensive rundown of its characteristics.

... oOo ...

Back in Huntsville, von Braun's colleagues made a toast to his Washington success.

"It's the extraordinary breadth of his intellect," young Redstone metallurgist William Lucas said "No matter what the subject or problem, he always gets straight to the heart of it."

Here, the proud employee took a moment to catch his breath before recounting his own dealings with his boss.

"When I first mentioned possible corrosion of missile material at coastal launch sites, von Braun was working at White Sands and wasn't particularly interested. But the second he got back from his holiday in Florida he was on to it.

"Drop everything Lucas," he ordered, "and start a program to tackle corrosion immediately My tooth-powder tin rusted through after only two days at Cocoa Beach. The salt air there is ferocious and if we're going to launch from Florida, we'd better come up with a solution fast."

THIRTY-EIGHT

MEANWHILE, HAVING MADE GOOD USE of the press, von Braun turned to television to get his message across.

"A Mr Walt ... Walter Disney called," one of his new secretaries came into his office to say.

Von Braun looked up from his desk in astonishment. Not at all surprised that the famous animator had phoned him, but that the girl with her vacant, brown eyes evidently hadn't a clue who Disney was.

"I suppose I should fire her," he said when his chief scientist, Ernst Stuhlinger, also complained of her work.

"But you won't," Stuhlinger replied, well acquainted as he was with von Braun's weakness for curvaceous blondes for whom he was prepared to overlook the absence of a brain.

"Well, what can I say?" Wernher threw back with a wink, "You'd think my happy marriage and religious beliefs would keep me faithful, but I have to admit that I find it hard."

This, to a degree, was understandable. Wherever von Braun went he was besieged by beautiful women – all of them predatory and prepared to do anything to attach themselves to his celebrity, which was a dilemma due to get worse now that his fame and face were to be broadcast on televisions around the world.

"Your private life is none of my business," Stuhlinger hastened to say. "I just want to know what's expected of us on Disney's show tomorrow."

To capitalise on the growing Space Age craze, Walt Disney was producing a new TV series called *Man in Space* in which von Braun and Stuhlinger were to star. Keen for good ratings, Disney was going to introduce the show himself with the promise that its hosts would prove more popular than Mickey Mouse.

The series did its job, and together with the *Collier's* articles, built enough momentum to kick-start von Braun's dreams, while realising one that Disney held dear: the creation of *Tomorrowland* at his fabulous, new fantasy theme park.

"It's all falling into place," von Braun said when in 1955, he was at last, formally made an American citizen.

At heart, he would always be German, but he had the sense to embrace the big change in his life, along with the one that suddenly happened at Redstone. The switch in its command and objectives came swiftly.

"You are to start, straight away, on a crash program to finalise your missile's development. It'll be renamed Jupiter-C," von Braun was ordered by his new boss, Major General John Medaris.

As a decorated war hero, the intractable officer with his slick, dark hair and moustache burst onto the scene with a riding crop in hand and a larger-than-life presence that rivalled von Braun's. Yet, that had nothing to do with von Braun taking an instant dislike to him. His response, therefore, was brusque:

"What's happened to Toftoy?"

Obviously, the general had been given the side-shuffle, which was shoddy treatment von Braun resented for the man he had always seen as a gentleman and friend.

Medaris, however, was unmoved.

"He was too soft for the job," he said in clipped reply as he offered a cigarette.

Whereas, you're all spit and polish and poised to be a gigantic pain in the ass, von Braun was thinking as he cupped his hands round the match flame to light it.

But first impressions could be wrong. Whether he liked to admit it, von Braun always functioned better under strong command, and within weeks he and Medaris were getting on like a house on fire, working with a set-up that suited them both. To parallel the special arrangement the air force had put in place to minimise red tape, the army doubled its budget and personnel to rush through the creation of its new Army Ballistic Missile Agency. With the indomitable Medaris at its head, it was aligned to Redstone Arsenal, yet operated separately and carried more clout. More importantly, it put all the US armed forces on a level pegging.

Still, it seemed that the Eisenhower government favoured the navy when it decided to back its more sleek-lined Vanguard project instead of the army's Redstone rocket to launch America's first satellite. Von Braun was furious:

"This isn't a beauty pageant!" he protested. "It's a contest to get a satellite into Earth's orbit and we – the army – are way ahead on this. Vanguard might look prettier, but it's a completely untested design."

The Russians agreed and were rejoicing. With the Space Race on in earnest, they too were about to launch their Sputnik 1 and could not believe that America was giving them the advantage by opting for the untried Vanguard over Redstone's tried and true.

"The US has no time to lose if it wants to be first into orbit," von Braun warned Washington, only to receive a patronising reply:

"We don't share your sense of urgency," they rang him back

to say. "No one is the least bit excited about a little man-made object floating around Earth."

"What a pack of idiots!" von Braun said as he slammed down the phone.

Fortunately, he was familiar with the stubborn short-sightedness of those in power. His dealings with Hitler had taught him to bounce back from the disappointment of decrees made by those who refused to see the light.

So he wrote back, with renewed optimism, to the congressional committee:

> *May I suggest, then, that we put in place our Project Orbiter as a back up to Vanguard in case it should fail?*

Their answer was swift and succinct:

> *Please confine yourself to weapons development.*

This was where Medaris stood up to be counted, treating von Braun and his team to a small sample of the guts that had brought him glory on the WWII battlefields.

"There's always been conflict between the US services when it comes to the space program," he said with a dismissive confidence. "So far, the army's seen the worst of it, but this time, I'm here to make damned sure it's not *our* program that bites the dust."

Von Braun's eyes lit up. Having a champion like Medaris on side meant that nothing was going to stop them.

They had been issued specific orders to forget all about satellite work, but they weren't about to do any such thing. It was no coincidence then that the 12 Jupiter-C's they were commissioned to build bore a striking resemblance to the souped-up Redstone rockets they had proposed for Project Orbiter. Their first test launch wa to be from Cape Canaveral, with the Jupiter's four-stage rocket containing a dummy satellite package in its nose.

Suspecting that von Braun was pulling a stunt to beat the navy's Vanguard to the punch, the Pentagon sent a stern order to Medaris:

Don't you dare!

The command was explicit, so their Jupiter-C blasted off with an inert fourth stage and no satellite on board, but neither were necessary to prove their point. The rocket set a record by reaching an altitude of 600 miles and travelling a distance of 3300. Any doubt about putting a satellite into space was quashed, and von Braun could not wipe the smug smile from his face.

CHAPTER

THIRTY-NINE

B UT THEN CAME A SHOCK bigger than Pearl Harbour.

No one believed von Braun when he said the Soviets were about to launch their first artificial satellite, but on October 4, 1957, when Sputnik 1 appeared overhead, America was horror-struck and utterly humiliated.

"I told you so," von Braun was tempted to say to Washington's big brass, but instead, he confined himself to President Eisenhower.

"We could have done it years ago if you'd only let us."

Short of admitting his own mistake, Eisenhower spoke for the entire country.

"Our failure to be the first in orbit is a national tragedy that's damaged American prestige across the globe. What can you do, von Braun, to repair it?"

He had thrown down the gauntlet, and true to his knight's heritage, von Braun rose to the challenge, the next day presenting the US political hierarchy with his pitch to have his Jupiter-C rescue the country's reputation.

"What we need most to make it happen is freedom from government interference and a ready flow of money. The scientific obstacles we face such as propulsion and atmospheric re-entry heat barriers will all fade away, but the cash barrier *never* will."

"Why have we allowed ourselves to lag so far behind the Soviets in space?" one senator interjected. "Just tell us what it will take for America to pull ahead."

Without missing a beat, von Braun turned to him and answered: "How much are you prepared to sacrifice for us to do it?"

For putting the politician on the spot, he received a round of applause, but the man came back giving as good as he got:

"We have two automobiles at home," the senator said. "I'll sacrifice my wife's!"

Von Braun laughed, but then put humour aside.

"Take warning, gentlemen. If you're not prepared to give us your full support now, then you'd better prepare yourselves to be affronted by the many Soviet 'firsts' to come."

His prophecy came true when a month later, Sputnik 2 orbited with a 1120-pound payload, including a dog named Laika. But America was still indecisive and its favoured Vanguard project could not get off the ground. Televised to a nationwide audience, the rocket rose just a few feet from Cape Canaveral's sand before it collapsed onto its launch pad in a roaring, red ball of flame.

"Well, that was embarrassing," the navy had to admit, while the press rubbed their faces in it further by renaming their Vanguard 'The Stayputnik'.

Suddenly the spotlight was back on the army.

"We're ready to direct your Jupiter-C team to prepare a satellite payload for launching if needed," the Pentagon conceded. "But with one condition: we're still not giving our full authority to launch."

In response to this unflinching absurdity on Washington's part, Medaris came back with an ultimatum of his own:

"If you don't give us your unqualified go ahead, right here, right now," he threatened Defence Secretary Neil McElroy, "then both von Braun and I will resign."

That was a chance McElroy wasn't prepared to take, so he gave the green light and Medaris went straight to von Braun's office to pass on the good news.

"Wernher," he said, his face beaming with joy as he flung open the door, "We're a go!"

... oOo ...

On January 31, 1958, America's pride was restored with the launch of its Explorer 1, the first spacecraft to detect the Van Allen radiation belt and to remain in orbit until 1970. It was an achievement so great that it spawned more than 90 scientific spacecraft in the Explorer series.

Medaris went to Cape Canaveral to watch the rocket take off.

"But you'll have to sweat it out at the Pentagon's Communications Centre," he told von Braun.

"*Why?*" Wernher argued, when after all his hard work it was only fair that he should see his baby fly first-hand.

"Because if it's successful, they'll need you there to speak to the press . . . so wear a dark suit."

"And if it's not?" von Braun snapped back scathingly.

"Then wear dark glasses and duck out the back door."

It was a success that went down in history and von Braun soon received a letter of congratulations from the British Minister of Defence, Duncan Sandys – the son-in-law of Winston Churchill, who as an Intelligence officer during WWII had instigated the RAF raid on Peenemunde. There was irony in that and it seemed the world had turned full circle when they became fast friends.

> *For yours is an achievement that surpasses all else,* Sandys wrote, *and will open to you, von Braun, the gates of Heaven.*

PART FOUR

HALFWAY TO HEAVEN

CHAPTER

FORTY

DUE TO VON BRAUN'S CONTENTIOUS ACTIONS during the war, some thought it debatable that he would ever pass through that pearly portal. To prove those people wrong, he had been working to remedy all that was awry in his life; using his enormous resources of energy, ingenuity and optimism to make something out of nothing. Aside from flying to the moon, his home town of Huntsville was his favourite project.

"You've been named the first recipient of Huntsville's Annual Distinguished Service Award," Maria rang his office excitedly to tell him.

Wernher was taken totally by surprise. "Really? By whom?"

She scanned down to the signature on the formal piece of stationery.

"By Huntsville's business leadership," she read out in her now perfect English. "For your constant participation in high-priority community interests."

It was a newly instituted award from what was once a dead-end town now thriving thanks to von Braun's input. Everywhere one looked in its streets his hand could be seen, from its state-of-the-art supermarkets and booming employment to the added refinement of its new symphony orchestra. Short of renaming the whole town in his honour, the award was the best its citizens could do to express their gratitude.

To have won the heart of Huntsville was an achievement that rivalled his rockets' success. Bursting with pride, Wernher picked up his pen:

> *I accept this award in all humility,* he wrote back.
> *But I want you to know that I've only just begun.*

It was easy to let such things go to his head, but soon he and America had the wind taken out of their sails when the Soviets successfully launched their record-setting 3000-pound satellite Sputnik 3.

Another slap in the face, yet still the US military services were busier battling between themselves than beating the real champions of the Space Race. When the navy's latest attempt to launch Vanguard again saw it fizzle within seconds of ignition, von Braun's army team rubbed salt into the sailors' wounds by successfully putting their Explorers 3 and 4 into orbit. That was immensely satisfying for von Braun but did not change the fact that they were merely playing catch-up, constantly running second to the Soviets.

To combat the frustrating state of affairs, the Defence Department decided to create the Advanced Project Research Agency to referee among the military services and their competing space proposals. None of its board members cared which of the services ranked supreme, just so long as one of them came up with the goods. The first stop on their rounds was Redstone, where von Braun was quick to open discussions.

"I don't understand our preoccupation for merely reacting to Soviet invention, when it's we who should be setting the benchmark by striking out on something innovative ourselves."

Having gone straight for the jugular, he got immediate action.

"What do you have in mind?" the delegates asked.

"I want to do studies on development of clustering engines for the first stage on our new Nova heavy-lift rocket."

There was a moment of mumbling among the delegates before one of them said:

"How much funding will you need?"

"How much do you have?" von Braun threw back.

"10 million is all we can spare."

"I'll take it."

In return for the financial favour, von Braun's big-booster work would lead directly to the Saturn family of heavy-duty space launch vehicles. Setbacks were bound to arise, but von Braun was never shy about admitting his mistakes or to confess to knowing nothing.

"Hang on . . . hang on, let's backtrack here," he said, interrupting project engineer Don Bowden's briefing about a critical valve problem with their Jupiter S-3D engine. "You've just jumped to lesson two and I haven't even had lesson one."

Bowden was astonished. Not because the world-renowned rocket scientist did not know what he was talking about, but because he was big-time enough to admit it.

"Never let your ego get in the way," von Braun explained when he saw the look on Bowden's face. "In our field, it's fatal to fake it and make the wrong decision."

Bowden admired him more for this than for any of his remarkable achievements.

Ego, however, was playing a big part in politics. The Soviets' constant boasting about their space supremacy was causing the US leaders considerable concern.

"Space exploration must be our nation's highest priority," Senate Majority Leader Lyndon B. Johnson said with the thump of an emphatic fist on his desk.

Because America was fed up with having to swallow its pride, his decree carried weight, and President Eisenhower sent Congress a proposal to establish a space agency, which was to become von Braun's first non-military employer. In July 1958 NASA was born, made up largely from the old National Advisory Committee for Aeronautics, NACA, headquartered at Langley, Virginia.

Von Braun was summoned to Washington.

"We want you and your Redstone team to move your operations to Langley," the agency administrator Keith Glennan said.

Here, von Braun had to be diplomatic because he knew that Medaris would strenuously object.

"Dr Glennan," he answered. "All we at Redstone really want is to stay put with the patronage of a very rich and generous uncle."

For the time being, they got what they wanted, but during the difficult transition of NASA's control over US space activities, von Braun had to continually make sure he was not left out of the loop. Despite staying rooted at Redstone, he took members of his team regularly to Langley as plans for Project Mercury and its one-man space capsules got underway.

Nothing, however, continued to run smoothly, and someone with ideas as strong as von Braun's was bound to clash with him. In this instance, it was NACA's Robert Gilruth, who as an aerospace engineer, was poised to become the first director of NASA's Manned Spacecraft Centre in Houston. Having worked in England as a plane designer during the war, he detested everything to do with Nazis and their V-2 rockets, which equated to detesting von Braun. When he took a lead role in their talks, Gilruth made no bones about it, but at the end of the day, had to concede that von Braun's plan of using his Redstone rockets to lift the first US astronauts into space on arcing, sub-orbital flights over the Atlantic, was the most viable. That concession came with a look of loathing that pushed von Braun into combat mode.

"I hear reports that you're talking to the air force about plans for some kind of two-man capsule," he said, calling Gilruth out on what was meant to be top secret. "Given that we're all meant to be working together, would you care to fill me in on the details?"

"No, I wouldn't," Gilruth answered with a contempt that brought von Braun's German blood back to the boil.

"Well, we'll see about that!" he said, fully aware that Gilruth and his cohorts were actively trying to keep him and his Huntsville team out of the new Gemini Project. Now that the truth was out, he went directly to headquarters to make sure that Redstone was at least assigned to the launch-vehicle-end of it.

Von Braun's operation already controlled army rocket launch operations at Cape Canaveral and testing at White Sands, but he wanted more and lobbied hard for astronauts and their training to be based at Huntsville. It was just one in a series of battles he waged against Gilruth – some won, some lost – but due to his dogged determination, his space centre grew to incorporate facilities at five locations in four southern states, including support activities at the Cape and a coast-to-coast network of project branch offices.

When it came to space, some said he was insatiable, whereas Gilruth always maintained that all von Braun wanted was everything.

"He's got that right," von Braun agreed, accepting Gilruth's insult as a compliment.

Houston and Huntsville would always be at loggerheads, with neither von Braun nor Gilruth happy to work together. Yet, as time went by, their mutual distrust slowly dissipated to a grudging professional respect. They would never be best buddies, but when the future Apollo project was put on the agenda, they were prepared to shake hands for the sake of posterity.

CHAPTER

FORTY-ONE

JUST WHEN VON BRAUN FELT HE was getting on top of things, he received shattering news.

My dear boy, his father wrote from Germany.
*I am sad to say that your most beloved mother has
passed away. I am bereft and completely alone.*

That was all the letter said, its words scrawled in a script bearing no resemblance to his father's more familiar, firm hand.

For a critical moment, Wernher couldn't breathe, as much incapable of taking in air as the shock loss of his kindred spirit. It took some time to pull himself together and to book a flight back to Germany, stopping short of saying he was flying 'home', even though he knew in his heart that was where he was going.

It had been 14 years since he had set foot on its soil, but his sad reason for being there made the familiar scent less sweet. He arrived to find his father and two brothers standing by the grave, the time that had elapsed since he had seen them melting to nothing at their coming together to mourn.

"How did it happen?" he asked Siggy, for his father was unable to speak.

"She was rushed to hospital for an emergency colon cancer operation just a few days ago," Siggy replied, his voice ragged with grief. "She died on the operating table."

Wernher's throat clamped tight at those intractable words of finality, He had to gather his courage to ask: "Did she suffer?"

"It she did, she didn't let us know," Siggy said simply. "Never once did our darling mother lose sight of her courage."

Looking down at her coffin, all four men wished that they could say the same of themselves, for their mother's sudden passing had shaken them to the core.

The baron, bent low over his cane, looked utterly broken and Siggy, Wernher thought, appeared worn out after his emergency trip from the West German embassy in London where he worked.

"How are you holding up?" Wernher turned to ask his little brother Magnus, who was fighting hard to control his emotions.

Only a few months before, he had come from his Chrysler office in Detroit to visit Wernher at Redstone, but since then, his mourning for his mother had aged him 10 years.

The men's reunion after such a long time apart should have been joyous, but they found it easier not to speak; and when his father's hand, clasped tight to his cane, began to shake, Werhner steadied it with his own.

The funeral was difficult enough, but when the press got wind of Wernher's presence and their flashing cameras and fast-talking journalists intruded on his family's mourning, he was incensed.

"Well what did you expect?" his father said, shrugging off any emotion that went beyond his own grief. "Now that you're a worldwide celebrity, it goes with the territory."

Fame and fortune, von Braun found out, was not all it was cracked up to be. Although it gave him the platform to do what he wanted, it aroused jealousy among his peers and unending demands from an admiring public; some of which came as a thrill, but more often as a concern.

Fan mail rolled in, most of it fawning, but some of it downright obscene:

> *Is it possible for one to attain sexual pleasure from sending up rockets?* one woman wrote in a letter scented with cheap perfume.

To this one, he sent no reply, but used it as an anecdote to brighten up a few boys' nights out. The 'hate' mail he received more frequently, however, was no laughing matter.

To the Father of the V-2 Missile in World War II, one was addressed, while others went into more vivid detail, coloured with expletives and threats of death.

Ever-persisting was the question:

> *Were you a member of the Nazi Party?*

"Dr von Braun has long since regretted and renounced Nazism," his assistant grew sick of writing in reply, while having to demand many retractions from newspapers that accused von Braun of involvement in the Holocaust and queried his swift shift of allegiance at war's end. One lead article asking:

> *Will he be off if a better opportunity than America presents itself?*

The answer to that was that von Braun was in America to stay; at this moment, living there as its star turn, which was rare for a man of science, let alone a former enemy.

... oOo ...

"When he's around, no one gives a goddamn about the Secretary of the Army!" said the Secretary himself, Wilbur Brucker, when pandemonium broke out at the National Air and Space Museum in Washington.

He, along with General Medaris and von Braun, were guest speakers at the first anniversary celebrations for the Explorer 1 launch into orbit. Supposedly the least important of the trio, von Braun had to wait till last, but the second he took to the stage, he was mobbed by the crowd clamouring for autographs. In the stampede, the more medal-laden Medaris and Brucker were shunted out of the way.

The mania seemed to go a tad too far when Notre Dame University presented von Braun with their Patriot of the Year Award, an accolade that raised a few eyebrows and prompted American Jews to get their own back by mocking von Braun's newly released movie biography: *I Aim at the Stars*, with the subtitle:

But sometimes I miss and hit London!

If it weren't so serious, von Braun would have found it funny. Better then, he believed, to play it safe and keep his focus on his work.

As an off-shoot of the Explorer series, their Juno II had just launched the unmanned Pioneer 4 spacecraft for a fly-by of the moon. It was to be the first satellite to go into permanent planetary orbit around the sun, which at last put America one up on the Soviets, whose Luna 1, launched two months earlier, had missed its planned lunar landing.

Just three months later, the US put its first passengers into space, treating monkeys Able and Baker to a 1600-mile suborbital ride in the nose cone of the Juno I rocket as a warm-up for the Mercury astronauts to come.

It was all-systems-go, but due to von Braun's and his team's success, the issue of them moving to NASA surfaced again. This time it was to the newly built and largest of their facilities – the Marshall Space Flight Centre at Redstone Arsenal. It was the US government's civilian rocketry and spacecraft propulsion research centre, designed to have von Braun as its first director. It was the second time NASA requested that he and his team move to work under their banner and the second time, Medaris strongly objected.

"Well then . . . the option is for them to go over to the air force," he was informed when he went to the Pentagon to complain.

That was all that needed to be said to make Medaris back off. The head of Air Force Systems Command, General Bernard Schriever, was his archrival and he'd be damned if he would do him any favours.

"There are worse things than losing von Braun to NASA!" he said as he stormed from the main office.

One way or another, von Braun didn't like being a pawn in America's military game, shuffled from pillar to post as if he were a second-rate citizen. It was a sore point that would stay with him forever in regard to his true allegiance and nationality.

Yet, with the inevitable move to NASA, a dinner party was held in his honour, attended by the rich and famous; one of whom stood to say:

"Dr von Braun, I enjoyed sharing this evening with you and I appreciate what you are doing for my country."

Von Braun's reaction was instant.

"Sir," he said. "It's my country too."

FORTY-TWO

IT WAS 1961 and America had a new President: WWII naval officer John F. Kennedy. Fresh blood gave hope of fresh endeavours, which was just as well, when despite von Braun having successfully shot another monkey into space in preparation for the Mercury-Redstone one-manned capsule, the Soviets went one better with cosmonaut Yuri Gagarin orbiting the Earth in Vostok 1.

After congratulating the Soviet Space Agency, von Braun went straight to the media to get his message across to the White House.

"It's the shot heard around the world,' he said in a nationwide broadcast. "We are going to have to run like hell to catch up."

"I'm right with him there," the President said as he turned off the television.

He was in dire need of something to distract from his Bay of Pigs disaster and happily, space stepped up to fill the bill.

"Space is the new ocean on which America must sail in a position second to none," Kennedy announced to the public.

Later, in private, he said to Vice-President Lyndon B. Johnson: "What we need is to seize the initiative with a dramatic new space goal . . . one that America can win! So, put out some feelers, will you. I want to move on it like lightning."

A lunar landing! was von Braun's instant response to the Vice-President's letter of inquiry. The decisive exclamation mark at the end of his sentence appealed to Kennedy, so he invited von Braun to the White House.

"No one is more tired than I am of America's second-place standing in the Space Race," Kennedy said as he offered him a glass of brandy. "But there's no escaping the truth that we're a long way behind."

Von Braun had a knee-jerk reaction on both counts. Considering Kennedy probably didn't know a rocket from a rabbit, how could he possibly claim to be the most tired in a race he was not personally running? What's more, the fact that they were behind was not due to any lack of technical expertise, but to the constant impediment of America's red tape and reticence.

He was not, however, prepared to debate the point and took up the challenge with his trademark optimism.

"Well, fasten your seatbelt, Mr President. I'm going to get you your blue ribbon by landing America on the moon."

That was a big boast von Braun had to scramble to back up. He started by putting astronaut Alan Shepard into a capsule called Freedom 7 atop one of his Redstone rockets at the Cape. It was to be boosted on a curving 15-minute ride, 116 miles up and back before splashing into the Atlantic and being recovered by an aircraft carrier.

When Shepard first set eyes on the small spacecraft he was horrified.

"You mean I'm supposed to fly in *that? I quit!*" he said in 10 percent jest and 90 stark terror.

Von Braun picked up on the fraction of humour: "What are you talking about Commander? You've never had it so good."

He and the seven astronauts hosted at Redstone got on famously. As a fellow risk-taker and aviator, von Braun identified with them and they liked him for it. It was hard for von Braun to believe that having conjured spacemen up in his imagination and written stories of them as a child, he was now walking among them and responsible for their lives.

"Don't you wish you were going up there with them into space?" a reporter asked at a news conference.

"Sure, why not?" von Braun answered. "But they've just told me I'm too fat."

It was far more important to have von Braun directing operations on Earth than thrill-seeking among the stars, and when the mission proved a success, he was proud that it was his reliable Redstone rocket that scored for the home team.

The launch was televised to millions, bar Shepard's small emergency segment that was edited out. With the entire journey expected to take only 15 minutes, his suit had no provision for the elimination of bodily waste. No one anticipated a launch delay of eight hours that would take Shepard, who was strapped in his seat throughout, to the extremity.

"I'm sorry," he said when he came to the end of his endurance and the liquid leak shorted out the medical sensors attached to track his condition in flight.

"Perhaps you could leave that part out when you talk to the President," he went on to suggest sheepishly to von Braun.

"I'll try," he answered with mock concern.

Yet, fun as it was teasing his friend, von Braun had no intention of embarrassing Shepard when he reported back to Kennedy.

"Granted, Shepard had a small hitch and it was no orbital mission," he covered up smoothly, "but at least, albeit briefly, we put a man in space."

Kennedy was excited, and being a man every bit as dynamic and determined as von Braun, he did not let him down.

"That's it," he said, "We're going for broke!"

It was a decision that made von Braun's heart skip a beat before he gave the President his personal guarantee:

"I promise you, that before the decade is out, there'll be American boot prints all over the moon."

CHAPTER

FORTY-THREE

AS THE SON OF ZEUS, it was Apollo's job to harness the sun to his chariot and drag it daily across the sky – a feat after which NASA's new space program was to be named. To align themselves with the gods, however, did not sit well with those more down to earth.

"Spending 40 billion to be the first to reach the moon is just nuts!" former President Eisenhower had argued in 1961.

Von Braun was used to that word being bandied about in regard to him and his hopes, and had learned not to take offence. Instead he said with enthusiasm:

"Some called Charles Lindbergh's solo flight across the Atlantic a stunt, but look what it did for aviation. Trust me . . . Apollo will be the wisest investment America has ever made. It'll fuel advances in science, technology and the economy at a cost, I can assure you, well under 40 billion. Even if we should find that the moon is made of green cheese, it will be worth every penny spent."

He thought it prudent at this point, not to mention that the moon was merely a pit stop on the way to his ultimate goal of Mars.

Baby steps, baby steps, he kept telling himself to get the Earth-bound non-believers over one hurdle at a time.

His next step, however, was rather a big one: the maiden test flight of his team's Saturn 1, which was the first in the series of three versions of heavy-duty space launch vehicles. The big rocket, with the clustered eight engines of its first stage, generated an almighty 1.3 million pounds of thrust and blasted off with resounding success.

It would have been worth celebrating had it not caused friction among the armed forces and various NASA facilities; something which became commonplace during the otherwise halcyon Saturn/Apollo era.

"Why aren't you using our Centaur missile's steering sensor as you were instructed?" Air Force Major General Donald Ostrander demanded of one of von Braun's team.

"Because we prefer to use the more reliable sensors our Redstone Guidance and Control laboratory have refined through years of research and development," aerospace engineer Walter Haeussermann answered. "After running full tests, we found extensive problems with your air force Centaur instruments."

Ostrander leapt red-faced from his chair: "This is totally uncalled for," he shouted. "Now get out of my office!"

Haeussermann returned to Redstone, and burning with indignation, handed in his resignation.

"What's this?" von Braun asked in surprise.

"I'm sorry, sir," Haeussermann answered, "but I will not tolerate being spoken to like that."

At the prospect of losing one of his best men, von Braun's lips thinned with resolve.

"Leave it to me," he said, before he scheduled a meeting with Ostrander. At the end of which, he walked from the office looking triumphant.

"Well?" Haeussermann asked, having had to wait outside.

"From here on in we'll be using our own sensors."

"But how did you swing it?"

"Just did as you did and threatened to resign if I didn't get my way. I knew Ostrander wouldn't want to shoulder that kind of onus. In fact, I'm reasonably sure he'll resign very soon himself."

It was just one of many NASA in-house battles, most of which had von Braun at their core due to the jealousy his celebrity status stirred and the resentment aroused by his aggressive push for new programs and bigger budgets to favour the Marshall Centre. For some of the NASA hierarchy, however, it was simpler than that. They just could never get beyond his Third Reich roots.

Houston's flight director, Chris Kraft, was one of them.

"I suppose he can't be blamed for being obnoxious after working with Hitler for so long, but my loathing of him is always simmering beneath the surface," he admitted to Robert Gilruth, who had been promoted from NACA to head of the Space Task Group at Houston's Manned Spacecraft Centre.

Having come to terms with his own animosity towards von Braun, Gilruth tempered his response with dismissive disdain:

"I wouldn't be too concerned about the strength of von Braun's Nazi convictions. So long as he gets what he wants, the man doesn't care for which flag he fights."

If this were true, then it went a long way to prove von Braun's innocence in regard to war crimes. It confirmed that he did not care about racial cleansing, the war itself or which side he was on, just so long as it facilitated his studies of space.

Strangely, the most unlikely of men believed him: Major General Samuel Phillips of the US Air Force, who was hired by NASA as the Apollo program director. Based in England as a fighter pilot during WWII, he saw the worst of the V-2 attacks and had personally escorted bombers on raids against Peenemunde.

"Having gone through all that, how could you possibly give von Braun the time of day?" Kraft asked when Phillips became von Braun's close friend.

"The way I see it, he did what he had to do for his country, as did we," Phillips answered. "And frankly, I've lived too long and seen too much to forever hold men accountable for the evil of others and the orders they were forced to obey."

While personal enmities persisted, NASA gave the go-ahead for a fifth engine first stage on the Saturn V, a monster of a machine that made everyone look up in awe.

"How can a beast that size possibly fly?" von Braun was asked.

It was hard to believe when the rocket stood 365 feet high, towered six storeys taller than the Statue of Liberty and weighed a whopping 6.5 million pounds at lift-off.

"That's some mother of a moon rocket," the newspapers said.

But von Braun strongly objected to putting that limitation on it, when for his Saturn V, the moon was merely a stepping stone to the stars.

"It's the most powerful rocket in the world . . . at least for the time being," he informed the press. "It's by no means the limit to which we can go, but it gives us the capability to do many things in space at the press of a button."

"After such an achievement, you must be proud of the remarkable loyalty and achievements of your German team," one reporter commented.

"I am indeed," von Braun replied. "Not only for their collective brilliance, but because they've stuck by me through thick and thin for an unprecedented period of time; some of them putting up with me since 1935."

It was important for von Braun, however, not to limit his praise to just his German colleagues.

"I've been fortunate twice over because of the wonderful array of young US-born scientists who've come on board and proved their worth. Their input has been invaluable."

Such diplomacy was appropriate, but wanting to spice up his article, the reporter pushed for more: "Yes, but surely there's no doubt that your German nucleus is smarter?"

Von Braun immediately rejected the compliment.

"Perhaps it appears that way because we old-timers have been working on these things for so long. We've had 12 more years to make mistakes and learn from them. What's important is that the young bloods of our team learn from us what they can, *while* they can."

Here, von Braun would have been horrified to know, he was much like Hitler in their shared preoccupation with time. Ever aware that theirs would run out fast, they both felt the obsessive need to achieve what they had to achieve at top speed and to impart their knowledge before it was too late. Von Braun, just like his old fanatical Fuhrer, thought nothing of keeping his people up all night to lecture them on new insights and to instil in them, his own extraordinary dreams.

CHAPTER

FORTY-FOUR

THOSE DREAMS WERE NOT LIMITED TO SPACE, when to von Braun any new frontier was fascinating. One of them was deep-sea diving; an activity, among many others, which he shared with his family and good friend, broadcast journalist Walter Cronkite.

"Everything to be said about space has already been said between us," Cronkite related when he was asked about von Braun in an interview. "But you should have seen his eyes light up at the challenge of designing a submarine to travel to the unknown depths of the ocean."

Catching the scent of a scoop, the reporter asked: "Do you think von Braun will make it his next project?"

Cronkite was sorry to disappoint him.

"Given half a chance, I'm sure he would, but let's face it . . . he's got his hands full trying to conquer the universe."

While he worked to that end, von Braun always took time out to enjoy a good joke, finding them funnier when done at the expense of unsuspecting friends. With his host of scientific achievements, some of them did not believe that he was also a skilled pilot, so he figured they had to find out the hard way.

"When you reach 7000 feet I want you to fake engine failure," he said conspiratorially to the veteran American fighter pilot who had taken to offering scenic flights over Mount Rushmore. "I'm playing a prank on my friends, so when you cut your engine, look scared and I'll take over."

The man baulked. "Not a chance buddy!"

There was nothing for it but for von Braun to come clean. At the risk of reviving bad feeling, he flashed his credentials.

"You know those Messerschmitts that gave you US flyboys a spot of bother during the war . . . well I was flying one of them."

That was enough to convince the man and after a moment of subduing past resentment, he took to the skies with von Braun and his two friends. As instructed, he cut the engine and feigned fear as they flew over the monumental rock face.

"Don't worry, I'll try to fly it myself," von Braun said, when to his friends' dismay, he took over the controls.

"*Goddamn, Wernher,* what do you think you're *doing!*" one of them shouted when von Braun abruptly turned the plane on its side to give them a better view of the stone presidents in profile – a waste of time when their eyes were squeezed shut in stark terror.

"*Oops!*" he said with his hands hovering hesitantly over the instruments. "Just give me a moment and I'll get the hang of it."

It wasn't until he threw the small plane into a professional loop and came in for a smooth landing that his friends caught on.

'You rotten bastard," one of them said sitting white-faced in shock, when von Braun turned in his seat and laughed out loud.

"Today's lesson, gentlemen," he said. "When a German says he can do something, you'd better believe it."

For that, he owed them a round of beer.

It was no joke, however, when flying to Washington later in the week, such an emergency became real and the lives of his passengers were put in his hands.

"Take the controls, will you Wernher," the regular pilot of their NASA plane said when he had to check their faulty radio transmission.

When the airwaves cleared, he requested clearance for landing and despite thick cloud cover, the control tower radioed back: *"Come straight in."*

Von Braun lowered the nose of the plane to go down through it, while at the same moment, up out of the clouds came the nose of a DC-3 head on.

"Shit!" the co-pilot swore, as with split-second timing, von Braun peeled the plane sharp right, evading collision with the dog-fighting skill of a WWII ace.

"I didn't think I still had it in me," he confessed, when still shaking from the experience, he was later lavished with praise.

For history's sake, it was fortunate that he did. In fact, when he stopped to think about it, he'd had quite a few near misses in his life; time and again being saved inexplicably from situations that should have been fatal. Given his far from exemplary past, he often wondered why God bothered to back him, but there was no longer any doubt in his mind that He did. The deeper his understanding of science, the more he realised how much he didn't know and the more convinced he felt that there was something greater "out there" beyond man's finite comprehension. He had often felt a strong sense that someone was watching over him, protecting and guiding his path until he fulfilled his purpose.

Such moments made him acutely aware of his weaknesses and misdeeds, and knowing that none of them could be undone, he had got into the habit of making amends whenever he could, regularly donating sizeable chunks of cash to charity, while giving more hands-on help to those he saw in need.

The most recent experience was during his holiday in Kathmandu, where from their hotel balcony, he and his family saw a bedraggled group of refugees, who in their flight from communist-occupied Tibet, barely had the strength to push their wooden wheelbarrow of meagre possessions.

"Oh Wernher, look at them . . . they're starving," Maria said, so appalled by their emaciated state that she turned to take her three children back inside to spare them the sadness.

Wernher, however, had seen such sights before. Not confined to a small group, but to the millions of displaced Jews in exodus from the horrors of the Reich. Back then, he had not been in a position, nor had chosen to do anything about it. He was not going to make that mistake again.

Without thinking twice, he crossed the road to greet them.

"Here, take this," he said, as he emptied his wallet and pressed a wad of money into each refugee's hand.

"It's not enough to merely feel compassion for others," he explained to Maria when they, themselves, were left without funds for the rest of their trip. "I know now that faith demands deeds."

He only wished he had cleared his conscience by learning this lesson 20 years earlier.

CHAPTER

FORTY-FIVE

AMERICA HAD AT LAST PUT A MAN INTO ORBIT, boosting Lieutenant Colonel John Glenn into three swings around the Earth.

"Finally, the US is where it belongs . . . in Space," von Braun said at the press conference.

During preparations for the historic flight, he and Glenn formed a friendship that was to last for life; one close enough for Glenn to send him a postcard while he was on holidays in Germany:

Dear Wernher,

Well here I am on your old stamping ground and there you are back in good ol' Huntsville USA. Gees, what a switch! I'd say: "Wish you were here", but I'm happier knowing that you're burning the midnight oil trying to blast us to the moon.

Glenn had got it half right. Much as von Braun wanted to concentrate on his work, distractions kept getting in the way. One of them he didn't mind so much.

"The bank's offered me a position on its board." he told Maria proudly. For him it was a point of principle, because his father-in-law, as a prominent banker, had always looked down on him, and he only wished he were still alive to see it.

Had he been, he would have also taken pride in his son-in-law's successful petition to the Alabama Legislature for a \$2million grant to build a space and rocket centre in Huntsville as an education facility; and for the fact that in between designing rockets to the moon, Wernher was earning extra pocket money by writing articles for *Popular Science* and constantly traversing the country to host speaking engagements; as always, working at a frenetic pace to ensure he gave his all to the world before fate saw fit to take him from it.

Meanwhile, President Kennedy came to check on the progress of Apollo.

"That's just wonderful Wernher! If I could only show this to the people in Congress," he bellowed at von Braun through the screeching, window-shattering static firing of a Saturn booster stage strapped to its test stand.

His hearty handshake left von Braun in no doubt of Kennedy's deep friendship and full support. If it continued, there would be no stopping him.

Two days later, the shocking news hit the headlines:

PRESIDENT SHOT DEAD
IN DALLAS

Von Braun took it hard twice over: the assassination put an end to what he hoped was now smooth sailing, and to the camaraderie of a man of like mind of whom he was very fond. Unable to cope with the sadness of attending Kennedy's funeral, he instead buried himself in his work.

"I know it's a day of national mourning, but would you mind

coming into the office to help with the backlog?" he asked his secretary.

The truth was that there was nothing much for them to do, and as she slowly tapped out non-urgent notes on her typewriter, von Braun sat in his office, intermittently picking up his pen and putting it down again to watch the memorial proceedings on TV.

"What a waste," he said to her when she took him in a cup of coffee. "What a tragic loss of a good friend and great leader."

Seeing his jaw grow tight with restraint, she discreetly left the room.

… oOo …

Kennedy was a hard act to follow, but the tall Texan who replaced him came as a pleasant surprise. Lyndon B. Johnson had been an earlier and much stronger advocate of space, *plus* he invited von Braun to his big ranch and gave him a five-gallon cowboy hat to keep. That, along with including him in a cattle muster, helped von Braun bounce back to form, and work on the Saturn/Apollo project steamed ahead.

At his Marshall Centre, no one looked at a clock, and while everyone worked seven days a week it seemed von Braun worked eight. So as not to miss a moment, he took his work home with him every night, leaving his chauffeur-driven car light on to read on the way, while doing the same in his constantly lit plane cubical when winging his way as a passenger to his many meetings in different cities and aerospace facilities across the country. All the while his eyes shone with zeal, but the dark circles under them showed that he never slept. Some saw it as unearthly energy, but his doctor called it 'burning the candle at both ends'.

"If you don't stop and get some rest, it's going to kill you," he warned.

But possessed with a passion, von Braun could only reply: "I can't think of a better way to die."

Time was ticking and with none to waste, he never sat still. While reading, he would be listening to foreign language tapes to improve his fluency; while eating lunch, he was doing cryptic crosswords; and in the one rare moment when he had nothing to do in his office, he started re-arranging its decor. When his secretary walked in to find him busily moving his model rockets back and forward from bookcase to desk, she rolled her eyes.

"Must you *always* be doing something?" she said. "Why don't you just sit down and relax."

Von Braun was too busy to even look up.

"Idle hands do the devil's work," he answered as he swivelled the silver, rocket replica on his desk to best catch the light.

His commitment to the Apollo project was commendable, but the fact that it also required the participation of nearly 400,000 people and 20,000 companies, drew an enormous amount of criticism.

"Why spend so much on the moon, when we need it here on Earth?"

It was a well-worn argument that always whipped von Braun into a fury. The fact that people refused to see the big picture and constantly needed it explained to them never ceased to amaze him.

"NASA's budget is not being spent on the moon," he reiterated for the 50th time, "but right here on Earth in the provision of new jobs, products and processes; to say nothing of the establishment of profitable companies and entirely new industries."

Given the American people's short-sightedness, he often

wondered how they and their allies won the war. One American, President Johnson, however, got it right, and after the fifth successful, unmanned test of a Saturn 1 rocket, he rang NASA Mission Control at the Cape.

"Does von Braun's cowboy hat still fit?" he asked the official who answered the call.

With phone in hand, the man scanned the control room to see von Braun at its centre swilling champagne.

"Mr President," he reported back. "Judging by the Cheshire grin on his face, I suspect it's now two sizes too small."

For von Braun, however, it was still a case of *win some, lose some*, because with each rocket success came his failure to completely sell himself and his supposedly guilt-free past to the public.

The Holocaust hung the sword of Damocles over his head, but at the same time, instilled in him a genuine concern for minority groups. To soothe his conscience he had joined the civil rights movement in the south and had spoken in support of school desegregation, voter rights and equal-opportunity employment. NASA was fully behind his initiative, keen as it was to improve Alabama's poor race relations so that their Marshall Centre and its contractors could attract top technical and management talent. Von Braun, however, was more hands-on in his campaign, actively hiring more people of colour and championing the cause of any of them who found themselves victimised.

"I want the reason why a member of your staff quit so suddenly," he demanded of one foreman, who as an unapologetic white supremacist, made no secret of his 'no blacks' policy, nor of the fact that he had no sympathy for the former employee who was hovering close to death in hospital as the result of a brutal bashing.

Given von Braun's history, the foreman felt on safe ground and spoke freely:

"I thought you, of all people, would understand," he answered, offending twice over for presuming to align himself with his boss and for his attempt to drag him down to his level.

The look on von Braun's face told the foreman he had said too much, but with no turning back, he finished what he had to say:

"Personally, I think you Nazis got it right."

Von Braun's blood came to the boil, surging like lava from the pit of his stomach to burn hot red in his face.

"Then you can pack your bags and get out!"

"I'll be expecting severance pay."

"Not if I have anything to do with it," he said, physically moving the man faster from his office with a hard push before slamming the door behind him.

In his efforts to clear himself of lingering war crime allegations, von Braun was taking risks – playing a dangerous game with men who had no concern for the law or human rights. He started by making a public stand against Alabama Governor George Wallace, who in his inaugural speech, proudly declared himself pro-segregation:

> *I stand for segregation now, segregation tomorrow, segregation forever!*

"Just add a little black moustache and he'll have it down pat," von Braun said scathingly when the man's speech was televised.

Comments like these made Maria very nervous when she knew Wernher did nothing by halves. Once committed to a project or an ideal, he would see it through and in this case, possibly make a target of himself. There was a protection of sorts in that he was high profile and less likely to be mugged in a back alley, but when the Ku Klux Klan burnt a cross in their backyard and Wernher struck out for revenge, she was truly concerned about their family's safety.

"Please do be careful," she pleaded with him, knowing even as she said it that there was no point when there was no moving him.

"I will not stand by a second time and let bad men get away with it," he declared to her and everyone else who would listen, taking a strong moral position that should have helped clear his name.

Yet still, his every public appearance attracted protest groups, Nazi salutes and shouts of *Sieg Heil!*

FORTY-SIX

K EEPING THE PEACE seemed impossible when rivalry between NASA facilities and their contractors ran rampant. Of peak concern was their prime contractor, Northern American Rockwell and the irascible president of its space division, Harrison B. Storms.

"They call me Stormy behind my back," he told von Braun when they first met, "And I don't mind one bit so long as it keeps them on their toes."

That was certainly where he kept von Braun for a year with their feud over the development of the S-2 second stage of Saturn V. Stormy liked sticking to his exclusive air force system that effectively dammed up the information flow on technical issues to von Braun and his team. Those at the Marshall Centre didn't appreciate being kept out of the loop and preferred their more efficient army protocol of keeping in intimate contact with its contractors at all times. Of far more concern to von Braun, however, was the danger of Stormy's power plant burning extremely volatile liquid hydrogen as fuel. It had the potential of going off like an atomic bomb and was an accident just waiting to happen.

"Old Stormy has to go," he caused controversy by saying at their next conference.

Yet, despite saying it straight to the man's face and drawing a gasp of surprise from all present, Stormy stood firm – at least until NASA decided to use him as a scapegoat and had him sidelined. Even von Braun was shocked by this unexpected move. Although he had the biggest axe to grind, he thought it grossly unfair that Stormy was set up to take the fall for the Apollo 1 spacecraft fire in 1967 and the consequent deaths of astronauts Gus Grissom, Ed White and Roger Chaffee, who were incinerated in the blaze. It was a horrible thing for which to be held accountable.

Considering the horrific circumstances, von Braun felt ashamed that he felt equally perturbed over a simple case of jealousy. It always riled him that his Huntsville Marshall Centre did not have Cape Canaveral's *countdown-to-take-off* glamour or the flash of Houston's *right-stuff* astronauts. He usually kept a lid on his envy, but when at a major function a film was shown making no mention of his Marshall Centre's key role in the Apollo project, he was enraged.

Promptly up and out of his seat, he intended to be all fire and fury, but when he saw the smug smiles on his rivals' faces, he wiped the floor with them using humour instead.

"I really should be angry about our Marshall Centre's blatant omission, but let's face it, compared to the razzle-dazzle of America's astronauts, our Saturn rocket has about as much sex appeal as Lady Godiva's horse!"

Laughter, he always found, was the best medicine, but two days later he could not raise a smile when fresh allegations of war crimes reared their head yet again.

"I saw von Braun abuse prisoners at Germany's Mittelwerk factory," one of those who survived it swore in court.

It seemed the monkey would never be off his back when

this grey area in his past kept surfacing. Its lack of definition along with the conspicuous absence of any documentation about his role in the Third Reich, spoke neither for nor against him.

Fortunately, there were a few who were keen to speak in his defence. One of them was his old friend from Germany Willy Ley, whose Jewish links and hair-raising escape from Nazi Berlin to America gave his testimony great credence. Another defender was one of his rocket team veterans, who said with his hand on the Bible:

"As Peenemunde's technical director, von Braun was working 400 kilometres from Mittelwerk and couldn't possibly have been in charge of its forced labour. His only participation was to inspect the quality of the end product. I know, for a fact, that von Braun specifically requested skilled German workers, but all of them had been drafted into the army and were being slaughtered on the Russian front."

The eye-witness accounts of him playing an active part in the abuse of prisoners could just as easily be explained away.

"You must remember," the same character witness continued, "that Wernher von Braun bears a striking resemblance to his younger brother, Magnus. Both of them visited the facility and one could easily have been mistaken for the other. A stranger's testimony to having identified him without an element of doubt cannot be relied upon."

NASA agreed and was certainly not prepared to condemn von Braun without solid evidence. Now that its top priority was Apollo 11, they simply could not afford to lose him.

But there were more barriers to come: Washington decided to cut back on its space program, and with the Pentagon refusing to listen to his protests, von Braun was forced again to go to the press and publicly air them.

"It's insanity!" he said, feeding the reporters their headline. "If this trend isn't reversed the nation might as well hang a sign on the moon saying: *'Kilroy was here'*. Slashing funds and limiting our stay there to only a one-night stand would be as senseless as building a railroad from New York to New Orleans for the sake of one trip."

Nonetheless, the Marshall Centre's Saturn V workload and staff levels started to decline and the limelight to recede.

"You know as well as I do that being at the beginning of the chain makes it our fate," chief scientist, Ernst Stuhlinger commiserated with von Braun.

They had good reason to worry, because as a research and development facility, their work on Apollo 11 was done well in advance of its launch date and now all the action was at Cape Kennedy.

What's next after the moon? those at Huntsville were left to wonder, knowing in their hearts it was Mars, but that Washington seemed set on clamping down on the very idea.

Meanwhile, the rivalry between Huntsville and Houston had grown fierce with each facility constantly fighting for funds and pre-eminence. Much to von Braun's annoyance, it was the public's perception that Houston, with its daredevil astronauts, was the hub of all space activity, while they at Marshall were merely their back-up crew. Worse still was to be patronised when Houston threw them a bone, conceding the design, development and production of a lunar roving vehicle.

"Something for you to gnaw on while we, at Houston, work on more important projects." von Braun could clearly read between the lines of the contract.

It was not wise, however, to make waves when Washington was closing its purse strings. Better than holding a grudge, von Braun believed, was for Marshall to make the most of it. And it did, with its usual flair putting Houston's nose out of joint when its Moon Buggy proved to be a scientific and public relations boon. For von Braun, though, it was still not enough.

"We must be involved in lunar soil analysis and other science programs," he insisted at a meeting between the two facilities when the division of labour on the upcoming Skylab and post-Apollo projects was being discussed.

"That's better left to Houston," his old sparring partner Bob Gilruth argued back.

So, the battle went on between them at every meeting – this most recent of which had von Braun say to his staff before it started: "Remember boys . . . we're heading into enemy territory."

Making light of it did not change the fact that the process dampened his spirits. So it helped at this time that he was awarded the gold Langley Medal; an enormous accolade that paid tribute to his string of achievements: his creative vision in advancing rocketry; his leading the way to America's first Earth satellite; and his technical leadership in development of the Saturn class of large launch vehicles.

In 59 years, the honour had only been awarded to 12 outstanding aviation and space pioneers. He was so moved when he gave his acceptance speech that for the first time in his life he could only find a few words.

"To join the ranks of the Wright brothers, Charles Lindbergh and the remarkable Robert H. Goddard means more to me than I can express."

CHAPTER
FORTY-SEVEN

THE BUTTON WAS ABOUT TO BE PRESSED for the critical first-countdown demonstration test of the Saturn V. Essential in that it would lead to the giant vehicle's first flight.

To that end, Peenemunde/Mittelwerk veteran Arthur Rudolph had been put in charge of the test and was positioned at Cape Kennedy Control Centre.

It was a resounding success, and filled with nostalgia for all he and Rudolph had gone through together over the years von Braun rang through from Huntsville to celebrate with his old friend.

"Congratulations Art!" he said when his call was put through to Mission Control. The sentimental moment he expected, however, turned to astonishment when Rudolph did not know who he was.

"Who is this?" he asked, not recognising von Braun's voice through the cacophony of noise going on around him.

"It's *Wernher*."

Due to the deluge of congratulatory calls Rudolph was receiving, he couldn't be bothered to mentally sift through the array of 'Werners' he knew, so he persisted:

"Werner who?"

"The only one spelt with an '*h*'!" von Braun was hot enough under the collar to shout down the line before he suspected Rudolph was playing a prank and came back in kind: "You son of a bitch . . . I'm the one who goes to Washington and gets all the money for you to play your funny games!"

It was an embarrassing mistake and finding it easier to play along with what von Braun supposed was a joke, Rudolph nervously laughed with the rest of those at the Cape who heard the hilarious conversation over the intercom.

... oOo ...

The fact that the Soviets were still the front-runners in space was not as funny, so it was a matter of urgency that America was first to the moon. The once-wounded Apollo project was back on track and Saturn V was up and flying, but still funding posed a problem. The Vietnam War, together with the civil rights movement and the recent assassinations of Martin Luther King Jnr and Robert Kennedy had knocked the nation sideways and drained much of its confidence and cash. Yet again, to von Braun's immense frustration, it was the Space Race that suffered. As was his practice when under pressure, he let loose in a media interview:

> *It's very difficult to run as fast as we can in the lunar program if America keeps building down rather than up. It's like being ordered to disarm while the war is still on. What we need is sustained support which doesn't blow hot and cold. Make no mistake . . . it does matter that America beats Russia to the moon. Who remembers the second man to fly the Atlantic Ocean?*

His words packed a punch and the USA hit back by taking several big strides in space.

In October 1968 Apollo 7 was launched atop a Saturn IB, for the first time carrying astronauts. At Christmas the Saturn Apollo 8 made history by flying astronauts Frank Borman, Jim Lovell and Bill Anders on 10 swings around the moon before bringing them safely home. It was a momentous achievement, and given its religious timing, all three men paid homage, while aloft, to whoever was hovering with them in the heavens by reading passages on creation from the book of *Genesis*.

At this point, Americans took time out to welcome Richard M. Nixon as their new president, before Apollo 9 and its astronauts were shot into an Earth-orbit shakedown test of the spacecraft's command service and lunar modules. Come May, it was a case of *'so near and yet so far'*; when another Saturn V boosted Apollo 10 into orbit to circle the moon in a dress rehearsal for the first lunar landing.

It's not fair, its astronauts were thinking, when close enough to nearly touch its cratered surface, they were instructed to turn and fly home.

As a fellow pilot and pioneer, von Braun understood their yearning, but he was now too old to be fitted for a space suit and was better placed directing operations on Earth.

His staff often thought a short trip to the stars by von Braun would temporarily spare them his relentless pursuit of perfection, which remained ingrained in his nature since his training at the Borsig Locomotive factory in Berlin.

"Near perfection is equivalent to disaster," von Braun drummed into his staff as he daily haunted the technical labs and drafting rooms to make sure everything was up to scratch. "Here at Huntsville, there's no margin for error."

But even as his team rolled their eyes, they knew it was

his irrepressible optimism and sense of humour that always motivated them; the latter of which forever failed to instil the 'fear factor' necessary to keep them all in line, but made him eminently likeable. Only one thing sparked his temper – the lack of commitment in others; but even then, he hated having to reprimand them for it.

"You do it," he often said to his deputy to spare himself the duty, which could have been construed as weakness, but instead, was seen as a chink in his Lancelot-like armour, which merely made him more human. For that, he was loved and respected, as he was for his democratic practice of empowering each member of his staff to play a part in every decision-making process.

In this instance, it was his secretary's decision to double back and answer the phone when by rights her work was done for the day.

"Yes, Dr Maxfield, I'll put you through," von Braun heard her say before the light lit up on his private line. He picked up the receiver, said hello and listened to what the man had to say:

"You've got to be kidding!" his voice then boomed through the office. "I don't care what the problem is. There's not a hope in hell that I'll be getting blood tests done tomorrow . . . *of all days!*"

Tomorrow was July 16, the day of Apollo 11's launch and the realisation of his life's dream. *Nothing* . . . not the Queen of England, the Pope or even the early signs of colon cancer was going to stop him being there.

... oOo ...

"Wouldn't you prefer to be *in* the rocket rather than just watching it all happen here on Earth?" he had been asked at a press conference two days before.

"I only wish I could fly to the moon," he answered wistfully, "but this grey hair of mine rules me out. At 57 I can no longer react like a young test pilot to emergencies with the precision, speed and accuracy needed."

Here, another more cynical reporter chimed in.

"But where is all this headed . . . to America's ultimate goal of militarising space?"

At this controversial question, von Braun stopped cold. No matter how high-minded his aspirations and achievements, it always came back to this.

"God forbid that warfare will spread to the heavens when we have ample capability to destroy ourselves here on Earth," he replied, grim-mouthed. "All I can say is that I'm so thankful for NASA's peaceful role and am so very, very glad that I'm out of weaponry."

The very mention of the word sparked flashbacks to his V-2s deadly role in WWII and in the hope of capitalising on the contentious subject, a sudden frenzy of questions flew at him from all directions. With their voices growing louder and more accusing, NASA's press secretary stepped forward to take over proceedings.

"As you must appreciate, ladies and gentlemen, Dr von Braun has a lot on his plate and is pressed for time. We'll allow just one more question before he leaves."

Fortunately, the reporter who raised his arm to ask it cut through the controversy to make it one of higher calibre:

"Dr. von Braun, how do you rank the impending Apollo 11 landing with other historical events?"

He did not hesitate: "With the importance of aquatic life first crawling on land."

… oOo …

It was in much the same state that he dragged himself from bed in the early hours of July 16, physically and emotionally exhausted from years of frenetic work and a night of pre-launch partying. As if the lead-up to this big day had not been demanding enough, he had felt compelled, at the last minute, to squeeze in a quick trip to the Greek island of Delos where he satisfied his superstition by visiting the Temple of Apollo to ask for his blessing.

In the dark, pre-dawn hours of July 16 it still remained to be seen if he had received it, and with the world asleep around him, all was eerily quiet in his motel room as he showered, shaved and dressed in suit and tie.

When he arrived at Launch Control at 4am, however, all that changed. There stood the Saturn V-Apollo 11 stack in the spotlight, a leviathan looming 40 storeys high, glowing luminous white against the black sky. 500 million people were waiting to watch the launch on televisions worldwide, while hundreds of VIPs, 3000 media representatives and one million more spectators were on site to see it firsthand. Among them, former President Johnson and someone far more important who had made a special trip from Germany for the occasion. When von Braun saw the man walking towards him, he couldn't believe his eyes and for a moment thought he was hallucinating. But when the warm hand of his old mentor, Hermann Oberth, reached out to shake his, it all became very . . . *wonderfully* real.

"Good luck, my boy," Oberth said. "I wouldn't have missed this for the world."

In the emotion of the moment, von Braun could barely speak, but finally found the words to insist that Oberth join him at Launch Control. For where else, he reasoned, did the Father of Rocketry and weaver of his dreams belong?

... oOo ...

Considering the circumstances, it seemed oddly restrained at the hub of the action. While the widescreen on Mission Control's wall was a constant reminder of the impending drama, the men and women working around it went quietly about their business, with headsets in place, talking in low tones as their eyes moved constantly from their desk computers to the big screen.

Beneath the deceptive calm, however, there was a hot, hidden tension. Like the rocket champing at the bit on its launch pad outside, the whole centre was silently seething as it held itself in wait for the burst of explosive energy to come. The hour von Braun had worked toward all his life was at hand. Acutely aware of the role he was about to play in it, he took his assigned seat, put on his headset and tuned in.

What if it should fail? he suddenly thought in panic as the final few minutes of talk went on between Launch Control and Apollo's astronauts. The mounting excitement was almost unbearable, and sick with worry, his heart broke into gallop, pounding so loud in his ears that it temporarily deafened him to the tense, fluorescently-lit reality going on around him.

T minus 10 seconds was the last thing he heard before a far brighter, white light encompassed him and an overwhelming sense of awe had him close his eyes to whisper: *Thy will be done.*

EPILOGUE

WERNHER VON BRAUN

THE PEOPLE OF HUNTSVILLE hoisted von Braun on their shoulders to celebrate his phenomenal success. It had cemented his name in history and made their town the proudest place on the planet.

The Eagle had landed and since Neil Armstrong's giant leap for mankind, the smile had not left von Braun's face. Yet, he could not have been more serious when he made his triumphant broadcast:

> *I do hope that history records the enormous implications of this lunar journey. We take pride in our American achievement, but share it in genuine brotherhood with all nations and all people.*

It was a perfect piece of diplomacy, given that he must have been tempted to claim just a little of the kudos for his fallen Germany. In the end, however, it was America that came good and had the right to rejoice. But when the star-studded exaltation passed and the ticker tape was swept from the streets, von Braun fell heavily back to Earth.

Man's first landing on the moon was a hard act to follow and having now proved its point, America was concerned about footing the bill for future space exploits.

"How many times do we have to prove it?" was the word from Washington, when with one lunar landing accomplished and another soon due, it was considering cutting some of the following nine flights planned.

Here we go again, von Braun thought with tired resignation. It seemed that he had spent his entire life drumming up interest and scrounging round for funds to get his show off the ground. Fortunately, Vice-President Spiro Agnew saved the day by devising a bold new report: *The Post-Apollo Space Program: Directions for the Future*. Because it was based on the Saturn-Apollo hardware and von Braun's ultimate goal of landing on Mars, it was logical that he should transfer to Washington to sell the 20-year package to the White House.

He was torn. He wasn't happy about leaving his old friends at Huntsville and was absolutely sure they wouldn't want him to go.

"Don't worry," the Pentagon assured him. "Until you make up your mind, we'll keep our job offer under wraps."

Somehow though, the rumours found their way to the Marshall Centre and his old associates were stunned.

"We can't believe you're leaving us," they said and, to be honest, nor could von Braun. However, unless he made his presence and ideas felt in the halls of power, everything they were working towards would slowly die.

"I feel like a captain deserting a sinking ship," he answered. "But, the reality is that it's *not* sinking and with me going back and forward from Washington to Marshall all the time, everything will go on just as before."

But it didn't and for those at Marshall, it was never the same. With him gone, it was like trying to carry on at Camelot without King Arthur.

Before he left, it was with considerable sadness that the whole town turned out to observe 'Wernher von Braun Day' and to formally open the new civic centre named in his honour. By the time von Braun was shaking hands with his old German comrades, tears were streaming down his cheeks.

Seeing as much made his wife, Maria feel a little guilty when it was she who put in the big push to make the move.

"I've endured this town for 20 years and now the children and I need access to a life broader and more cultured than Huntsville can offer."

This was countered by better advice from another who was more in the know:

"It'll be unwise for you to go to Washington, Wernher. They'll eat you alive."

In the end, family came first and feeling that he could hold his own, von Braun moved confidently to the capital. He had no idea, when he walked full of hope to his new office, that the closed doors he passed in the hallway housed others full of spite and malice, whose chronic jealousy of his celebrity and resentment of his Nazi past was destined to bring him down. They would not like the sound of his convivial laughter in the corridors, the bags of fan mail he would receive, or the stream of famous people who would come to visit him.

"It goes against the grain when there's every chance he's got away with murder," the strong contingent of Jewish employees among the staff thought.

At first von Braun coped well with the brewing bad feeling, but the rot set in when the man who hired him retired. Those now in charge made their sentiments clear when he presented his submission: *Space Programs in the Year 2000.*

"I can't believe that Nixon and Congress knocked it back," said his associate on the project, NASA Administrator Tom Paine.

Both he and von Braun were devastated; Paine to the extent that he handed in his resignation, while von Braun held back on being so rash, not realising the mood in Washington was now set on deep freeze and a calamitous change in his fortune was on its way.

It came in the guise of Austrian-born Jew George Low, who took over as NASA Administrator. Within days of making himself comfortable in his new leather chair, von Braun became *persona non grata*. Not only did Low never forgive his Nazi connection, but he worked diligently on behalf of Houston colleagues to make sure that von Braun got his just deserts for having constantly one-upped them over the years.

With the two strong men who had backed him no longer on staff, von Braun was without support and Low hung him out to dry. Despite working only two doors down the corridor, he never granted von Braun a private appointment or made him a part of any staff meeting.

Stop talking space exploration and stick to the script was all the contact Low made in a memo, which effectively stripped von Braun of his favourite subject and of the impact of his dynamic ad-libbing.

On the plus side, von Braun was pleased to know that the Skylab project he had helped conceive at the Marshall Centre was materialising and that his new focus on the practical benefits of satellites was being taken seriously. Day by day, however, he was actively being left out of the equation, with almost all his colleagues in Washington making sure that he was never again given the opportunity to shine.

"How's your work going up here?" he was asked by a Huntsville colleague who ran into him in a Washington bar. It was the first time he had seen von Braun with a drink in his hand but without a smile on his face.

"Well John," he answered glumly. "I've found out that in Washington I'm just a guy with a funny accent."

When his old military boss from Peenemunde, Walter Dornberger, heard of his predicament, he contacted Wernher immediately with only one thing to say:

"Never give up!"

But sick of his fast downhill slide at NASA, von Braun finally did. He handed in his resignation and took up the position of vice-president for engineering and development at Fairchild Industries in Germantown. There at least, its president, Edward Uhl, admired him and encouraged him to pursue space projects he thought were important; namely, making inroads into the practical applications for satellites, while selling one of them – the ATS-6 – to India.

Von Braun was a man who could never sit still but was finally forced to when he attended Fairchild's obligatory medical examination.

"X-rays have shown strong evidence of cancer," the doctor told him. "You'll need immediate surgery and a course of radiation therapy."

"It's so strange," von Braun's old US Army boss John Medaris said when he heard the bad news. Now having exchanged the stars on his officer's epaulettes for a small crucifix pinned to his priest's collar, he was more attuned to the cosmos and the meaning of life. "I always thought von Braun had nine lives. He's escaped so many life-threatening scrapes, it's awful to know that cancer's finally got him."

But a wider view would have shown that it was actually his dream that killed him.

On the day before Apollo 11's launch, his doctor had told him there were polyps on his colon that needed immediate removal. But in the excitement of the moment, he chose to ignore the advice, even though the same disease had killed his mother.

Instead, von Braun carried on, and in July 1975 he made a final visit to the Kennedy Space Centre to view an outdoor rocket exhibition. Moved, as he always was, by the immensity of their size and destination, he said to a friend:

"Will you take my photo in front of the Saturn V?"

He then paused before adding: "Because I may never be here again."

Von Braun did not lie when he said his sole ambition was space, but some would say that he sold his soul and cost America too dearly to achieve it.

"So, what was *your* cut from the billions of dollars spent?" he was asked scathingly by the press. But the reporter was put to shame when he found out that for all von Braun's energy, genius and contribution to mankind, he received a paltry annual salary of $35,000. Apart from finding funds for space, money never mattered to him.

No one believed that von Braun was dying when it seemed he would live forever, but in the early hours of Thursday, June 16, 1977, he passed away at the age of 65.

A London newspaper read:

NAZI V-2 GENIUS IS DEAD!
Good riddance to the man whose bomb
struck terror into the hearts of millions.

The New York Times was nearly as brutal:

ROCKET PIONEER WITH DARK PAST DIES

The world will probably never know the whole truth of the man; whether there were sins for which he should have been held accountable. But perhaps the scales of justice would have weighed up more fairly if at least one headline had read:

**THE MAN WHO OPENED THE GATES
TO THE UNIVERSE IS GONE.
TO HIM, WE PAY TRIBUTE.**

At his own request, Baron Wernher von Braun was buried in a private ceremony attended by only family and close friends. His headstone was simple, chiselled with just his name and favourite psalm.

BARON MAGNUS VON BRAUN
WERNHER'S FATHER

Magnus Alexander Maximilian Freiherr von Braun, born on February 7, 1878, was a German civil servant and conservative politician whose career spanned the German Empire, World War I and the Weimar Republic. He served as the Federal Minister of Nutrition and Agriculture and *Reichskommissar* for Eastern Aid in the cabinet of Chancellor Franz von Papen, a position he kept under Chancellor Kurt von Schleicher until January 1933.

After the Nazis came to power on January 30, 1933, the baron moved to his manor in Silesia, but when it became part of Poland after World War II, he was expelled to Western Germany.

He followed his son, Wernher to the United States in 1947, but returned to Germany in 1952, where he died, aged 94, at Oberaudorf, Bavaria. He had lived from the reign of Kaiser Wilhelm I to the age of lunar exploration, and in his last letters compared his son with Kepler, Galileo and Copernicus.

Wernher made the difficult decision not to attend the funeral because he did not want the prospect of his presence there to spur the same ruckus that happened at his mother's burial in 1959. He visited his father's grave a month later to privately pay his respects during a speaking tour of Austria.

BARONESS EMMY VON BRAUN
WERNHER'S MOTHER

Baroness Emmy Melitta Cécile (von Quistorp) von Braun was born in Creznow in 1886 and died of colon cancer in 1959 in München, Bayern, Germany. Her death came as a hard blow to Wernher, as he and his mother were very close and it was she who most encouraged his dreams of space. Contrary to the account given in this book, Wernher did not attend her funeral because he knew his presence there would turn it into a media circus. Nevertheless, the very anticipation of his possible attendance resulted in just that. In early 1960 he went to her grave to say goodbye in private.

SIGISMUND VON BRAUN
WERNHER'S OLDER BROTHER

Baron Sigismund von Braun was born in Berlin in 1911. He was the older brother of Wernher and Magnus Jnr and the father of politician Carola von Braun and cultural theorist Christina von Braun.

After an apprenticeship in 1934, he studied law with a scholarship from the German Academic Exchange Service for a year at the University of Cincinnati in America. In 1936, he was an attaché in the German Foreign Service and until April 1937 was the personal assistant of the German ambassador in Paris. Due to a dispute with Baldur von Schirach he was reassigned to Addis Ababa. He joined the Nazi Party in October, 1939, but the date and details of his denazification are unknown.

In 1943 he became legation secretary of the embassy to the Holy See in Rome, where he remained until 1946. After internment in Germany he occasionally worked in the private sector, first as an assistant at several Nuremberg trials, then at the Wilhelmstrasse trial against Ernst von Weizsäcker. In 1954 he entered the diplomatic service of the Federal Republic of Germany, and in 1970 became Secretary of State. Living 22 years longer than his younger brother Wernher, he died at the age of 87 on July 13, 1998.

MAGNUS VON BRAUN (JNR)
WERNHER'S YOUNGER BROTHER

Born in Greifswald, Germany, in 1919, Baron Magnus 'Mac' von Braun was the youngest of the three von Braun brothers. He was born nearly a decade after his two older brothers who had come of age before the Nazis took power in Germany. Unlike them, Magnus had a National Socialist adolescence. While the older brothers can be seen as having joined the Nazi Party for reasons of professional advancement, Magnus signed up with ideological commitment.

At 13, he participated in the Hitler Youth organisation and experienced a secondary school environment and curriculum adapted to fascism. His politicised early years naturally influenced his character. Even after the war Magnus stood apart from Wernher by his displays of arrogance and aristocratic pretension, duly noted by the army officers who kept files on both men after their 1945 immigration to the United States. In later years, the recorded sightings of von Braun during brutal occurrences at the Mittelwerk factory were thought more likely to be Magnus than Wernher because of their striking physical resemblance and Magnus' stronger commitment to Nazism.

In 1955, after living in Huntsville for a time, Magnus began a career with Chrysler in Michigan – first, in the missile division and then in the automotive. He relocated to Britain, working in London and Coventry as Chrysler UK export director before retiring in 1975. A few years later he returned to America, living in Arizona until his death in 2003.

GENERAL KARL BECKER
GENERAL OF THE ARTILLERY
CHIEF OF ARMY ORDNANCE OFFICE

Karl Heinrich Emil Becker, born in 1879, was a German weapons engineer who advocated and implemented close ties of the military to science for purposes of advanced weapons development. He was the head of the Army Ordnance Office, senator of the Kaiser Wilhelm Society, first president of the Reich Research Council, the first general officer to be a member of the Prussian Academy of Sciences, as well as being a professor at both the University of Berlin and the Berlin Technical University.

He was an early and key supporter of the development of ballistic rockets as weapons. The military-scientific infrastructure he helped implement supported the German nuclear energy program, known as the Uranium Club.

Due to being depressed over heavy criticism from Hitler for shortfalls in munitions production, he committed suicide in 1940 and was given a state funeral.

MAJOR GENERAL WALTER DORNBERGER
ARMY ARTILLERY OFFICER, ENGINEER
AND LEADER OF THE V-2 PROGRAM

Born in 1895, Dornberger's career spanned the two world wars and a subsequent, successful career in America.

At an internment camp after the war, the British bugged Dornberger, who in conversation with another German officer said that he and Wernher von Braun had realised in late 1944 that things were going wrong and consequently were in touch with the General Electric Corporation through the German embassy in Portugal, with a view to coming to some arrangement.

Dornberger was interrogated for war crimes and after two years imprisonment in England was sent to America as part of Project Paperclip. There he worked for the US Air Force for three years, developing guided missiles.

From 1950 to 1965 he worked as vice-president of the Bell Aircraft Corporation, where he played a major role in the creation of the North American X-15 aircraft and was a key consultant for the Boeing X-20 Dyna-Soar project and the creation of the space shuttle. During his time at Bell, there was some friction between him and von Braun, because he recruited several engineers from von Braun's Huntsville team for his air force projects.

He retired to Mexico and later returned to Germany where he died in 1980.

ROLF ENGEL
ROCKET TECHNICIAN AND AIRCRAFT MANUFACTURER

Born in 1912, Engel worked with von Braun at the 1930s Rocket Flight Centre and followed him to Peenemunde. He later joined the SS and led its Rocket Research Centre for Jet Propulsion in Großendorf near Gdansk. In the 1950s he was hired as head of an Egyptian rocket program, but it failed due to missing components. Engel died in 1993 in Munich.

CONSTANTINE GENERALES
MEDICAL SPECIALIST

Dr Constantine D.J. Generales was a medical internist and a specialist in biomedical research and space medicine who lived in Manhattan. He was a native of Athens who came to the United States as a child.

As a graduate of Harvard, he met and befriended von Braun during a trip to Europe, and largely due to their friendship went on to study for his medical degree and a doctorate in philosophy from the University of Berlin. Despite serving in the United States Army Air Corps during World War II, he and von Braun remained friends for life and von Braun named his son, Peter Constantine, after him. Generales died in 1988 at the age of 79.

ROBERT GILRUTH
AEROSPACE ENGINEER AND AVIATION/SPACE PIONEER

Robert Rowe Gilruth was born in 1913 and was the first director of NASA's Manned Spacecraft Centre, later renamed the Lyndon B. Johnson Space Centre. He worked for the National Advisory Committee for Aeronautics from 1937 to 1958 and its successor NASA, until his retirement in 1973.

When President John F. Kennedy announced that America would put a man on the moon before the end of the decade in 1961, Gilruth was 'aghast' and unsure that such a goal could be accomplished. He was integral to the creation of the Gemini program, which he advocated as a means for NASA to learn more about operating in space before attempting a lunar landing.

The Apollo program was soon born and Gilruth was made head of the NASA centre that ran it – the new Manned Spacecraft Centre (MSC) where he served as director until his retirement in 1972. During that time, he oversaw a total of 25 manned space flights, from Mercury-Redstone 3 to Apollo 15.

Gilruth died in Charlottesville, Virginia, at the age of 86.

MAJOR JAMES HAMILL
US ARMY ORDNANCE CORPS OFFICER

James P. Hamill was born in 1919. His contributions to the Ordnance Corps played a major role in the United States' missile and aeronautical technology as it exists today.

Hamill worked as a member of the Ordnance Technical Intelligence during WWII.

His significant contribution came in 1945 when his team discovered a large number of V-2 rocket parts in an underground factory in Germany. Hamill was put in charge of the mission to gather these rockets parts and ship them to the United States for testing. Because of his success in doing so from within the Russian sector, and due to his handling of the captured German scientists, Hamill placed the United States years ahead of other countries in the rocket program, which culminated with the landing on the moon.

Hamill rose to the rank of colonel and retired from active duty in 1961. He died in 1984 at the age of 65.

RUDOLF HERMANN
SPECIALIST IN WIND TUNNELS AND AERODYNAMICS

Dr Hermann was born in 1904, and in 1937 became director of the supersonic wind tunnel at Peenemunde. After the compound was bombed, plans to build a Mach 10 hypersonic wind tunnel facility at Kochel were accelerated. Hermann became its director. When he received Hitler's order to destroy all documents, he ignored them and hid all wind tunnel documents and components to pass on to the US at war's end. In 1945 he became a consultant for the US Air Force and in 1951, a professor of aeronautical engineering at the University of Minnesota. He became the first director of the Research Institute at the University of Alabama in 1962, dying in Huntsville in 1991.

HELMUT HOELZER
ROCKET ENGINEER

Helmut Hoelzer was born in 1912, and as head of Peenemunde's Guide Beam Division, was brought to the United States under *Operation Paperclip.*

In 1940 his team developed a guide-plane system that greatly advanced space exploration technology. Hoelzer's 'mixing device' was used to provide V-2 rocket-rate measurement instead of rate gyros. Hoelzer built an analog computer to calculate and simulate V-2 rocket trajectories, while he and his team also developed the Messina telemetry system. He died in 1996 in Huntsville Alabama at the age of 84.

DORETTE KERSTEN
VON BRAUN'S WARTIME SECRETARY

In 1941, at the age of 20, beautiful blonde, blue-eyed Dorette Kersten became one of von Braun's secretaries. She was later to marry one of the other rocket experts, Rudolf Schlidt, but she said of von Braun:

"All the girls were attracted to him. He was young and looked like a Greek god in the way he walked and carried himself. He was a genius and yet he was playful and sportive."

When she and von Braun worked long hours together, he sometimes would suggest that they take a relaxing bike ride or go for a sail in a borrowed boat.

"Otherwise, it was strictly business between us," Dorette said, *"but von Braun could certainly switch on the charm at will."*

"I always have two secretaries," he once said to her with a grin, *". . . a pretty one and a prettier one."*

Still, Kersten was a 100 percent committed to the job.

"Which wasn't hard," she said, *"when he was more committed still and had such charisma. He was always a kind boss who never criticised."*

CHRISTOPHER KRAFT
AEROSPACE ENGINEER

Christopher Columbus 'Chris' Kraft Jnr was born in 1924. As an engineer and manager at NASA, he was instrumental in establishing the agency's Mission Control operation.

In 1944 Kraft was hired by the National Advisory Committee for Aeronautics (NACA), the predecessor organisation to the National Aeronautics and Space Administration (NASA). He worked for over a decade in aeronautical research before, in 1958, joining the Space Task Group, a small team entrusted with the responsibility of putting America's first man into space. Assigned to the flight operations division, Kraft became NASA's first flight director. He was on duty during such historic missions as America's first manned spaceflight, first manned orbital flight and first spacewalk.

At the beginning of the Apollo program, Kraft retired as a flight director to concentrate on management and mission planning. In 1972, he became director of the Manned Spacecraft Centre (later Johnson Space Centre), following in the footsteps of mentor Robert R. Gilruth.

More than any other person, Kraft was responsible for shaping the organisation and culture of NASA's Mission Control.

WILLY LEY
SCIENCE WRITER AND SPACEFLIGHT ADVOCATE

Willy Otto Oskar Ley was born in 1906 and went on to become a German-American historian of science who helped to popularise rocketry, spaceflight, and natural history in both countries.

The German rocketry fad that Ley played a big part in promoting culminated with Fritz Lang's 1929 film *Die Frau im Mond (Woman in the Moon)*. Although Hermann Oberth is often credited as the main technical consultant on the film, Lang said of Ley's key role: *"The work he did on the space models and their trajectory to the moon was so amazing and accurate that the Gestapo confiscated all models of the spaceship and all foreign prints of the picture."*

When the Nazis seized power Ley's situation became increasingly desperate. Although having been brought up as a Lutheran, there was Jewish blood on his father's side. To make matters worse, Ley had an established reputation as an international scientist who openly shared and popularised technical information about rocketry, while his articles continued to be republished by foreign newspapers throughout 1934.

In January 1935 Ley fled to America where he continued his friendship with von Braun and spoke up on his behalf when his possible part in war crimes was being questioned.

Ley died in 1969 at the age of 62, only a couple of days before the Apollo 11 moon landing. The crater *Ley* on the far side of the moon was named in his honour.

MAJOR GENERAL JOHN B MEDARIS
COMMANDER OF THE ARMY BALLISTIC
MISSILE AGENCY

John Bruce Medaris was a US Army officer born in 1902. In the 1950s, during his leadership of the Army Ballistic Missile Agency (ABMA), the agency developed the Redstone Jupiter-C and Saturn boosters.

Although the navy's Vanguard was the official satellite program, Medaris encouraged von Braun to continue development in case Vanguard failed. When news of Sputnik1's launch was broadcast, von Braun said to Defence Secretary Neil McElroy:

"For God's sake, let us do something. We can put up a satellite in 60 days."

Medaris knew that the jet propulsion laboratory would need more time to prepare what became Explorer 1, so he admonished von Braun by saying: *No Wernher, 90 days.*

Medaris retired from the army in 1960. His dedicated efforts in the engineering and scientific fields related to guided missile development marked him as one of the nation's leading authorities on the evolving US space program.

Medaris was ordained an Episcopal priest in 1970 and was honoured in May by the National Space Club and the Smithsonian Institution for his vision and leadership in the early days of the space program, as well as for his work in public awareness of the promise of the Space Age.

He died in Tennessee in1990 at the age of 88.

RUDOLF NEBEL
SPACEFLIGHT ADVOCATE SPOKESMAN FOR SPACEFLIGHT SOCIETY

Rudolf Nebel (1894-1978) was a spaceflight advocate active in Germany's amateur rocket group VfR (Spaceflight Society) in the 1930s and in rebuilding German rocketry following World War II.

He served as a fighter pilot in WWI and pioneered the use of unguided air-launched signal rockets in 1916. He was an early member of the Spaceflight Society, and acting as the group's spokesman, sought sponsorship from the Reichswehr as well as from individuals as diverse as Adolf Hitler and Albert Einstein.

He had a difficult relationship with Artillery General Karl Becker who distrusted his showmanship and temporarily cut off the army's official contact with him. When Becker later offered to bring the rocketeer team into a strictly controlled army rocketry project, Nebel refused, saying that he and his colleagues had invented the technology and that the army would "choke us with their red tape". Conversely, Wernher von Braun accepted the offer. During WWII, von Braun tried again to have Nebel join them, but by then the SS regarded Nebel as untrustworthy and had von Braun cease his attempts.

Nebel died in Düsseldorf at the age of 84.

HERMANN OBERTH
GERMAN MATHEMATICIAN AND PHYSICIST

Born in 1894 in Romania, Hermann Oberth moved to Germany at the age of 18. Along with America's Robert Goddard and Russia's Konstantin Tsiolkovsky, he was considered as one of the founders of modern astronautics.

In 1929 Oberth conducted a static firing of his first liquid-fuelled rocket motor. The engine was built by Klaus Riedel in a workshop space provided by the Reich Institution of Chemical Technology, and although it lacked a cooling system, it did run briefly. He was helped in this experiment by 18-year-old student Wernher von Braun, who later said of him:

> *Hermann Oberth was the first, who when thinking about the possibility of spaceships, grabbed a slide-rule and presented mathematically analysed concepts and designs. I owe to him not only the guiding-star of my life, but also my first contact with the theoretical and practical aspects of rocketry and space travel. A place of honour should be reserved in the history of science and technology for his ground-breaking contributions in the field of astronautics.*

Oberth, whose obsession with space began with his boyhood reading of Jules Verne's *From the Earth to the Moon*, died in Nuremberg in 1989.

EBERHARD REES
ENGINEER AND ROCKET PIONEER

Eberhard Friedrich Michael Rees was born in Germany in 1908 and later became an American citizen. Rees arrived at the Army Research Centre Peenemunde in the spring of 1939 and managed V-2 rocket fabrication and assembly. He served as Wernher von Braun's deputy from World War II through to the Apollo program.

Rees was in the first group of *Operation Paperclip* rocket scientists brought to the US by the Army Ordnance Corps in October 1945, serving first at the Army Aberdeen Proving Grounds, then at Fort Bliss, and in 1946 to 1950 at the Redstone Arsenal. In August 1957 his team developed the ablative heat shield.

After serving as deputy director of development operations for the Army Ballistic Missile Agency Rees became the Marshall Space Flight Centre deputy for technical and scientific matters in 1960 and directed the Lunar Roving Vehicle program.

In 1970 Rees was appointed as the director of the Marshall Space Flight Centre in Huntsville, Alabama, from which he managed the Skylab space station development and construction. He retired from NASA in 1973 and died in Florida at the age of 89.

KLAUS RIEDEL
MACHINEST AND ROCKET PIONEER

Klaus Riedel was born in Germany in 1907 and was a member of the Spaceflight Society. His work there resulted in the Mirak and Repulsor rockets, which were tested at his family farm.

He was involved in many early liquid-fuelled rocket experiments and after the VfR disbanded in 1933, he was invited by Wernher von Braun to join him in the army's rocket program at Peenemunde Army Research Centre. Riedel's position there was head of the test laboratory and his work seems to have been mostly concerned with developing the mobile support equipment for the V-2.

In 1944, he was killed in a car accident two days after his 37th birthday.

WALTER 'PAPA' RIEDEL
ROCKET ENGINEER

Walter J.H. 'Papa' Riedel was a German engineer who was the head of the Design Office of the Army Research Centre Peenemunde and the chief designer of the A4(V-2) ballistic rocket. The crater *Riedel* on the moon was co-named for him and the German rocket pioneer Klaus Riedel.

From May 1937, following the transfer of the rocket activities from Kummersdorf to the army's new rocket establishment at Peenemunde, Riedel headed the Technical Design Office as chief designer of the V-2 ballistic rocket.

At the end of WWII Riedel was held in protective custody at the US Third Army's internment camp at Deggendorf, after which he was employed by the Ministry of Supply Establishment at Trauen. When this organisation was disbanded in 1946 Riedel emigrated to England to work initially at the Royal Aircraft Establishment, Farnborough, and later, from 1948 until his death in 1968, at the Ministry of Supply Rocket Propulsion Department in Buckinghamshire.

In 1957, Riedel became a British citizen.

ARTHUR RUDOLPH
ROCKET ENGINEER

Arthur Louis Hugo Rudolph, born in 1906, was a German rocket engineer who was a leader in developing the V-2 rocket for Nazi Germany. After the war he went to America as part of *Operation Paperclip*, where he became an integral part of the US space program. He worked within the US Army and NASA, where he managed the development of several systems, including the Pershing missile and the Saturn V moon rocket.

When in 1984 the US government re-opened investigations about his possible involvement in war crimes, von Braun was no longer alive. Had he been, there was a good chance this investigation would not have happened. After much debate over the issue and due to his concern for the welfare of his family, Rudolph agreed to renounce his United States citizenship and to leave the US in return for not being prosecuted.

Over the years there was much controversy as to his guilt and whether he had been wrongly victimised. In 1989 Rudolph applied for a visa to attend a 20th anniversary celebration of the first moon landing, but was denied by the State Department.

He died of heart failure in Hamburg in 1996 at the age of 89.

ERNST STEINHOFF
ROCKET SCIENTIST

Steinhoff was a glider pilot who held distance records and had the honorary Luftwaffe rank of flight captain.

He went to the United States as part of *Operation Paperclip* and after working at Fort Bliss until 1949, moved to Holloman Air Force Base where he also worked closely with White Sands Missile Range in New Mexico. He focused on guidance control and range instrumentation throughout his career. He was awarded the Decoration for Exceptional Civilian Service in 1958 for his contribution to the US rocket program and in 1979 was inducted into the New Mexico International Space Hall of Fame.

Steinhoff is credited as one of the first pioneers to popularise the concept of space resource utilisation for Mars exploration. He became the first chairman of Working Group on Extraterrestrial Resources (WGER).

He died in New Mexico in 1987 at the age of 79.

ERNST STUHLINGER
ATOMIC, ELECTRICAL AND ROCKET SCIENTIST

Ernst Stuhlinger was born in 1913 in Niederimbach, Germany. After being brought to the United States as part of *Operation Paperclip* he developed guidance systems with Wernher von Braun's team for the US Army and later worked as a scientist for NASA. He was also instrumental in the development of the ion engine for long-endurance space flight and a wide variety of scientific experiments.

After retiring from NASA in 1976 Stuhlinger became an adjunct professor and senior research scientist at the University of Alabama in Huntsville, holding this position for the next 20 years. In 1978 he was at the University of Munich for six months on a Humboldt Fellowship. Stuhlinger was especially proud of winning this award as an American scientist.

Starting in 1990, Stuhlinger and American space scientist Frederick I. Ordway III collaborated on the two-volume biography: *Werhner von Braun: Crusader for Space.*

In it, Stuhlinger downplayed claims that von Braun had mistreated prisoners working on the V-2 program during the war and reiterated as much in a newspaper article:

Yes, we did work on improved guidance systems, but in late 1944 we were convinced that the war would be over before they could be used on military rockets and that those rockets would be aimed at the moon, not London.

In 2004, when he was 90, Stuhlinger helped to raise funds to preserve a Saturn V rocket display at Huntsville, Alabama. He died in 2008 at the age of 94.

BERNHARD TESSMANN
GUIDED MISSILE EXPERT AND CHIEF DESIGNER OF THE PEENEMUNDE TEST FACILITIES

Bernhard Robert Tessmann was born in 1912. He worked on guided missiles during WWII, and later for the United States Army and NASA. He was involved in the basic planning for the Army Research Centre Peenemunde, moving there in late 1936 to supervise construction and conduct first engine testing at Test Stand I. Tessmann worked on wind tunnels, then on thrust measuring systems for V-2 engines.

He was a key man in securing the V-2 legacy at the end of the war. When von Braun became afraid the SS would follow the Fuhrer's 'scorched earth' policy and destroy the tons of precious V-2 documents and blueprints, he instructed his personal aide, Dieter Huzel, and Bernhard Tessmann to hide the documents in a safe place. It took three trucks to transport the 14 tons of paperwork to an abandoned iron mine in the isolated village of Dornten, where they carried them by hand into the powder magazine.

Tessmann was transferred to the United States for *Operation Paperclip*, where he worked the rest of his life with the rocket team, first at Fort Bliss, White Sands Missile Range and then Huntsville. In 1960 he became a deputy director of the test division at NASA Marshall Space Flight Centre.

He died in Huntsville in 1998 at the age of 86. The Ilse and Bernhard Tessmann Music and Foreign Language Scholarship is awarded at the University of Alabama, Huntsville.

ADOLF THIEL
GUIDED MISSILE EXPERT

Born in 1915, Adolf Thiel was a German expert in guided missiles during WWII. He joined von Braun's team at Peenemunde where he was involved in developing the V-2 rocket. He went to America as part of *Operation Paperclip* and worked with von Braun's group at Fort Bliss. He supervised the preliminary design of the Redstone missile and other short and intermediate-range ballistic missile systems.

Thiel was one of the main dissenters among the Peenemunde Paperclippers who did not like von Braun's high-profile salesmanship when it came to their scientific pursuits. Knowing, however, that he could never stop von Braun from spreading his dreams of space to the public, he had this to say of him:

> *"Von Braun could charm the pants off you. He was a real glory hound, but he never sought it for himself . . . only to advance space exploration."*

During the late 1950s Thiel was program manager for the Thor ballistic missile, which became the first-stage launch for the Explorer spacecraft. He was director of space projects for the aerospace division of Thompson Ramo Wooldridge (TRW) when it developed Explorer VI and Pioneer V. He oversaw all TRW's space programs during the 1970s, and having served as an executive consultant on NASA planning groups, was named a fellow of the American Astronautical Society in 1968. He died in Los Angeles at the age of 86.

WALTER THIEL
ROCKET SCIENTIST

Dr Walter Thiel was born in 1910 in Breslau. In 1936 General Dornberger asked Thiel to move his fundamental rocket research to Kummersdorf, where all topics regarding rocket engines were assigned to him, as were further advances on propulsion which Thiel managed in a very short time. In 1940 he became deputy director of the Peenemunde HVP Organisation under von Braun.

When the A-4 started to show its military qualities and the Nazis demanded its mass production, Thiel and many fellow scientists became exhausted and unhappy at Peenemunde. Work overload, pressure to succeed and the change over from a research unit to a production facility started to take its toll. Thiel refused to declare the rocket engine ready for mass production. In a letter to von Braun, sent during a trip to a health farm, Thiel described the Aggregat 4: " . . . *as more of a complicated lab product than a mass item . . .* ".

Thiel handed in his resignation, but Dornberger's rejection of it turned out to be fatal.

On August 18, 1943, the Royal Air Force launched a bombing raid of Peenemunde.

The entire Thiel family died in a slit trench in front of their home in Karlshagen.

In 1970 a moon crater was named after him, and Thiel was one of the first pioneers to be inducted in the Space Hall of Fame in Alamogordo, New Mexico, in 1976.

MAJOR GENERAL HOLGER TOFTOY
US ARMY OFFICER

Major General Holger Nelson Toftoy, born in 1902, was a United States Army officer linked to early rocketry such as the Redstone missile.

In 1944 he became chief of the Army Ordnance Technical Intelligence team assigned to Europe to seek out and evaluate captured enemy ordnance weapons and equipment. His orders were to acquire and ship 100 operational V-2 rockets to White Sands Missile Range in New Mexico for testing. He assigned Majors William Bromley and James Hamill to salvage what missiles they could, all of which were put in hastily requisitioned rail cars.

Knowing that the US Army was planning to add guided missiles to its weapons program, Toftoy went to Washington to recommend that the German scientists be brought to the US for interrogation and possible employment. By September 1945 the first group of scientists, including von Braun, arrived in the United States under Toftoy's leadership. Not long after, Toftoy was transferred back to Washington and assigned responsibility for direction of the army guided missile program.

In 1952 he became Deputy Commanding General of the Army Ordnance Missile Command at Redstone Arsenal and in 1958, was named Commanding General of Aberdeen Proving Ground, Maryland.

Toftoy died in 1967. He was buried in Arlington National Cemetery with full military honours. A commemorative plaque was placed in Big Spring Park in Huntsville, nicknaming him 'Mr Missile'.

OPERATION PAPERCLIP
GERMAN ROCKETRY RECRUITS

AERONAUTICS AND ROCKETRY

Hans Amtmann

Herbert Axster

Erick Ball

Oscar Bauschinger

Hermann Beduerftig

Rudi Beichel

Anton Beier

Herbert Bergeler

Magnus von Braun

Wernher von Braun

Walter Burose

Adolf Busemann

GN Constan

Werner Dahm

Konrad Dannenberg

Kurt H Debus

Gerd De Beek

Walter Dornberger

Gerhard Drawe

Friedrich Duerr

Ernst R G Eckert

Otto Eisenhardt

Krafft A Ehricke

Anton Flettner

Alfred Finzel

Edward Fischel

Karl Fleischer

Anselm Franz

Herbert Fuhrmann

Ernst Geissler

Werner Gengelbach

Dieter Grau

Hans Gruene

Herbert Guendel

Fritz Haber

Heinz Haber

Karl Heimburg

Emil Hellebrand

Gerhard Heller

Bruno Helm

Rudolf Hermann

Bruno Heusinger

Hans Heuter

Guenther Hintze

Sighard F. Hoerner

Kurt Hohenemser

Oscar Holderer

Hans H Hosenthien

Walter Jacobi

Erich Kaschig

Ernst Klaus

Theodore Knacke

Siegfried Knemeyer

Heinz H Koelle,

Gustav Kroll

Werner Kuers

Hermann Kurzweg

Hermann Lange

Hans Lindenberg

Hans Lindenmayer

Lippisch R Lusser

Alexander Martin

Helmut Merk

Joseph Michel

Hans Milde

Heinz Millinger

Rudolf Minning

Willi Mrazek

Hans Multhopp

Erich Neubert

Gerhard Neumann

Hermann Oberth

Hans von Ohain

Robert Paetz

Hans Palaoro

Kurt Patt

Hans Paul

Arnold Peter

Theodor Poppel

Werner Rosinski

Heinrich Rothe

Ludwig Roth

Arthur Rudolph

Friedrich von Saurma

Edgar Schaeffer

Martin Schilling

Helmut Schlitt

August Schulze

Albert Schuler

Walter Schwidetzky

Ernst Steinhoff

Wolfgang Steurer

Ernst Stuhlinger

Kurt Tank

Bernhard Tessmann

Adolf Thiel

G von Tiesenhausen

Werner Tiller

JG Tschinkel

Arthur Urbanski

Fritz Vandersee

Richard Vogt

Woldemar Voigt

Theodor Vowe

Herbert A. Wagner

Hermann Weidner

Walter F Wiesemann

ARCHITECTURE

Heinz Hilten

Hannes Luehrsen

ELECTRONICS: GUIDANCE SYSTEMS, RADAR AND SATELLITES

Wilhelm Angele

Ernst Baars

Josef Boehm

Hans FichJtner

Hans Friedrich

Eduard Gerber

Georg Goubau

Walter Haeussermann

Otto Heinrich Hirschler

Otto Hoberg

Rudolf Hoelker

Hans Hollmann

Helmut Hölzer

Horst Kedesdy

Kurt Lehovec

Kurt Lindner

JW Muehlner

Fritz Mueller

Johannes Plendl

Fritz K Preikschat

Eberhard Rees

Gerhard Reisig

Harry Ruppe

Heinz Schlicke

Werner Sieber

Albin Wittmann

Hugo Woerdemann

Albert Zeiler

Hans K. Ziegler

MATERIAL SCIENCE

Claus Scheufelen   Rudolf Schlidt

MEDICINE: BIOLOGICAL/CHEMICAL WEAPONS AND SPACE MEDICINE

Theodor Benzinger   Richard Lindenberg   Hubertus Strughold
Johannes K Buttner   Walter Schreiber   Erich Traub
Rudolf B Konrad

PHYSICS

Gunter Guttein   Helmut Weickmann   Friedwardt Winterberg
Gerhard Schwesinger

Time puts a limit on us all. We can overcome all other dimensions, but in turn, we are overcome by time

– Wernher von Braun

AUTHOR'S NOTE

There were many brilliant minds involved in the Apollo Project, but this story is dedicated to the one among them whose brain and brilliance sold the concept to the world and made it a reality.

BIBLIOGRAPHY

(IN ALPHABETICAL ORDER)

With special thanks to Michael J. Neufeld, Bob Ward and Wayne Biddle for their words and wide research.

DARK SIDE OF THE MOON
BY WAYNE BIDDLE
W.W. Norton & Company Inc.,
New York, New York, 2009 USA

DR SPACE
THE LIFE OF WERNHER VON BRAUN
BY BOB WARD
Forward by John Glenn
Naval Institute Press
Annapolis, Maryland, 2005 USA

VON BRAUN
DREAMER OF SPACE, ENGINEER OF WAR
BY MICHAEL J. NEUFELD
Vintage Books
A Division of Random House, Inc.
New York, New York, 2007 USA

WUNDERWAFFEN: THE HISTORY OF ROCKETRY
HITLER'S DECEPTION
http://v33v.tripod.com/ww2.html
Copy and Edit: Levi Bookin
Researched and compiled by: Walther Johann Von Luepp